Tros of Samothrace: 4

City of the Eagles

TROS OF SAMOTHRACE: 4
City of the Eagles

Talbot Mundy

LEONAUR

Tros of Samothrace 4: City of the Eagles
by Talbot Mundy

Published by Leonaur Ltd

Material original to this edition and this editorial selection
copyright © 2007 Leonaur Ltd

ISBN: 978-1-84677-187-3 (hardcover)
ISBN: 978-1-84677-188-0 (softcover)

http://www.leonaur.com

Publisher's Notes

The views expressed in this book are not necessarily
those of the publisher.

Rome: 54 B. C.

*I have failed often at what I attempted, and at the time
I have learned from failure nothing except not to flatter it
by calling it the end. At its worst it is but a beginning of
some new phase of destiny. But looking backward, as when
remembering night at daybreak, I have learned what gives
me courage to look forward. I perceive that failure more
often than not is the fruit of a man's forgetfulness of his
own importance in the Eternal Plan.*

—FROM THE LOG OF TROS OF SAMOTHRACE

Summer twilight deepened and the bats began to flit among
the tombs and trees that lined the Via Appia. Dim distant lights
irregularly spaced, suggested villas, standing well back from the
road amid orchards and shade-trees, but the stench of trash-
heaps and decaying ordure overwhelmed the scent of flowers,
and there was a dirge of stinging insects irritating to seafaring
men. The slaves who bore Tros's litter flapped themselves with
olive twigs, muttering and grunting as they bent under their
burden.

Beside the litter, cursing unaccustomed sandal-straps that
chafed his swollen feet, limped Conops, with the tassel of his
knitted seaman's cap dangling over the empty socket of his right
eye. With his left hand he held the litter, and with the stick in his
right hand he kept prodding the wretched contractor's slave in
front of him, throwing him out of step and then abusing him in
half the languages of Asia Minor.

On a horse behind the litter, looking like a centaur—for he rode magnificently—Orwic led twelve Britons, who marched leg-wearily with short spears over their shoulders; they wore a rather frightened look and crowded closely in the ranks. Behind them came a two-wheeled cart piled high with luggage held down by a net. Two Northmen were perched on top of the pile, and behind the cart trudged four-and-twenty other Northmen, battle-axes over shoulder, targets slung behind them. They swung from the loins like men well used to it, although there was a hint of a deep-sea roll, and more than a suggestion in the northern song they hummed of wind, waves and battle on a surf-enthundered beach.

A beacon many miles away behind—where one stage-contractor was giving warning to the next one beyond the skyline, that a personage was coming southward and would need relays of horses—gleamed on the narrow road and made imagination leap the shadows in between; the Via Appia ran as straight as an arrow and twenty weary miles resembled one.

In front, the lights of Rome blinked sparsely. There was a house on fire that threw a red glare on the belly of a cloud and showed in silhouette the roofs of temples and the outlines of two hills edged with buildings, like the teeth of a broken saw. There were temple lights, and over one or two streets where the night life swarmed there lay a stream of hazy yellow. Here and there a light showed through an upper window, and there was a suggestion rather than the sound of babbling tongues; Rome looked, in the near distance, like a crouching monster, and the ear deceived itself with what the eye conveyed.

In the shadows of the tombs and cypresses that lined the road lurked men—and occasionally women—who peered at the litter and vanished at the sight of so many armed men. Runaway slaves, almost numberless, lived in the shadow of terror cast by stenching gibbets, on which scourged human bodies writhed or rotted near every crossroad; there had been a recent and, as usual, sporadic outburst of official morals, so the runaways were rather less bold and more hungry, lurking in the neighbourhood of villas and the north- and south-bound traffic, but afraid to try conclusions with the passer-by.

"Master," said Conops at last, thrusting his ugly head in through the litter curtains, "take advice from me for once and let us find an inn. There are enough of us to throw out all the thieves who occupy the place—"

"Aye, and to make a meal for nearly half the bedbugs!" Tros interrupted. "No more inns, little man! Rot me such dung-heaps! Am I a Carthaginian ambassador that Rome should not provide me with a decent place to sleep? I tell you, Conops, here, unless a man considers his own dignity, none thinks he has any."

"Would we were safely at sea again!" Conops grumbled, leaning his weight on the litter and kicking at one of the bearer-slaves, whose slouching irritated him.

"We are near Zeuxis' house. I see it yonder," Tros said, leaning through the curtains. "Bid the bearers turn where that tree, like a broken ship's mast, stands against the sky."

"Zeuxis sounds like a Greek in foreign parts," said Conops gloomily. "Commend me rather to a crocodile! Not for nothing, master, was I born in Hellas. Keepers of Roman inns are like their bedbugs—one can crack them between thumb and finger. But a Greek—has this Zeuxis a master?"

"He is a distinguished Roman citizen," Tros answered. "Furthermore, I have a hold on him."

"Poseidon pity us! A Greek turned Roman is a wolf with a woman's wits! Better give me the pearls to keep!"

"Keep your insolence in bounds, you ignorant salt-water fish! Go forward—lead the way up the path beyond that broken tree; try not to behave as if you were selling crabs out of a basket! Spruce yourself! Erect yourself! Up chin, you dismal looking dog! Put your knife out of sight! Shall Zeuxis' servants think we are Cilician pirates? Swagger forward now, and ruffle on the manners of a nobleman's retainer!"

Conops did his best, shaking the dust from his kilted skirt and straightening his cap, but he limped painfully. Orwic, recognizing climax, ordered out a great ship's lantern from the cart and sent one of the Britons running forward with it; he thrust the lantern into Conops' hand and ran back to his place in the ranks as if ghosts were after him, whereat Orwic laughed.

The lane by the broken tree was unpaved and dusty but there was a row of recently set cypresses on either hand; their height, a grown man's, intimated that the owner of the villa at the lane's end had not occupied it long, but he was advanced in his notions of living. There was gravel in the ruts, and there were no pigs sleeping in the shadows. The lowing of cows in the distance suggested affluence, and as the lane lengthened there began to be neat walls on either hand, built of the broken rubble of older walls well laid in pozzolana.

The lane ended at a high gate swung on masonry posts surmounted by marble statuary, whose outline merged itself into the gloom of overhanging trees. A grille in the wooden gate was opened in answer to Conops' demand to know what the owner of the house would say to keeping the most noble and famous Tros of Samothrace waiting in the dark. The slave behind the grille remarked that he would go and see. During the short pause, all of them, including Orwic's horse, flapped savagely at swarms of gnats.

Then the great gate swinging wide, revealed the porch of a Greco-Roman villa, newly built, its steps about two hundred paces from the garden entrance. Parchment-shaded lanterns cast a glow over the columned front, making the stucco look like weathered marble. There was a burst of music and an almost overwhelming scent of garden-flowers, as if the gate had dammed it and now let it pour into the lane. A dozen slaves came running, six on each side of the path, and behind them Zeuxis strode, combining haste with dignity, extending his arms in welcome as Tros rolled out of the litter and stood blinking at the lamplight.

"Tros of Samothrace—as welcome as Ortygian Artemis!" he cried in Greek, gesturing dramatically at the full moon rising like a mystery between the treetops.

"May the goddess bless your house, and you!" Tros answered. "Greeting, Zeuxis!"

They embraced and Tros presented Orwic, who rather embarrassed the Greek by leaping from his horse and also embracing him in the British fashion.

"All Rome would fight to kiss him if they knew how he can drive a chariot!" Tros said, half apologetically. "He is a barbarian prince."

"A prince among your followers—prosperity! The more the merrier, friend Tros, and the surprise adds zest. My house is yours; enter with your friend and take possession."

He led Tros by the arm, but paused to study him keenly in the lamplight on the porch, where slaves fawned and a steward prodded them to make them more obsequious.

"You have aged ten years in two," he remarked, "and yet—I will wager you bring good news."

Tros only grunted. Zeuxis led the way into a hall, of which he was comically ashamed. The walls were painted with scenes from the Iliad, done recently and too spectacularly. There the steward took charge of Tros and Orwic, leading them away to a bathroom, where slaves sluiced and kneaded them for half-an-hour and other slaves brought blue-bordered Roman clothing in place of their travel-stained Gaulish costumes. The luxury made Orwic talkative and it was an hour before they rejoined Zeuxis, in an anteroom beside the dining-room that faced on a tiled courtyard in which a fountain played amid flowers and young girls moved with calculated grace. There was music somewhere, not quite loud enough to make the fountain-splash inaudible.

"You must excuse my house," said Zeuxis. "I have baited it to catch some Roman buyer who has made a fortune selling war material. I am afraid the penalty you pay for coming unannounced is to wait for dinner, while the cook makes miracles. Why didn't you send word, you spirit of unexpectedness?"

Tros signified with a frown that he would prefer to keep silence until the slaves had left the room but Zeuxis laughed.

9

"My slaves will have your story from your followers. You may as well talk at your ease!" he assured him.

"I have only one man who can speak any language your servants know," Tros answered. "If your craftiest man—or woman—can get one word out of Conops, Rome is welcome to it. I sent no word because I trusted none to carry it."

The Greek leaned back in a gilded chair, looked humorously into Tros's eyes, took a goblet from a slave and held it while another poured the wine. Then he rose and, spilling a libation to the gods, smiled at Tros over the brim of the goblet.

"I see you understand the Romans," he remarked, and, having sipped, sat down again.

He was a handsome Greek with quantities of brownish hair curled artificially, his age perhaps not over forty, but not less than that. The care with which the wrinkles had been smoothed out from his face, and the deliberately studied youthfulness of gesture rather hinted that he might be older than he cared to seem. He had an air of artificial daintiness; there was a sapphire on the middle finger of his left hand that sparkled wickedly, calling attention to the delicacy of his fingers, which looked more capable of handling drawing instruments than weapons.

The contrast between him and Tros was as great as could be imagined between two men of the same race. Zeuxis' smile suggested cynicism and ability to reach a given goal by going around obstacles, which Tros would simply smash.

There was a desultory conversation for a while, because the slaves were Greek. Orwic, knowing neither Greek nor Latin, watched the scantily clad girls and after a while confined his interest to one, whose movements were deliberately calculated to enchant him. When the steward announced that the meal was served he followed Zeuxis with such manifest reluctance that the Greek laughed.

"Tell your barbarian friend not to leave his heart here. She shall wait on him at dinner."

The dining-room was classically elegant, its walls adorned with paintings of the Muses and divided into panels by Corinthian half-columns of white marble. The furniture was Alexandrian. The food, cooked by a slave from Syria, was carried in by Greek girls.

There was no sign of Zeuxis' wife; Tros guardedly remarked on it.

"She is at my country place in the Aventines," said Zeuxis. "Like many another foolish fellow I married youth and beauty instead of experience and domestic virtue. Beauty, in Rome, arouses greed; if possible one steals it; failing that one buys. If neither, then one gets the lawful owner into difficulties and converts him to a Roman point of view—which means, to look the other way. So I have sent my wife to the Aventines in charge of a virago who, current rumour has it, is a midwife; you will have noticed, however, that rumour frequently exaggerates. Meanwhile, my difficulties disappear and trade is excellent."

Lolling gracefully on his couch at the head of the table, with Tros on his right hand, Orwic on his left, toying with the food rather than enjoying it, he kept up a running comment for the steward's benefit, not often praising the skill with which the viands were made to resemble something they were not, more often explaining how they might be better.

"My Syrian cook is an artist," he complained to Tros. "In Alexandria they might appreciate him. Here in Rome you must be vulgar if you wish for popularity. Food must be solid, in gross quantities and decorated like the Forum with every imaginable kind of ornament, the more crowded and inappropriate the better. Rome proposes to debauch herself with culture; so I have to crucify a good cook's soul and train girls how to misbehave. I was cursed with vision when I came into the world; I foresee the trend of events, and I know I must swim with the stream or go under; so I try to guide the Romans decorously along the line of least resistance. They began by being wolves and they will end by being pigs, but that is for the gods to worry over, not me. I am a contractor. I arrange banquets. I decorate interiors for equites who grew rich lending money. You know the system, of course? The tax-farmers drain the treasury of con-

11

quered provinces, compelling them then to borrow at twenty-four percent compound interest; when accumulated interest amounts to half-a-dozen times the principal, the inhabitants are all sold into slavery. Most of my girls were obtained in that way. Damnable? Undoubtedly. But I might be a slave myself if I had stayed in Greece instead of coming here and flattering that rich rogue Crassus. He had me made a Roman citizen, although I might have had the same favour from Pompeius Magnus. Do you know how Crassus made his money? With a fire-brigade. There are some who say he also kept incendiaries. His men monopolized the putting out of fires by always arriving first on the scene in great numbers and fighting for the privilege. Soon nobody else dared to put a fire out. Crassus' men would simply stand by and let the place burn until the owner was willing to sell it to Crassus for a song. Then out would go the fire, Crassus would restore the place and let it out at rack-rents. He has the trick of money-making.

"But he is mad; he covets military honours. He has gone to fight the Parthians. He is envious of Caesar's fame. Caius Julius Caesar, if he lives, will ruin both him and Pompey, but they say Caesar has the falling sickness. I have also heard said that his sickness is the result of slow poison secretly administered by one of his lieutenants in the pay of some patrician. Caesar is a patrician; but he has made all the other patricians loathe him by his systematic pandering to the plebes. He sends gladiators for the games and corn-doles—that might not matter so much; they all do it. His worst offence is the money he sends from Gaul to buy the election of candidates who keep Rome in political torment. He also sends presents to senators' wives, and keeps a swarm of paid propagandists, who sing his praises to the crowd at every opportunity. Caesar has brains. One of the brightest things he ever did was to marry his daughter to Pompey. She is a charming woman. Consequently, Pompey has to pose as Caesar's friend, whatever his feelings may be—not that they are particularly secret—he says little, but every one knows he thinks Caesar a dangerous demagogue."

Zeuxis gossiped gaily through the meal, doing his best to loosen Tros's tongue and reversing usual procedure, ordering the finer qualities of wine brought as the meal progressed. Orwic, unaccustomed to such subtle vintages, drank copiously and before the meal was over fell asleep. Tros's taciturnity only increased as he listened to Zeuxis' chatter. He had almost nothing to say until the meal was finished and Zeuxis wanted to leave Orwic in the woman's care.

"Zeus!" he exploded then. "Sober, a man needs help to save him from the women. Drunk, not all the gods together could protect him! And besides," he added, looking straight in Zeuxis' eyes, "I myself will tell you all you need to know. If you have a slave woman who knows Gaulish, keep her for some necessary business."

Four slaves carried Orwic to a bedroom and Tros sent for Conops to sleep on a mat at the foot of the bed.

"Not that I doubt your honour, Zeuxis, I am thoughtful of it. This handsome cockerel recovers like a Phoenix from the ashes of a feast. Not remembering where he is, he might remember, nevertheless, that he is a king's nephew—which means a king's son, less the need of self-restraint. Conops knows how to manage him."

Conops' one eye glinted meaningly as he met Tros's glance and nodded. Hideous though he was, it took no augury to guess that Zeuxis' women had been making love to him for information; he made a gesture with a clenched fist that meant, and was interpreted to mean, "they have learned nothing from me!"

Zeuxis led into a room where gilded couches with a low wine-table set between them gave a view through an open window into the lamp-lighted courtyard, where a dozen girls were posing near a fountain.

"Shall they dance?" he asked.

"Aye—into the River Lethe! Let a slave set wine in here and leave us," Tros suggested.

Zeuxis laughed, dismissing the girls with a wave of his hand. The slaves retired. Tros strode to the curtain drawn on rings across the doorway and jerked it back to make sure none was listening. Then he glanced into the courtyard and at last sat down on the window-ledge, whence he could talk while watching both the courtyard and the corridor beyond the now un-curtained door.

"I am honoured!" said Zeuxis, bantering him. "These must be deadly secrets you intend to pour forth. Come and drink; this wine of Chios was reserved for Ptolemy the Piper. I was able to acquire it because Ptolemy came to Rome to borrow money when the Alexandrians drove him off the throne. He gave a feast to a number of Roman senators, for which I was the contractor and, though they lent him money, he has never paid my bill. I shall have to repay myself by roundabout means. The senate is forever obedient to the money-lenders. Mark my words—they will send Caesar or Marcus Antonius one of these days to collect. Drink! Ptolemy the Piper knows good wine, if nothing else. The old fool gave his note to Caesar for seventeen and a half million sesterces to persuade him not to veto sending Gabinius and Rabirius to Egypt."

Tros reached under his tunic and produced a little bag tied tightly with a leather thong. He bit the thong loose, glanced into the bag, tied it again and tossed it into Zeuxis' lap. The Greek weighed it, eyed it curiously, opened it at last and poured nine pearls into his hand. His eyes blazed.

"Plunder?" he asked.

"My gift," said Tros.

"By Aphrodite's eyes! By all the jewellers of Ephesus—these are better than the pearls that Pompey took from Mithridates. There are no such pearls in Rome," said Zeuxis, rolling all nine on the palm of his hand and stirring them with a sensitive forefinger. "They are matched! Tros, they are priceless! Whom do you wish to have murdered?"

"Are you a contractor in that trade, too?" Tros asked him sourly.

"No, but since Sulla's time one can always hire that sort of tradesman. Nobody is safe in Rome without an armed band at his back. Do you wish me to introduce you to a Roman who will work himself, for a consideration, into the necessary right-eous frenzy? And who is the victim to be? Some one important, or my wits deceive me as to the value of this present."

"When I must kill, then it is I who kill," Tros answered. "I could buy nine senators with those nine pearls."

"You force me to admire myself!" said Zeuxis. "Have you any more of these?"

"Nine more for you, of nearly the same weight if—when my venture is successful."

"Tros, you deal a dreadful blow against the inborn honesty of Hellas! Whom do you wish me to betray to you, and why?"

"Yourself!" Tros answered. "One who did not know me might propose to play me false. But you will not commit that indiscretion. I have chosen you to assist me in a certain matter."

"You oblige me to pity myself!" remarked Zeuxis. "A king's nephew and a king's pearls? Rome is no playground for kings; they come here begging, or to walk in triumphs and be strangled afterward. Whoever befriends kings in Rome—and yet—friend Tros, these pearls are irresistible! Have you come like a messenger from Pluto to arrange my obsequies?"

"I come from Britain."

"Britain? The end-of-the-world-in-a-mist, where Caesar landed with the famous Tenth and ran away again by night? Hah! How the patricians gloated over that defeat! I was decorating Cicero's new villa at Pompeii and I overheard him telling what the senate thought of it; they were overjoyed to learn that Caesar is not invincible."

"But he is," said Tros. "He is invincible unless we can—Those pearls are in your hand because he shall not be invincible!"

Politics

A man forgets his own importance, but he magnifies want and the mystery of the many moods of want, his own included. He forgets that his wants and his fears and his perplexity are unimportant, but his own importance is eternal and changeless, whereas wants continually change, and fear is the illusion of which wants are brewed like foul stink from a wizard's kettle.

If a man can remember his own importance he is saved from many unimportant but demeaning deeds. His dignity, should he remember his importance and the unimportance of his fears and wants, directs him to a right course, though it may seem at the moment lacking in profundity of rightness.

—FROM THE LOG OF TROS OF SAMOTHRACE

Zeuxis stared, his shrewd imaginative eyes growing narrower under slightly lowered lids. He was not one who attempted to conceal emotions; he preferred exaggeration as a safer mask. But Tros's face, as he sat still on the window-ledge, was a picture of iron resolution, unafraid although aware of danger. Zeuxis was aware of an excitement he could not resist.

"I have a friend who is a king in Britain," Tros began, but Zeuxis interrupted.

"Kings are no man's friends."

"I helped him against Caesar. He helped me to build my ship. Caswallon is his name."

"Did he give you these pearls? Beware! King's gifts are expensive."

"I had those from the druids."

"Ah! You interest me. I have talked with druids. Caesar sent a dozen of them in a draft of prisoners from Gaul. One had a beard that nearly reached his knees. He was so old he had no teeth. It was hard to understand him, but he knew Greek and could write it. I befriended him. The others were sold as secretaries, but since that old one was a hierarch they were to keep him to walk in Caesar's triumph; the weight of the fetters killed him before long—that and the stink of the dungeon; he was used to open air. There was a new aedile making a great bid for popularity. I was one of three contractors who had charge of the games he squandered stolen money on, so I had plenty of opportunity to talk with that old druid. I used to go down to the dungeons whenever I had time, pretending to look for some one who might make a showing against an enormous bear they had sent from Ephesus—bears usually kill a man with one blow, whereas what the spectators want is to see a fight. It was thought, if a man with a knife would defend himself against the bear for a few minutes that aedile might be very popular.

"I didn't find a man to fight the bear. I did not want to; I was interested in the druid, he talked such charming nonsense with such an air of authority. He told me, among other things, that Caesar is an agent of dark forces that will blot out what remains of the ancient Mysteries and make Rome all-powerful for a while. He said if Caesar dies too soon those forces will find some one else, because their cycle has come, whatever that means, but meanwhile Caesar is in the ascendant because he typifies the spirit that asserts itself in Rome. So if you think as much of the druids as I do, Tros, you will think twice before you oppose Caesar."

"I have thought twice, and the second thought was like the first," Tros answered.

"Think a third time. Rome is violent, strong, cruel, split up into factions, yet united by its greed. They have had to postpone

17

the elections. Pompey does nothing—I tell you, Caesar is inevitable! Let us flatter Caesar and grow rich when he has made himself master of the world!"

"Those pearls are worth a fortune," Tros reminded him.

"There is no such thing as enough," said Zeuxis. "There is too much and too little, but enough—who ever saw that? You have given me nine pearls. I covet nine more. I am Greek enough to know I must pay a usurer's price."

"No, you may give them back."

Tros held his hand out. Zeuxis poured the pearls into their little leather bag and slipped it into a pocket underneath his sleeve, where no one would have suspected a pocket might be hidden.

"What do you propose? A revolution?" he asked. "That would bring Caesar down on us. He conquers Gaul for money and to make himself a reputation. He corrupts Rome into anarchy so as to have the city at his mercy when the time comes. I could guarantee to start a tumult the day after tomorrow, but as to the consequences—"

"If Caesar should descend on Rome, he could not also invade Britain," Tros answered.

"But you might destroy Rome. Pompeius Magnus hates luxury and corruption—for other people. There is nothing too good for himself. He would rally the patricians to fight Caesar's faction to the death. That might mean ruin for all of us. I am a parasite. I fatten on rich men's ignorance. There would be plenty of ignorance but no wealth after a civil war, whichever side should win."

"Let Rome rot. Who spoke of revolution?" Tros retorted. "I am here with thirty men to find some way of bridling Caesar. I would not give one pearl to buy a Roman mob. They would sell themselves for two pearls to the next man, and for three pearls to a third. But I have bought you, Zeuxis! Tell me how to put a stick in Caesar's wheel."

Zeuxis studied Tros's face over a goblet's rim.

"I prefer not to be crucified," he answered. "There is only one way to control Rome—through a woman."

Tros exploded. His snort was like a bison's when it spurns the turf.

"No truck with women! Let Caesar manage the senate with his presents to the cuckolds' wives. I play a man's game."

"Fortuna ludum insolentem ludit!"

Zeuxis filled his goblet, smiled and let the lamplight show the colour of the wine.

"Ptolemy the Piper, king of Egypt, is a drunkard," he remarked. "I said nothing about women. I said 'through a woman'!"

"Lord Zeus!"

"But the very gods and goddesses love one another, Tros. However we may think of women in the mass, one woman brought you into the world and one bore me. One woman supplies the key to any situation. For instance, Caesar's daughter has kept him and Pompey from each other's throats."

"I will not stoop to such practices," Tros answered.

"I have known men who were forced to rise to them!" said Zeuxis. "I only mentioned Julia by way of illustration. She is too ill to be of any use to us. I was thinking of another woman— Helene, daughter of Theseus, a musician, who came with old King Ptolemy from Alexandria. She is the scandal and the admiration of all Rome. The sons of newly rich equites wear flowers filched from her garland and brawl about her in the streets, while their fathers defy even the Vestal Virgins in refusing to let her be expelled from Rome. Some say she is a spy for Ptolemy; others that she seeks revenge on Ptolemy and plots to send the Roman eagles into Egypt. The truth is, she has genius and seeks enjoyment. She adores sensation. It was she who posed to Timonides of Corinth for the new statue of the Venus Genetrix; his workshop was so thronged with visitors that he removed the unfinished statue all the way to Tarentum, but when he did that she refused to go there and the statue is still unfinished. She rides in a gilded litter, as she isn't a slave and they can't prevent it. Recently she offered to drive her own quadriga in the races. When the aedile refused to permit that she offered to fight Juma, the Nubian gladiator. Some think she might have beaten him, but the Vestal Virgins would not hear of such a scandalous proceeding. She understands that stirring of desire is much more profitable than to satisfy it. For a pearl or two we might persuade her to amuse herself immensely for our benefit. By Heracles, I have it!"

Zeuxis rose dramatically, one hand raised, as if he plucked a great idea from the ether, but Tros watched him without enthusiasm. "Let us send the girl to Caesar."

"Trash!" Tros answered. "I could dig that thought from any dunghill. Caesar is not Paris, son of Priam—he is Caesar. He would take, but the woman is not born who can seduce him. Caesar smiles once, and the craftiest surrender to him like ice to the sun. I know him. Five times I have met him, and he—almost—won-me! I admired his brilliance. He has intellect. He recognizes strength on the instant, or weakness equally. He can read men's character as I read wind and sea; and he can use the rogue or the weakling as I use puffs of wind to fill my sails. But he prefers to match his strength against the strongest, even as I love conquering the storms. Five times I have met him. Three times I have beaten him. Each time he has offered me command of all his fleet. I laughed."

"I remember your father also was mad," remarked Zeuxis. "Why in the name of all the mysteries of death should you reject the friendship of a man like Caesar? That is wanton waste of golden opportunity! And you a Greek from Samothrace! Have you not sense enough to realize that fortune favours Caesar? Will you flaunt your prejudices in the face of Providence? I tell you, Caesar will inevitably be master of the world unless an accident prevents."

"Then let my name be Accident," said Tros.

"In the name of the immortal gods who turned their backs on Hellas when the Romans came, let us be wise men and swim with the tide!" Zeuxis urged. "You and I are not heroes. Caesar is. We might destroy him, as I have seen dogs drag down men in the arena; but the dogs did not turn into men; nor should we become Caesars. Tros, I tell you, we should let this Caesar burst a breach for us in fortune's walls and follow in with him. Success is sweet! I drink to it! Failure is bitter; lo, I hurl my dregs at it! Men live longest who know enough to follow fortune's favourites."

Tros snorted, thumping a fist down on his thigh. He glared at Zeuxis as if eyes could burn him up.

"Aye, gods have turned their backs on Hellas. She is dead. I live!" he answered. "I measure life by strength of living, not by days and nights and lustrums. Failure? A beached fish for it! Riches? There isn't a rogue in Rome who mayn't be as rich as Crassus if he has the luck. What is worth having in this life? Dignity and friendship, Zeuxis! Courage to stand by a friend! Vision and will! The choosing between right and wrong! The pluck to take the weaker side—the obstinacy to persist—rebellion against the wrong thing—action! Those are life."

"Then why not be the friend of Caesar?" Zeuxis argued. "Friendship should not be squandered on unworthy people. If choosing is the gist of life, choose wisely! Caesar will give you action; and if the apparently weaker side amuses you, choose his. He is all-powerful in Gaul, no doubt; but here in Italy Pompeius Magnus has the gage of him at present—or so the senate thinks, and so think nearly all the equites and the patricians—and so thinks Crassus, or he never would have gone to Asia to try to wrest a triumph from the Parthians. Select the cause that seems the weaker at the moment; then—success?—suppose we call it opportunity for further effort. You are a young man. You may outlive Caesar. It would be no mean memory that you were Caesar's friend. If he should have rewarded you—"

"With what?" Tros interrupted. "Money? The stolen gold of Gaul! Employment? Holding in subjection ravished provinces, or possibly off-standing pirates who are no worse than himself and only seek to glean where Caesar harvested! Honours? He has no honour. He has avarice, energy, skill; he can arouse the sentiment of pauper-soldiers driven from their farms by cheap slave-labour enslaved by himself from looted provinces. But honour? He serves out honours as he feeds his legions, from the commissariat. He keeps faith when it pays him, and because it pays."

21

"By the forsaken gods of Hellas, Tros, I think we all do that," said Zeuxis. "You have paid me to keep faith with you, and since you whetted my discretion with one gesture of royal extravagance, why not confide in me a little? You spoke of a ship. Where is the ship? Where did you land in Italy?"

"I landed at Tarentum. My ship is at sea," Tros answered. "She will come for me to Ostia, where Conops shall quarter himself in order to hurry to me with the news of her arrival. I found me a pilot in Gades who knows Roman waters; and I have a Northman in charge of the ship, whom I trust because he and I fought until we learned the temper of each other's steel."

"Caesar has a way of knowing what his enemies are doing. Does he know you are in Rome?" asked Zeuxis.

"He knew I left Gades for Rome. I had a brush with him in Gades. I won from him authority to use all Roman ports. I have a letter from him, signed and sealed."

"He knows you are his enemy?"

"He does."

"Then that letter is worth exactly the price of damaged parchment! I suppose you haven't heard how Cato proposed to the senate to revive Rome's reputation by sending Caesar in fetters to the Usipetes and Tencteri. Caesar broke his word to them and violated the law of nations; but how much support do you suppose Cato aroused? Men simply laughed. There is only one way to win influence in Rome—that is, purchase it in one way or another. If you buy with money in advance, the danger is that your opponent will out-buy you. Besides, how can you compete with Caesar? His agents Balbus and Oppius have spent sixty million sesterces in buying up old buildings alone, to enlarge the Forum. Prices—any price at all; but 'Vote for Caesar!' If any senator wants money he goes through the farce of selling a house or some worthless work of art to Caesar at an enormous price, so as to avoid conviction of receiving bribes. The plunder from Gaul provides work at unheard-of-wages for the artisans, who would undoubtedly accept your bribes but would also continue to pocket Caesar's wages; they look to Caesar to go on enriching them forever, whereas you would only be a momentary opportunity.

"The better method is to entertain them, which is almost equally expensive. You would find the competition deadly. But there is this to be said; the mob will be faithful as long as nine days to whoever gives it a good thrill. After that you must think of another new thrill—and another one. Keep Rome entertained and you may even nominate her consuls."

Tros rose from his seat on the window-ledge and paced the room, his hands behind him and the muscles of his forearms standing out like knotted cords.

"You know Cato?" he demanded.

"Surely. Only recently he had me driven from his door. I represent the decadence he makes his reputation by denouncing—the ungrateful, vain, old-fashioned snarler! He is the best man in Rome and politically the most contemptible, because he means exactly what he says and keeps his promises. Pin no hopes on Cato."

"Cicero?"

"He owes me money for his new house. I have a little influence with him. But he is much more heavily in debt to Caesar. Cicero measures gratitude by bulk; he will even praise bad poetry if rich men write it."

"Marcus Antonius?"

"Profligate—drunk—insatiable—rash—a Heracles with a golden voice, in love with popularity. He knows how to win the mob's plaudits—and at present he favours Caesar."

"Have you the ear of Pompey?"

"Nobody has. He has the best taste of any man in Rome, so he is naturally disgusted with politics. He glooms in his country villa, where even senators are turned away. Pompey half imagines himself super-human but half doubts whether his good luck will continue. I believe he is losing his grip on himself. He recently refused to be made dictator on the ground that there is no need for one, but I think the fact is, he has no policy and doesn't know what to do. His wife is ill, and if she should die he might come out into the open as Caesar's enemy, but at present he makes a show of friendship for him.

"His intimates flatter him out of his senses; and because of his easy success in the war against the pirates and his aristocratic air of keeping his intentions to himself he is the most feared man in Rome. But the mob believes Caesar will bring fabulously rich loot out of Britain, which makes the moment inauspicious to oppose Caesar; and though Pompey loathes the rabble he likes their votes. Who wouldn't? Also, I think he honestly dreads a civil war, which would be inevitable if he should announce himself as Caesar's enemy. You have no chance with Pompey."

Tros came and stood in front of Zeuxis, frowning down at him, ignoring a proffered goblet of wine.

"Have you the ear of any one in Rome who would serve my purpose?" he demanded.

"I have told you—Helene of Alexandria." Tros snorted again, but Zeuxis went on:

"At the moment she is keeping rather quiet because three days ago two factions of young fools fought about her with their daggers in the Forum. Two sons of equites were killed and half-a-dozen badly hurt. Cato was furious. She must be nearly bursting after three days' seclusion. She likes me because—well, to be candid with you—she influences business and draws fat commissions. The best advice I can give you is to see Helene."

Tros scowled and stroked his chin.

"Tomorrow morning. Why not? It will be a novelty that will stir her craving for amusement. You arrive at the door of her villa with a handsome young barbarian prince, exactly at the moment when she is ready to burn the house over her head with boredom. Flatter her—amuse her—praise her—bribe her—and she will ruin Caesar for you if it is possible to do it."

Tros groaned aloud, shaking his fists at the painted ceiling—

"O Almighty Zeus, am I never to be disentangled from the schemes of women?"

"You are forgetting Leda and the swan," said Zeuxis. "Even Father Zeus himself has had entanglements at times!"

Helene

*I have seen many a man ape humility by magnifying
the importance of his office and denying his own claim to
be more than a servant. But his office is what he makes it,
as a ship is what her builder makes her and behaves as her
master directs. If a ship's crew is unseamanly, I know her
master's character, no matter what his chastity of homage to
the ill luck that he bids me witness. If I see a city foul with
lewdness, I know its rulers' character, no matter what their
mouthings about the sanctity of office and the grandeur of
their institutions.*

—From the Log of Tros of Samothrace

Three hours before dawn Tros awoke Orwic to discuss pro-
posals with him.

"Cato is the noblest Roman of them all. He is incorruptible.
This woman Helene is Rome's paramour. Cato's party is in con-
tempt because it is old-fashioned and honest. Which shall it be?
Shall we attack Rome's weakness or ally ourselves to strength?"

"Try both!" Orwic murmured sleepily. "What difference does
it make to me? I know no Latin. I can neither make love to a
woman nor address the senate! It appears I can't drink! That fellow Zeuxis' wine has made my head feel like a copper kettle."

Orwic fell asleep again. Tros went to his own room, where he
lay cudgelling his brains. He could foresee nothing. It was possible he was in danger of his life, equally possible that Caesar's
enemies might leap at every opportunity and stage a demonstra-

tion that should force Caesar to abandon his attempt on Britain. Should he adopt a subtle course or the direct one of appealing bluntly to such men as Cato, Cicero and Pompey?

Zeuxis, on the other hand, with pearls in mind, sent a slave with a letter in haste to Helene's villa. Three hours after daybreak two of her litters, borne by slaves in her livery and with a eunuch in attendance, waited in front of Zeuxis' porch.

By that time Zeuxis and his guests had breakfasted under the awning in the fountained courtyard. Already Zeuxis was deep in his affairs—mercurial, excited—giving orders to his foreman in an office whose walls were hidden behind drawings and sheaves of estimates. There was a staff of nine slaves busy figuring at long desks. A stream of tradesmen and subcontractors poured in and out, all chattering. But Zeuxis abandoned business when he heard that those litters had come.

"Tros, fortune smiles on us!"

He ordered his own chariot brought—an extremely plain affair, unpainted, drawn by mules.

"Lest I arouse cupidity! My customers would be annoyed if I looked rich. Rome is still a strait-laced city—except for the rich Romans!"

Refusing to explain, he almost dragged Tros into the first litter and waved Orwic into the other. Tros found himself on scented cushions behind embroidered silk curtains through which he could see but remain unseen. An escort of men armed with staves went before and behind and a eunuch, modestly arrayed, but strutting like a peacock, led the way for a while in the dust of Zeuxis' chariot. Zeuxis drove full pelt to have a first word with the lady who had sent the litters, and was shortly out of sight.

They passed into the city through a swarming crowd of slaves and merchants, skirted the Mons Palatinus by a smelly street between brick houses, crossed the Tiber by a wooden bridge, where slaves of the *municipium* stood guard at either end to put out fires and regulate the traffic, and emerged into a zone of trans-Tiberian villas, where hardly a house was visible because of densely planted trees and high walls, and the only gaudy ostentation was displayed on decorated gate-posts. There was much less traffic over-river, although chariots, often preceded by men on horseback and usually followed by breathless slaves on foot, were driven recklessly, their drivers shouting to foot-passengers to clear the way; and there were countless slaves carrying provisions and merchandise for sale.

There were no armed men in evidence, but the high walls of the villas suggested fortifications and the general impression was of jealously guarded privacy.

The villa occupied, but not owned, by Helene faced the Tiber between higher walls than ordinary, above which the trees had been topped to make them spread into impenetrable masks of dusty green. On the high gate-posts were portraits in colour intended to convey a sort of family likeness of the succession of Romans who had owned the place—and lost it to a money-lender, from whom Helene had rented it.

Her slaves were at the gate, all liveried. An impudent Cyprian eunuch, in canary-coloured robes and wearing his mistress' portrait on a copper disk hung from his neck, commanded that the gate be opened, saluting the litters as they passed in, but tempering civility with a leer that made Tros's blood boil; and almost before the gate had slammed again his squeaky voice was raised in vinegary comment on the impatience of the slaves of certain equites who sought admission with letters and gifts to be delivered into the fair Alexandrian's hand.

"Tell your masters that my mistress will receive gifts when it pleases her. Has none brought any gifts for me? What sort of persons are your masters? Paupers? Plebes? Ignoramuses? What are they?"

The villa was built in the style that had grown fashionable when the Roman legions had brought their plunder home from Greece. It was faced with columns looted from a temple in Boeotia. Stolen statues—fawns, Bacchantes, Naiads—grinned, danced and piped under every group of trees, so that the grounds looked like the entrance to an art museum; it would have taxed even the ingenuity of a Roman money-lender to find room for one more proof that culture can be dragged in with a team of oxen.

But within there was something like taste, although the cornices were far too richly ornamented and the paintings on the walls were garish. Some woman's hand had draped the place with Babylonian embroidery, so rich that it challenged attention and threw overcrowded elegance into comparative obscurity. The art of Alexandria had overlaid confusion of design.

However, there was no time to admire the hangings. There was laughter, the echoing clash of weapons and the thumps of bare feet leaping on a marble floor. There was a glimpse along a marble corridor of gardens leading to the Tiber. The eunuch drew aside embroidered curtains to reveal a sunlit court surrounded by a balcony. Young Romans lounged against the columns, laughing and applauding; in the midst of one side Zeuxis sat amid a group of women, to whom he appeared to be giving intricate instructions. In the midst of the mosaic, sunlit floor, half-naked and aglow with exercise, Helene fought with net and trident against a Nubian armed with a blunted sword. There were great red splotches on her skin where he had smitten her, but he was backing away warily, circling toward her right to keep clear of the sharpened trident that she held in her left hand.

Suddenly, as Tros strode in, she lunged with the trident. The Nubian dodged and tried to smite her with the flat of his short weapon. She ducked, leaped, cast her net and caught him, spinning her trident and driving its blunt end with a thump against his ribs. Then, clinging to her rope, she spun herself around him, keeping him tight in the toils and prodding him until he yelled for mercy while the onlookers shouted applause.

"*Hic habet!* Punish him! Don't spare him!"

She did not cease until the Nubian went down on his back and she had put her foot on him, holding up her trident in imitation of a victor at the games, amid cries of "Kill him!"—"No, wait—whose gladiator is he? He might cost

28

too much."—"I'll pay for him. Go on, Helene—see if you can kill him with the trident—only one thrust, mind!—it isn't so simple as it looks."

She laughed down at the gladiator, breathless, prodded him again and turned away—caught sight of Tros and Orwic with their backs to the curtained entrance, and came running to them.

"Which is the king's nephew? Which is Tros?" She looked at Orwic longest as he took her in his arms and kissed her; which was perfect British manners but, to put it mildly, unconventional in Rome. The sons of Roman equites roared their astonishment, loosing noisy volleys of jests, but Orwic kept her in his arms and kissed her three times before she could break free.

"This is the king's nephew!" she assured them in a strident laughing voice that made the courtyard ring. "The other—"

Tros raised up his hand in greeting and the banter ceased. He was dressed as a Roman; except for the gold band on his forehead and the length of his raven hair he might have been a Roman of the old school, conscious of the debt he owed his ancestors.

"—this other doubtless is the uncle!" said Helene. "I expected Tros of Samothrace. All hail, thou king of an end of the earth! Helene welcomes you to Rome, where even Ptolemy had to wait on Cato's doorstep! Isis! You have dignity! What muscle! Do you seek a queen, most terrifying majesty? Or is the nephew to be married? I abase myself!"

She curtsied to the marble floor, the rhythm of her movements bringing a burst of applause from the gilded youths, who cried to her to repeat it, some urging her to dance—all anxious to attract her attention to themselves. Zeuxis left the women who surrounded him and, stepping forward into the sunlight, cried out:

"Pardon, mistress! Noblemen, your pardon! This is the most noble Tros of Samothrace. His friend is a royal prince whose name is Orwic."

"Not a king?" Helene gasped in mock astonishment. "Lord Tros, that Greek fool told we you were no more than a sailor! Kings go to Rome's back-doors, but I see you are neither a fool of a king nor a louse with a vote for sale!"

Again she curtsied, three times, throwing back the dark hair from her forehead with a toss that suggested blossoms nodding in the wind. Then:

"Equites!" she cried, addressing the youths who had begun to swarm around her. "Favour me by entertaining them until I have bathed and dressed."

She ran off through a door between two Doric columns, followed by the women who had been surrounding Zeuxis. Zeuxis came forward again and introduced the Romans, reeling off their names as each one bowed with almost perfect insolence, restrained, however, within bounds by recognition of Tros's strength of character and muscle and air of being somebody who might have influence. They tried to talk to Orwic, but, as he could not understand them and disguised embarrassment behind an air of aristocratic boredom, they were obliged by curiosity to turn to Tros again.

"I am from Hispania," he answered, telling half the truth. "I have brought despatches from your imperator Caesar," he added, which was more than half an untruth. "To the senate? No. What would Caesar say to the senate?"

They all laughed at that. Whatever their opinions of Caesar, none pretended that he held the senate in respect. They began to ask news of Caesar, eagerly inquiring what the prospect was of his invading Britain and how true it might be that the Britons made their common cooking-pots of gold. So Tros seized opportunity and told them about Britain, saying it was nothing but a miserable, foggy island full of trees, where no wealth was and the inhabitants fought valiantly because there was nothing to make peace endurable.

"Then why does Caesar talk of invasion?" they protested.

"Possibly he talks of one thing and intends another," Tros retorted. "It is known that he prepares an army, and I have heard something about ships. However, which way will tomorrow's wind blow? How many miles from Gaul to Rome? If I were a young Roman I would watch to see Pompey's eagles gather. These are wild times. Stranger things might happen than that Caesar should propose to himself to seize Rome."

But such talk only vaguely interested them. They had the absolute contempt for politics peculiar to rich men's sons. The youngest of them had seen the mob made use of to reduce itself into submission. They had all heard gossip about Caesar. They considered Pompey vastly his superior. However, Caesar had significance.

"Caesar has sent three more shiploads of wild animals from Gaul," said one of them. "There are to be games to celebrate his recent victories. They are to surpass anything ever seen in the Circus Maximus. Crassus' agents have sent bears from Asia. There will be nine elephants. From Africa Jugurtha has sent fifty coal-black savages from the interior, who look fit to fight even our best gladiators. And there are two hundred and ten criminals in the dungeons, some of them women; they talk of slaughtering the lot in one melee—give them a taste of the hot iron, and a spear or something to defend themselves, and turn the wild beasts loose on them! There is rumour of a promise of freedom for the last man and the last woman left alive—but that may be only talk to make them try hard."

An older man, Servilius Ahenobarbus, waxed scornful:

"Any one in his senses would rather see two good gladiators fight than watch a thousand people butchered," he objected. "Fie on you, Publius! Are you degenerating? Such stuff is all very well for the rabble. I can smell them in my nostrils as I think of it! Can't you hear the snarl and then the yelp as they watch women being ripped by a bull? Caesar has sent bulls from Hispania. But you forget the best part—two days' chariot racing."

"Phaugh! A safe and pretty spectacle for Vestal Virgins!" Publius sneered. "I have heard Britons fix swords to their chariot wheels. Now, if they would have a race—quadrigas, say—with swords fixed to the wheels, wolves loosed at the horses and fifty or sixty prisoners of war in the way, tied in groups, to escape if they could, I would call that a spectacle! Wait until I am old enough and they elect me aedile!"

"Ah! Then at last my turn will come! You will let me fight then, won't you, Publius?"

Helene danced forth from her dressing-room in a chlamys made of Chinese silk from Alexandria, with a wreath of crimson flowers in her hair and a girdle that flashed fire as its opals caught the sunlight. She was better looking clothed; the drapery softened the lines of her too athletic figure and the wreath offset the hardness of her eyes—delicious dark-grey eyes that, nevertheless, could only half conceal the calculation in their depths. She was mentally weighing Tros.

She turned suddenly toward the Romans, laughing in their faces:

"Nobiles, who loves me? Who will hurry to the slave-market and buy Thracian grooms for my white team? Those Armenians I have are useless; I will sell them for farm-work."

There was a race to be first to find suitable Thracian slaves. The Roman youths cut short the courtesies and ran to find their chariots. Helene took Tros by the hand.

"And now those fools have gone we may talk wisdom," she said, looking almost modest. "Zeuxis tells me you have come from Britain and desire my influence—although I have not altogether understood him. Come."

She led into a room which formerly had been the atrium, which she had refurnished and disguised with hangings until it resembled nothing Tros had ever seen. There was crimson cloth with golden dragons; there were gilded cornices and curtains made from beads of ivory; the feet sank silently into rugs of amber and old-rose; the couches, the chairs and the very foot-stools were of ivory inlaid with gold. There was a smell of incense.

"Go!" she ordered, and the lurking slaves vanished.

Tros prodded the hangings. He opened a closet. He drew back the curtains that covered a doorway. He looked through the window and listened for breathing from behind some potted shrubbery through which he could not see. Then, striding to where she had thrown herself on an Egyptian couch of ivory and crimson cloth, he looked down at her dark eyes and, with his hands behind him, challenged her:

"I heard you say you wish to fight. Do you desire to fight me? With any weapon? With your wits?"

She shuddered.

"You look too much like Zeus!" she answered, rallying her impudence. "I understood you came to ask a favour of me."

"Whose slave are you?" he demanded.

She sat upright suddenly. She tried to look indignant but her eyes betrayed her; there was fear in their depths. She nearly spat the answer at him.

"I was born free! I am the daughter of Theseus the musician."

"And was Theseus free?"

She nodded. Words were choking in her throat. Her fingers moved as if she sought a weapon.

"Since when were the musicians at the court of Ptolemy free men?" Tros asked. "I have seen you dancing at the court of Ptolemy. You are the girl who danced when Ptolemy Auletes played the flute. Are you Ptolemy's slave?"

"I am free!" she insisted. Coiled on the couch, looking up at him, she suggested a snake in the act of striking. All the laughter was gone from her eyes, all her impudence.

"I am a silent man," said Tros. "I listen."

He began to pace the floor, his hands behind him, presenting his broad back toward her as he turned, to give her time to recover her self-possession; but she had no sooner regained a little of it than he snatched it from her, to convert it to his own use.

"Understand!" He stood in front of her again. "No panic-stricken yielding that broods treachery! Use reason. Judge me, whether I am one whom you can sway; or whether I am one who will betray you, if you keep good faith."

"Master of men, you are cruel!"

"I am just," Tros answered. "I will do you no harm if you yield to me."

"My body?" Her eyes lighted; her lips quivered in the faint suggestion of a smile.

"That for it!" He snapped his fingers. Instantly her whole expression changed; resentful, sullen.

"What then?" she asked. "Yield what?"

"Your secret!"

"I have no secret. I am the daughter of—"

He stopped her with a gesture. "Shall I go?" he asked, and turned toward the door.

She flinched at the veiled threat—sprang from the couch and stood between him and the doorway.

"I have influence," she said. "I dare to fight you one way or the other! Knife against knife, or cunning against cunning! If we make a bargain, you shall keep your share of it or—"

Tros thrust his thumb into the little pocket in his tunic and drew out a pearl of the size of a pea—a rosy, lustrous thing that looked incongruous as he rolled it on the palm of his enormous hand. She curled her lip scornfully.

"I could have pearls from Pompey. I can have anything in Rome my heart desires."

But Tros produced another one, and then a third. Her eyes changed subtly, though she still defied him, standing like an Amazon at bay. Tros was watching her eyes.

"I gave nine of these to Zeuxis. You shall have eighteen."

"For my secret?"

"No. I know your secret. There is only one man who would dare to risk burning his fingers in your flame. You are Caesar's spy."

"Liar! Rabirius sent me to Rome!"

Tros laughed. Rabirius was Caesar's money-lender—possibly a third as rich as Crassus, with perhaps a thirtieth of Crassus' manhood—an avaricious rat with brains enough to recognize his limitations and not vie with great men but play into their hands and pocket fabulous commissions.

"Sit down!" Tros commanded, pointing to the couch. He returned the pearls to his pocket. Then, as she obeyed him, "Judge whether I know your secret."

She set her elbows on her knees and clasped her chin, staring at Tros as if he were a prophet reading off her destiny.

"Caesar will need limitless fountains of money when he

makes his bid to be the master of the world. He invaded Gaul to make a reputation and for practice in playing off men against men. He married his daughter to Pompey to keep Pompey quiet. He encouraged Crassus to make war on Parthia, that Crassus might bleed Italy of men and leave none but Pompey and the idle rich to stand between him and ambition. Seeing far into the future, he sent agents into Egypt who should stir the Alexandrians against their king. So the Alexandrians drove out Ptolemy; but it was too soon; Caesar was not ready. Who was it then but Caesar who, in return for a promise of seventeen million sesterces, agreed to defy the Roman senate and send Gabinius with troops from Syria to restore Ptolemy to the throne, along with Rabirius to control Ptolemy's exchequer? Now you say you are the agent of Rabirius. That may be. But I think you are the slave of Caius Julius Caesar."

"What if I were? Is that your affair?" she answered.

"Aye! Caesar might learn too easily what I intend! You may report to him about Rabirius. You may tell him all the secrets of these young patricians who babble their fathers' treacheries in your ears. But concerning me you will be as silent as the tomb in which they bury Vestal Virgins."

"Caesar," she said, "is a terrible man to trifle with."

Tros nodded.

"Aye. I know him. His slaves keep watch on one another as well as on such Romans as he mistrusts and such provincials as he hopes to use. But since the gods, against my will, have guided me to your house, you shall run that risk of not informing Caesar!"

"You will injure him?" she asked.

"Nay. I will let him conquer Rome and leave the Britons to themselves!"

"You are his friend?"

"I am here to save Britain from Caesar."

Helene stood up, laughing, her eyes blazing. She defied him: "Do you dare to kill me in my own house? How else shall you gag me now I know your secret?"

"Gag you? I will make you garrulous!" Tros answered. "You shall find a way to make me famous in a city where such infamy abounds that no voice can be heard above the din! To Caesar you shall send word that Tros of Samothrace has prophesied Rome shall be his. Vanity may make him think he has persuaded me at last to love him."

"Many honest men love Caesar," said Helene.

"Aye, and many love you," Tros answered, "but not I. You shall have your choice of playing my game or explaining what you are, and why you are in Rome, to Cato. Now choose!"

"Cato?" she answered. "Are you of Cato's party?"

"No," he answered, "but I have a speech for Cato's ear that shall include you one way or another. Shall I say you are the agent of Rabirius and Caesar's spy—for I can prove it to him!—or—"

"Say Helene is your friend," she answered. "Cato is an old fool, but he is dangerous."

She looked keenly into Tros's eyes, and then laughed with a little breathless catch of nervousness:

"Tros, few in Rome would not like to say Helene is—"

"I am one of those few," Tros interrupted.

"Did you never love a woman?" she asked—curiously. His blunt rejection of her offer pleased her. By the light in her grey eyes he knew that she had made up her mind to conquer him.

"I am of Samothrace."

As he intended, she jumped to the conclusion he was an initiate under a vow to refrain from women.

"I will show you deeper mysteries than the Samothracian," she said with a confident toss of her chin and a laugh that had hypnotized many a man. "If I trust you, you must trust me."

"I have pearls. And you will do well to obey me," Tros retorted. "Be alone when I return from interviewing Cato."

Marcus Porcius Cato

*There are some men so enamoured by a half-seen truth
that they devote their energy to quarrelling with untruth
rather than to proving the little they do know. They are
like slaves with fans, who drive out through one window
flies that return through another. Stern men and unforgiv-
ing, they are so intent on punishing the evil-doer that they
have no time to practice magnanimity. Such men forget,
or never knew, that cruelty and justice mix no better than
fire and water, but that one extinguishes the other, leaving cruelty or justice. I have never seen one such man who
favoured mercy rather than his own delight in the importance of his fear of self-respect. Self-importance gives them
no time for importance.*

—From the Log of Tros of Samothrace

Nowhere on earth was it easier to make mistakes than in Rome,
nor more difficult to recover from them. It was a city where a man
might do almost anything, including murder, with impunity, provided he went about it according to precedent and did lip-serv-
ice to institutions and conventions. Above all, a foreigner needed
discretion. Too often foreigners had trailed behind the chariots
of Roman generals, in the celebration of those triumphs over
foreigners that made Rome affluent; too many thousands of alien
slaves were doing the work of animals and pandering to Rome's
depravity; it was too usual to attribute treachery to foreigners in
order to provide excuse for new campaigns, and it behoved the

37

alien to study his deportment shrewdly, with an eye not only to the mob's continuously cultivated craving for excitement, but also to the prejudices of the privileged. Privilege was of the essence of Rome's government.

Aware of all that, nevertheless, Tros fell immediately foul of custom. Wishing to avoid curiosity that Orwic, with his fair moustache and unusual manners, almost certainly would have aroused, he accepted the use of Helene's litters and her personal attendants to convey him to the Forum, where Zeuxis assured him he would almost certainly find Cato. He was conscious of having offended Zeuxis by not permitting him to overhear the conversation with Helene. He knew the Greek's mercurial temperament, as capable of malice as of generosity and of leaping in a moment from one extreme to its opposite. But he did not expect Zeuxis' resentment to be quite so swift. The malicious smile with which Zeuxis watched him get into the extravagantly decorated litter made no impression on him at the time.

"You will cause quite a flutter in Cato's bosom. There is nothing like a favourable introduction!" said the Greek.

And for a while it looked as if Zeuxis had meant exactly what he said. As the litters approached the city they became the objects of such attention that the liveried slaves had hard work to make progress through the crowd. Helene's notoriety had not been lessened, nor her popularity diminished by the recent brawling in the Forum for the right to walk beside her litter through the streets. Her recent offer to fight with net and trident in the Circus Maximus had become common gossip; it had been nobody's affair to circulate the news that the authorities had instantly forbidden such a scandalous proceeding. The crowd wanted to be scandalized and gloated at the prospect of Helene's doing it.

It was known too, that she had a four-horse team to enter in the races that would precede the three days' butchery of men and beasts in the arena; the possibility that she might drive the team herself had raised her popularity to fever-heat. The mere sight of her well-known litter forcing its way toward the Capitol was enough to block the narrow streets and draw attention even from the orators who were trying to work the crowd into electioneering frenzy wherever there was room for fifty men to stand and listen.

It was easy to see out through the litter-curtains, although next thing to impossible to recognize the litter's occupant, so all the way to the Forum Tros received the adulation that would have amused and thrilled Helene to the marrow of her being. It disgusted Tros. He loathed it. It revolted him to have to use a woman's notoriety to further his own plans. But it seemed safer to trust to Helene's influence than to make experiments with Rome's senators, or senators' wives, who might be less notorious but not less treacherous. No one—probably not even Caesar—knew the long reach of Caesar's spies and Caesar's money.

But he hated the scent of the goose-breast-feather cushions. The stifling city smells annoyed him and the din of city traffic—street-vendors' cries, the tumult of electioneering factions skilfully incited to frenzy by men whose only claim to public office was cupidity and the ability to pay the necessary bribes, yells of the charioteers who found the street blocked, clangour of the armourers in dim basement workshops, hoarse pleadings of the auctioneers disposing of the loot from far-off provinces, shouts of the public announcers, the yelping of dogs and the overtone, blended of all of it:

"Buy! Buy! Buy!"

Rome was for sale to the craftiest bidder. That was the key to the din. The offspring of seventy races were hawking their hearts in the market, to the buyer with the keenest brain and longest pocketbook.

Midsummer heat had driven all who could afford it to the seaside or to mountain villas—that, and bedbugs incubated in the crowded, dark slave-quarters and the rack-rent tenements. The orators were well dressed. There were equites in dusty chariots arriving post-haste from the country to investigate alarming rumours, but the crowd had the shabby, ill-tempered appearance it assumes so swiftly when the fashionable element withdraws. Hot nights and too much politics—slaves over-worked and free men unemployed—enormous and increasing wealth of one class, poverty and irresponsibility increasing for the other—corn-doles, open bribery, free entertainment at the expense of demagogues—postponement of the elections because the senate was afraid of mob-rule—Caesar's agrarian laws designed to curry favour with the populace, and the impossibility of enforcing them in the face of the landowners' opposition, or of earning a living on the land in competition with the cheap slave-labour of the large estates, had all combined to arouse irritation, uncertainty and the expectation of a riot such as even Rome had never seen. Almost the air itself seemed ready to take fire. Men's faces wore the ugly look that precedes violence.

And Rome herself was ugly-drab with the colour of smoky bricks and vegetable refuse—ugliness enhanced by the beginnings of adornment. There was marble here and there; and there were statues, some decapitated, some half hidden under crudely smeared electioneering posters, that suggested dignity forgotten. From between its ugly wooden scaffolding the marble of Pompey's enormous new theatre shone in the baking sunlight, hinting at the only method by which Rome was likely to emerge out of her filth. It was against the law to build a theatre of anything but wood; so, as all men knew, including they who should enforce the law, Pompey was building behind screens of wood that should be torn down in a night at last and lay bare a magnificent defiance of the law. And all men knew that none, unless possibly Cato, would dare to call Pompey in question. Men laughed at the senate's helplessness, while they reviled the senate for not fostering tradition.

As the litters neared the Forum, where the shop-fronts and the open wine-shops looked drab in the dust from buildings being torn down by Caesar's agents and the thud of falling masonry resounded like the tumult of a siege, the crowd grew denser. Roofs, temple steps, the shop-fronts, upper windows, all were thronged with agitated sightseers, some crying out the names of candidates for public office, some reviling Cato, others—evidently led by unseen agents—shouting for Pompeius Magnus and dictatorship.

The crowd was so dense that even two lictors preceding a praetor's deputy were brought to a halt. Rather than challenge the crowd in that temper they preferred to follow the two litters, for which the crowd made way. They recognized Helene's livery and there began to be an ovation. One of those strange moods that capture crises spread like a contagion; there was humour in the thought of humouring Helene, who had to stay at home three days because of gross infractions of the public peace of which she was the cause, and of dishonouring the praetor's representative.

The crowd, it seemed, was there to vilify the praetor—to inspire him with such dread as should prevent him from interfering with electioneering bribery. They began yelping at the lictors and at the sacred official who strode behind them with his toga concealing the lower half of his face. Then suddenly some genius conceived the thought that Helene had been arrested and was being brought before the praetor for examination. Mockery turned to anger. That was interference with the citizens' amusement and intolerable.

"Rescue her!"

The shout came from an upper window. It was echoed by a hundred voices from the street. Stones began flying, picked from the debris of the houses Caesar's agents were demolishing. An angry faction, seizing opportunity to pounce on their political opponents, surged between the litters and the praetor's representative and in a second there was a street fight raging. The two lictors, theoretically sacred in their persons, raised their fasces over the official's head and hurried him to safety in the nearest house, while a troop of young patricians, asking nothing better than excuse to terrorize the mob, charged on horseback from a side-street in the direction of the Capitol. They were only armed with daggers but they swept the mob in front of them, and in a sort of back-eddy formed by that onslaught the two litters swayed into the Forum, where the bearers set them down beside a statue on which men swarmed and around which sweating men were packed like herrings in a barrel.

Tros emerged out of the litter and by sheer strength scuffled himself standing-room. He shouted to Orwic to stay where he was, but the Briton at the risk of daggers fought his way beside him. They were facing the temple of Castor and Pollux, whose platform was thronged with patricians, one of whom was trying to address the crowd while others roared for silence, and no single word could be distinguished from the din. There was a sea of arms and hot, excited faces where the patricians tried to win the mob's attention. On the opposite side of the Forum, where the shutters had been raised on money-changers' windows and every statue held its crowd of men like corpses on a gibbet, other orators were roaring themselves hoarse. There were cries of:

"Who defeated Spartacus?"

"Pompeius Magnus! Let him be dictator!"

"Who conquered Asia?"

"Pompeius Magnus!"

"Down with Cato! He assails our liberties!"

"Caesar! Gaius Julius Caesar! The most generous, the most capable, the most glorious—Caesar! Caesar! Memmius!"

The last was Caesar's candidate for consul.

Cheers, groans, cat-calls drowned the efforts of each faction to popularize their favourite. There were scuffles and fist-fights going on in thirty places simultaneously, but there was no room for a general melee; public peace was preserved by the utter impossibility of concerted action where men were fainting for lack of breathing room and could not rally to their friends or reach their enemies. A young patrician, standing high above the crowd's reach on the balustrade that flanked the temple platform, was amusing himself by flinging copper coins, but none dared stoop to pick them up for fear of being trampled underfoot. Six others in a group yelled "fire!" to try to cause a stampede, but that failed because it was impossible to move in any direction.

The only un-invaded steps were those of the praetor's office, guarded by a row of lictors, whose fasces, vertically held in front of them, were still such sacred symbols of Rome's majesty as even that crowd dared not violate. The building, wedged between the massive temple of Castor and Pollux and a smaller one, more delicately built, that showed the influence of Greece, was blunt, uncompromisingly Roman, dignified and solid, raised above the level of the Forum on a concrete base that formed the platform and provided cells for prisoners as well as offices. Its brick-work, unadorned since Sulla's day when the stucco had been damaged in the rioting and afterward removed entirely, gave a gloomy, ancient aspect to the building that was only partially brightened by the stucco columns recently erected to support a roof over the platform. On wooden boards on either side of the open door were public proclamations, and on the platform was a table and a chair, but no man seated at it. That platform was the only vacant space in sight; even the bronze beaks of the rostra, at the Forum's farther end, were invisible behind a swaying sea of faces.

Suddenly the din ceased. There was silence as if Rome had caught her breath. The hammering of demolition stopped abruptly and the dense crowd swayed as every face was turned toward the door of the praetorium.

"Cato!"

It was a murmur, but it filled the Forum. He came slowly through the open door, the purple border of his toga emphasizing the dignity and matter-of-factness of his stride. He had a tablet in his right hand, which he studied, hardly glancing at the crowd, and he appeared entirely to ignore the half-a-dozen men who followed him, three on either hand. He was a round-headed, obstinate looking veteran, in contrast to their elegance and air of self-advertisement; the more they postured and acknowledged themselves conscious of the crowd, the greater seemed his dignity.

"Citizens!" he said abruptly. Even breathing ceased. There was a dead, flat silence—noncommittal. No man seemed to expect pleasantries. "It is your inalienable privilege to elect the officials of the Republic by ballot. However, certain individuals, ambitious to hold office for their private gain, have set the disgraceful example of bribery, corrupting public morals and preventing the election of such candidates as will not, for the sake of honesty, or can not purchase votes. This scandal I regard it as my duty to abolish. There shall be no bribery while I am praetor. I have caused to be deposited with me by each of these candidates for office whom you see before you a sum of money from his private fortune which would ruin any of them should he forfeit it. This money will be forfeited into the coffers of the state in the event of proof of bribery. So cast your ballots at the time of the election honourably, as becomes a Roman citizen, each voting for that candidate who seems to him to merit confidence."

He made no gesture—simply turned, looked sharply at the six men on the platform, and strode sturdily in through the door. There was a moment's silence, then a man laughed. Agitators, scattered at strategic intervals, cackled cynically until all the crowd was laughing. Cries from over near the rostra broke on the babbling din:

"This upstart believes he is Cato the Censor! He will abolish the games next! He will have us all eating turnips and wearing sackcloth!"

But the crowd, as volatile as mercury, had seen the humour of the situation. It turned its laughter on the candidates for office, booing them until they followed Cato in a hurry. There was a surge then as men were hustled off the rostra to make room for orators who sought with shout and gesture to claim the crowd's attention. But the mob would have none of them; it began melting, pouring along the Via Sacra, spreading the news of Cato's master-stroke and carrying the din of laughter down the narrow streets until all Rome seemed aroar with monstrous humour. Before Tros could straighten out his clothing, mussed by the crush of the crowd, the whole Forum was empty except for groups of arguing politicians. All except two of the lictors retired, and they sat at ease on stools on either side of the praetorium door.

"They are used to squalls—well used to them!" said Tros, and taking Orwic by the arm he bade the litter-bearers follow him to the praetorium steps and wait there.

As he reached the top step he met Cato face to face. The Roman, with only one slave following, stopped, framed in the doorway and stared at him hard, then glanced at the sumptuous litters and their slaves in Egyptian livery.

"Those slaves are better dressed than many a Roman," he remarked, with a sarcastic gesture answering Tros's salute. "Who are you?"

"Praetor, I am Tros of Samothrace. I seek audience with you alone."

Cato's florid, stubborn face grew wrinkled as a dry smile stole along his lips.

"You are an alien," he said. "You think the business of Rome may wait while I listen to your importunities?"

"Aye, let Rome wait!" Tros answered. "Caesar has the reins of fortune in his hand."

"You are Caesar's messenger?"

"I am Tros of Samothrace and no man's messenger. I seek an audience with you."

"Enter."

Cato turned his back and led the way along a narrow passage into a square room lined with racks on which state documents were filed with parchment labels hanging from them. There were several chairs, two tables and one secretary, bowed over a manuscript. Cato dismissed the secretary. He stared, glanced suddenly at Orwic and sat down.

"Be brief," he said abruptly.

Tros made no haste. He studied him, mistrusting ordinary methods. There was nothing subtle about Cato; the man's elementary simplicity and downrightness expressed themselves in every line. His windy grey eyes, steady and keenly intelligent, betrayed unflinching will. His wrinkles spoke of hard experience. The iron-grey hair, worn short, suggested a pugnacity that was confirmed by the lines of mouth and chin. His hands, laid calmly on his knees, were workmanlike, un-jewelled, strong—incapable of treachery; the voice, well modulated, courteous but carrying a note of irony and incredulity.

A little too much bluntness and Cato would construe it as a challenge; the merest hint of subtlety and he would close his mind. Too much politeness would stir suspicion; rudeness he would take as an affront to Roman dignity. Exaggeration he would instantly discredit; under-statement he would construe literally. He was difficult. Tros would have preferred a man more vulnerable to emotion.

"I am from Britain," Tros remarked at last. "This is a prince of Britain." He nodded to Orwic, who saluted with aristocratic dignity.

"You have come in very gaudy litters," Cato answered. "Whose are they?"

"Helene's. Lacking other means of—"

"Can't you walk?" asked Cato. "I am praetor. I invariably walk."

"I can walk when I will," Tros answered. "Having no lictors to make me a way through the crowd I did well to borrow litters that the crowd would let pass. It is of no importance how I came. I will speak of Caesar."

"You carry tales against him? I have heard them all," said Cato. He closed his mouth tight, as a man does when he reins impatient horses.

"I come to prevent Caesar from invading Britain," Tros insisted, leaning forward to watch Cato's eyes. "If he succeeds against the Britons, what will be his next move? Rome."

Cato nodded. "Caesar," he said, "is the first sober man who has designed to make himself the master of Rome. Sulla was a drunkard. So was Marius. Caesar drinks deep of the hog-swill of flattery. He is drunk with ambition. But that does not give you the right to conspire against the Republic."

"I will help you against Caesar!" Tros said, rising, and began to pace the floor, as always when he felt excitement surging in his veins. Three times he strode the room's full length and back again, his hands behind him, and then stood, looking into Cato's face.

"Alien," said Cato. "I am praetor. Caesar is a Roman general."

Tros snorted.

"You split hairs of morality while Caesar cuts throats! Listen! You love Rome, and you hate Caesar. Not I. I haven't Rome to lose nor all the plunder of a hundred provinces to make me fearful. You set the welfare of the state above your own. I set the welfare of my friends above my own; and I love Britain, where a king lives whom I helped to resist Caesar when he made his first raid on the island."

"Island?" said Cato. "We are told it is a mainland greater than all Gaul and Hispania."

"Mainland!" Tros snorted again. "A small, misty, wooded island, whose inhabitants can neither harm Rome nor enrich her treasury! A mere island, whose inhabitants are brave men. Caesar, while he gains time, seeks to build a reputation. But I have heard how Cato, staunchest of all Romans, resolutely sets his face against wars when there is no excuse for war. They say there is no other public man who has dared to defy the Triumvirate. Therefore, I have made my way to Cato, at my own great risk."

"And the price?" asked Cato, looking sourly at him.

Tros exploded like a grampus coming up for air, then turned and paced the floor again.

"Cato!" he said, turning to him suddenly. "They packed you off to Cyprus to get rid of you, and all the world knows what happened. You found an island ruined by the money-lenders, and you left it in a fair way to recovery. I have heard how you flung the taunt in Pompey's face that, notwithstanding you dealt honestly, you brought more money back from Cyprus for the Roman treasury than Pompey brought from all his plundering of Asia. So you know what Roman rule means in the conquered provinces. I tell you, I have seen Gaul writhing under Caesar's heel. Where I have known fair cities, there is wasted land and broken walls. I know a place where there are thirty thousand men who lack a right hand, simply because Caesar is ambitious. I have seen the gangs of slaves go trailing out of Gaul to replace Romans on the farms of Italy and force your free men to enlist in Caesar's and Crassus' legions. And you ask me my price?"

Cato eyed him undisturbed, his hands palms downward on his knees. No gesture, not a fleeting trace of an expression betrayed what thought was passing through his mind.

"Give me the right to call myself Cato's friend!" Tros urged, lowering his voice dramatically. "If I thought Rome held a hundred Catos, I would—"

Cato interrupted.

"Your opinion of me is unimportant. I am the praetor. That woman, Helene, whose litters you use, is a prostitute. You flaunt her impudence in Rome's face."

"Prostitute?" Tros retorted. "All Rome is given to prostitution! What does one more matter? I am told you wish to prosecute Rabirius for his chicanery in Egypt. Leave Helene to me and I will strip Rabirius as naked as when he yelled himself into the world! I will prove to you Caesar supported him, prompted him, pocketed a fat percentage of the money he stole and now makes use of Helene to watch Rabirius—and you—and others. She is one of Caesar's ablest spies. Touch her, and you bring down Caesar on your head! Leave her to me, and I will hamstring Caesar! Give me ten days, and you shall know about the war that Caesar plans!"

Cato took a tablet from the table and wrote swiftly. Then he laid the tablet back, face downward on the table.

"Caesar has authority," he said, "to declare war or to make peace in Gaul."

"Britain is not Gaul," Tros answered. "Neither is Rome Gaul."

Cato rapped the table with his knuckles. The secretary entered, took the tablet and went out again.

"Caesar has reported to the senate," said Cato, "that the Britons are constantly helping the Gauls to rebel."

"In the name of all the gods, why not?" Tros thundered at him. "Should a brother not defend his brother? There are Gauls and Britons who belong to the same tribe, share the same king and till land on both sides of one narrow sea. And did your ancestor sit idle when Hannibal invaded Italy, because forsooth, he had not yet reached Rome? Do you, another Cato, wish to grovel before Caesar? He will use the strength of Gaul and Britain against Rome, when he has glutted his ambition in that corner of the world. He is a madman! Stir up Gaul behind him! Let Gauls and Britons learn that there are men in Rome who sympathize. Give them but that much encouragement,"—he snapped his fingers—"and Caesar shall have his hands full!"

Cato, spreading out his knees with both hands resting on them, leaned back; he had done with arguing.

"No Roman praetor can lend his influence to the defeat of Roman arms," he said. "But I will do what can be done to bring the senate to a proper view of these things—"

"Phaugh!" Tros's fist went like a thunder-clap into his palm. "And two-thirds of the senators accepting Caesar's bribes! The other third opposing him because they think Pompey might put more money into their pockets! Cato, do you set this wolf-brood's appetite above fair dealing? Are you—"

"I am a Roman," said Cato.

"You shall see Rome fawning at Caesar's feet!" Tros answered, his eyes glowing like a lion's.

The line of Cato's lips grew tighter and then flickered in a hard smile.

"And by whose authority do you come here, riding in prostitutes' litters to hurl threats at me?" he asked. "Are you a Roman citizen?"

"I come by Caesar's leave," Tros answered, pulling out a parchment from his breast. He flourished it indignantly. He showed the seal and signature. "I won it! Three times I have had the best of Caesar and—"

He checked himself, aware that he had lost his self-control, whereas the Roman had not.

"Well—and what?" asked Cato.

But the thought that had flashed across Tros's mind was noth-

ing he could safely tell to any one of Cato's unimaginative temper; even in the heat of indignation he knew better than to run
that risk.

"And I will save Britain from him," he said lamely. Then,
recovering his self-possession, "You go prattle to the senate—if
you can make them listen without paying them to sit still!"

He saluted in the Roman fashion and Cato stood up to return the salute with an air of being glad the interview was over.
He ignored Orwic—merely nodded to him, as he might have
done to a familiar slave, and Orwic flushed, not being used to
rudeness even from his equals. As they left the room the Briton
growled in Tros's ear:

"Is that truly one of Rome's great men?"

"Rome's greatest! Iron-headed, and as blind as a boulder resisting the sea! Born out of his time! He loves the Rome that died
before the days of Marius and he is mad enough to think Caesar
can be tamed by quoting law! I have a thought, though."

For a minute Tros stood gazing at the Forum and its groups
of politicians vehemently gesturing. Helene's eunuch bowed.
He waved the man away.

"I will walk. Here—" He tossed him money. "Tell your mistress to expect me." Then, as he took Orwic's arm and they de-
scended the steps together, "I have a thought that quarrels with
inclination. I must study it. Keep silence."

Side by side they walked along the Via Sacra between rows of
graceless statues, Orwic copying the stride that gave the Romans
dignity when dignity of motive was the last thing in their minds.
Tros strode like Hercules, observing nothing, with a frown above
his eyes like brooding thunder.

"Of what do you think?" Orwic asked him at last, when
they had bumped into so many people that apology had grown
monotonous.

"Of my father's prophecy," Tros answered. "With his dying
breath he foretold I should struggle against Caesar but that I
should serve him in the end."

"Against Britain?" Orwic asked, startled, puzzled.

"Nay. He knew I will betray no friendships. But—why not against Rome? Do you and I care whether Rome licks Caesar's feet? This Tiber-wolf bred Caesar—let the cub's teeth make her suffer for it! If we offer Rome to Caesar he may turn his fangs away from Britain!"

"If we offer to do it he can laugh," said Orwic. "How can two-and-thirty men give Rome away?"

"The gods give and the gods take," Tros retorted. "Men are agents of the gods."

"But who knows what the gods intend?"

Tros turned that over in his mind a minute, doubting nothing except whether words could possibly convey his meaning to a man whose language he had learned but recently.

"The gods—they know," he said at last. "Men guess. And he who guesses rightly there and then becomes the edged tool of the gods."

"But how guess?" Orwic wondered. "If we had a druid with us—"

"He could tell us no more than we see," Tros interrupted. "Let us see Rome. If the heart is rotten, let us foretell death or a physician. I believe the gods purge evil with its offspring, and it may be Rome is ripe for Caesar, who will be a drench that will burn Rome's belly. He may fail. She may vomit him out. She may swallow and smother him. Murder—"

"But—but—"

Orwic stared at the crowd—three-fifths of them slaves from the ends of the earth—for the Romans were taking their ease in the midsummer heat. Even the half empty streets sent up a roar like the voice of a cauldron, and the baking heat suggested future on the forge. There was a thunder where the rubbish of demolished buildings tumbled down the wooden chutes into the carts. The sun shone through a haze of dust and, as the wind whipped up a cloud of it, there came down a narrow street, like spectres, nearly a hundred men all chained together, staggering under blocks of marble.

"Those are Jews," said Tros. "They are the fruit from Pompey's harvest in Jerusalem. Unless you and I act wisely we shall see Caswallon led in triumph, and the Britons building Caesar's Rome under the whip."

He was talking merely to keep Orwic silent. He wanted to think. He stood frowning, staring at the most dignified building in old Rome—the temple of the goddess Vesta, with the residence of the Vestal Virgins close behind it and, beyond that, the official home of the Pontifex Maximus.

Julius Nepos

I have used life wondering at marvels—aye, and look-
ing for them. But I know no greater marvel than the virtue
readily discernible in some men, whose calling is vile. Their
vileness is beyond coping with; it would be wiser to swim
in Leviathan's sea and try to cozen him, than to bargain
with such men's vileness. For they know their vileness and
they understand its channels; he who understands it not is
as a sheep to a wolf. But their virtue to them is precious,
and they understand it not. Touch such men's virtue and
uncomprehending they respond, as a blind ship responds to
a touch of the helm though all the gales of Neptune buffet
and her nature bids her drift before them.

—From the Log of Tros of Samothrace

Tros led on, ignoring the crowd; but even in polyglot Rome there were limits to the strangeness that could pass without excit-ing notice. If they had been slaves no citizen would have lowered himself by paying them attention, but they took the middle of the way like noblemen, although no servants followed to protect them from assault or from the importunities of wounded veterans.

So they were followed by small boys, who mimicked Tros's Herculean swagger and made moustaches for themselves of street dirt out of compliment to Orwic. Traders tried to drag them into shops where Crassus' oriental plunder was beginning to seek sale. They were bellowed at by leather-lunged slaves who stood on stone blocks advertising brothels. Insolent gangs of gladiators in the pay of men grown newly rich called to them out of wine-shops, where maimed ex-soldiers clamoured for the dregs of each man's drink. They were pestered by touts from lawless gambling-dens, thieves' auctions and even by slaves who were trying to sell themselves.

It was hours before Zeuxis found them, still wandering about Rome, visiting the temples and the great wooden arenas where the gladiators practiced, under the eyes of gamblers studying their chances and the betting odds. Zeuxis arrived on foot, sweat running from him, breathless and so agitated he could hardly speak. His slaves supported him, wiping his face with handkerchiefs until he thrust them aside at last and, stepping between Tros and Orwic, seized Tros's arm.

"What have you done? What have you done? One day in Rome and this already! They have seized Helene! She was taken by the praetor's men! They wrapped her in a hood for fear the crowd might recognize her. One of her slaves followed and declares he saw her hustled into the praetor's prison. There is a guard put on her house and men are searching it! A few of her slaves have run, but most of them are lined up in the garden; telling all they know. It was by the merest luck the praetor's men did not find me in the house—I had just left. One of the slaves escaped and overtook me. I have found you by describing you to people in the street and—gods of Hellas!—what a wanderer you are! I have followed you all over Rome."

Tros tried to calm him, but the Greek appeared to have no nerve left. He said he did not even dare to return home until he knew the praetor's men were not invading his house. He had sent a slave to see.

"They have no right to interfere with me—I am a Roman citizen, but a man's rights—Tros, Tros, you have brought me ill luck!"

"Where shall we go?" Tros asked. A crowd was gathering. "If they should find my Northmen at your house—"

"That's it, that's it!" exclaimed Zeuxis, wringing his hands. "Your wretched, bearded, battle-axing, drunken, quarrelsome barbarians! The praetor will accuse me—here, this way!"

Slapping a slave's wrist, who tried to calm him with affectionate remonstrances, he slipped through the crowd and led, panic-stricken, down a dozen evil-smelling lanes where the rubbish from tenements was dumped and mangy dogs snarled at the passer-by, until at last an alley opened into a nearly circular space that had been repaved with rubble from an ancient wall. There was a well in the centre, protected by masonry constructed from the fragments of crude statuary, and though the buildings around the enclosure were tidy enough and there were no heaps of stinking garbage, they were mean, small, solidly and crudely built, with heavy, tall flat stones instead of arches over all the doors. It was a section of the oldest part of Rome.

Zeuxis struck at a door whose cypress planks were scarred by a hundred years of violence. He struck repeatedly, but faces peered through many a narrow window before the door was opened cautiously and a man thrust out his head. He had iron-grey whiskers that met underneath his chin. Chin and upper-lip were shaven. His nose was discoloured by criss-cross purple veins. Extremely bright eyes glittered from under shaggy brows and his grey head, bald in the middle, was like a tangled mop.

"Zeuxis?" he said. "Volatile, venomous, vicious, effeminate— enter! You would never come here unless you were in trouble! Come in and amuse me. I suppose you have offended Cato. I know Cato better than to try to coax him, but you may as well tell me the news—the news—the news."

His voice echoed under the vaulted ceiling of a passage lighted dimly by one candle stuck on an iron bracket. On the walls of the passage were weapons, shields, helmets; some seemed to have come from the ends of the earth; there were Parthian scimitars, clubs studded with iron, three-headed spears and wave-edged daggers, long-handled hooks for dragging down a horseman, nets, tridents and swords by the dozen, of every imaginable shape and length.

Fire glowed on a hearth in a room at the end of the passage. There was something cooking on the coals and acrid smoke, that made the eyes smart, clouded among beams from which hung odds and ends of recently washed clothing. On the walls of the room hung garments of extraordinary richness, gruesomely suggestive of the spoils of horrible victories—more weapons—and a brazier in a corner, with an iron of peculiar shape beside it. Over the hearth, where smoky images of wax stood on a shelf in gloom, was an extremely heavy, short, broad-bladed sword. There were benches and a table, but the furniture was meagre, unpainted and such as the poorest citizen of Rome might have possessed.

"I introduce you to Julius Nepos," said Zeuxis, seeming to recover self-possession when the old man slammed the door and bolted it. The only light came from the smoky hearth and from a window, high up in the wall, which seemed to open on a courtyard. The heat was so great that the candles set on brackets on the walls had drooped in drunken curves and there was tallow on the flag-stone floor beneath them.

Tros bowed and Orwic copied him, but both men felt an impulse of reserve. Old Nepos noticed it.

"Be seated," he said gruffly. "I have cut the heads off nobler men than you. I have slain kings."

He seemed to think that made him anybody's equal. He glanced at the garments that hung on the walls—his perquisites; and having laid claim to distinction, he grew genial and grinned—pulled off his sandals and shirt, revealing a torso and arms like Vulcan's, all lumpy with muscle, the colour of bronze, and sat down on a creaking bench.

"This is the man," said Zeuxis, "who refused to be Sulla's headsman and yet Sulla spared him. He was formerly the chief instructor of the public gladiators, and not even Sulla dared to—"

"Oh yes, he did," Nepos interrupted. "He deprived me of my privileges. I might have starved; only when Cato became praetor he ordered Sulla's informers rounded up; and then he sent for me and had me cut the heads off most of them—a miserable brood!—nine-and-thirty in one afternoon, and a pleasanter death than they earned! If Cato had listened to me they would have died in the arena, fighting one another, with the beasts to clean up the survivors; but Cato thought they were too cowardly, although I told him a hot iron will make anybody fight. So I beheaded them. I killed two hundred and eleven altogether, and good riddance!"

His face looked something like a satyr's as he leaned forward to observe Tros. There were no signs of ferocity about him—rather of a philosophic humour, slightly cynical but tolerant. He struck the table with his fist and called for wine, which was brought in by a woman less agreeable to look at than himself. She had thick lips and most of her teeth were missing; her figure was shapeless, her arms like a fighting man's and her greasy hair like Medusa's. But it was good wine; and she provided lumps of bread to eat with it, breaking them off from the loaf with fingers that looked capable of tearing throats.

"And so now you are in trouble," remarked Nepos, eyeing Zeuxis comically. "You believe because I am a friend of Cato I can get you out of it. Isn't that so? Well, I tell you Cato doesn't like you, Zeuxis. Has he caught you cheating the public treasury over some contract for a spectacle?"

"He has arrested Helene," said Zeuxis.

Nepos suddenly sat upright, swallowed wine and snapped his mouth shut.

"So it is Cato who is in trouble, is it?" he said. "Obstinate old tamperer with hot irons! Fool! She'll wreck him! The mob loves her. What will he do—have her thrown to the beasts? Old imbecile! They'll leave the benches and throw Cato in, in place of her! There are some things Cato can't do, praetor though he is."

"How teach him?" wondered Zeuxis.

"Oh, he's teachable," said Nepos. "You couldn't have taught Sulla anything, or Marius—and Pompey won't learn nowadays, since flattery went to his head. But you can teach Cato what the crowd will have and what it won't have. Cato believes in the voice of the people. He'll hear it! As I've told him often, all they care for is money, doles of corn and entertainment. Cato sat there, on that bench, last night. He likes me because I talk good sense and never flatter him.

"I like Caesar, who knows how to rule; but I told Cato now is the time to throw in his lot with Pompey, and increase corn-doles and give astonishing spectacles, if he hopes to stand in Caesar's way. But Cato hates Pompey nearly as much as he does Caesar, so that's mutual. Pompey detests him for going bare-footed and poking his nose into public accounts. So he has bagged Helene, has he? Well, we'll have to save him from that predicament! You can't tell me Helene isn't Caesar's woman. Caesar can't afford to let his spies become disorganized. He'll kill Cato! He hates him. He'd love an opportunity to turn on him. Cato is a fool. I love him better than a brother, but he's a fool—he's a fool—he's an old fool—and that's worse than a young one!"

Zeuxis shrugged his shoulders.

"He is honest, which is much the same thing!"

"No, he isn't," said Nepos. "He is proud and obstinate. There's no such thing as honesty."

There came a hammering at the outer door and Nepos' wife admitted one of Zeuxis' slaves, who delivered his news breathlessly:

"The praetor's men have not come near the house. But the freedman Conops went to Ostia, so now there is none who can control the lord Tros's barbarians, who are afraid because of their master's absence and are threatening to go and look for him."

Instantly Julius Nepos seemed to throw off twenty years. His muscles tautened. Even his voice grew younger:

"Barbarians? What sort?" he asked. He glanced shrewdly at Orwic, who resented the appraisal and frowned haughtily. Tros sat still, acutely conscious of a tingling in his spine.

It was Zeuxis who answered: "Northmen—whatever that is. They are a breed never before seen in Rome, having red beards; and they fight with axes. But some are Britons and resemble Gauls. That one"—he pointed at Orwic—"is a prince among the Britons."

"Are they free men?" Nepos asked.

Instantly Tros lied to save them. If he had answered they were free men, nothing would have been more simple than to bring some charge against them. Then, as aliens unrepresented by an influential advocate, they might be condemned and sentenced to the arena.

"Slaves," he remarked, compelling his voice to sound casual. But his fist was clenched and Nepos noticed it.

"I have seen too many die, not to know when a man is afraid, friend Tros," he said, a lean smile on his face. "Good gladiators bring a high price. Men who fight with axes would be something new. They might be matched against the Mauritanians. Pompey would buy them. It would be a short way into Pompey's favour. That way we could approach Pompey, who is difficult to reach. We might persuade him; he would be glad to make trouble for Cato. And by releasing Helene he would again put Caesar under obligation."

Zeuxis chuckled. His superficial subtlety was stirred by Nepos' argument; he saw all sides of it, if not the inside.

"Dionysus! Excellent! Nothing ever was more accurate! Julius Nepos, you are fit to govern Rome; you understand Pompey and Caesar so well! Tros, have you not understood him? Pompey and Caesar lavish favours on each other, while they watch each other like cat and dog. Each hopes to be able to accuse the other of ingratitude when the time comes that they quarrel openly at last. Pompey will compel Cato to set Helene free, and he will tell all Rome he did it to oblige Caesar. He likes nothing better then to get Cato into difficulties with the Roman mob, because he knows that if it weren't for Cato's blunders and lack of tact the old man might be dangerous. Pompey will jump at it! Sell him your Northmen, Tros!"

Zeuxis leaned back and enjoyed the alarm that Tros could not conceal. He knew the Northmen were not slaves. He knew Nepos—understood the old man's combination of ferocity and amiable instinct.

But Tros's subtlety could under-dig the Greek's. He was at bay. He had his men to save, which stirred his wits. And he was not afraid Zeuxis would utterly betray him so long as there were pearls to be obtained by other means than downright treachery.

"The notion is good," he said, rising. "I will visit Pompey. Where is he?"

"As I told you, his wife is ill. You will have to drive out to his country villa, where senators wait at the gate like slaves for the chance of a word with him."

"No," said Nepos. "Pompey comes to Rome tonight. How do I know? Never mind. There are those who must go to Pompey and beg favours; but there are others whom not even Pompey the Great dares refuse if they send for him, no matter at what hour."

"The Vestal Virgins," Zeuxis said, and shuddered. "May the gods protect us from entanglements with them! This mob, that worships venery, adores those virgins and will kill you if they frown. But what should Pompey have to do with them?"

"Doubtless he brings gifts. Possibly he begs a favour for his wife," said Nepos; but he did not look as if he thought that was the reason. He was sly eyed.

"Where will he lodge?" Tros asked him.

"In his own house. Look you now—men have made worse friends than myself, and I love Cato, who is much too obstinate a man to be persuaded. We must get that Helene out of Cato's hands, if we want to keep Cato from being mobbed. Once or twice already they have nearly killed him because he did something stupid—once it was closing the brothels and once it was stopping payment of illegal bills on the treasury. So if you want my friendship, go you to Pompey and ask him to overrule Cato. You will either have to flatter him or buy him. Better both! For twenty gladiators of a new breed he would give you almost anything you ask. Cato will yield; he will have to. That will save his skin, which is what I want, and it may also force him into Pompey's camp, which would be good politics. But never mind politics. Get Helene released and you'll find my friendship worth more to you than Pompey's or any other man's in Rome."

Tros had made up his mind. Orwic, who had learned to recognize the symptoms, strode to the door and opened it. Tros, with a jerk of his head, beckoned Zeuxis. The Greek, too, recognized finality.

"Zeus sneezes and the earth quakes!" he remarked, then took his leave of Nepos, winking and making suggestive movements with his hand when he was sure Tros could not see what he was doing. Nepos' face as he answered Tros's salute was an enigma.

It was dark when they emerged out of the maze of lanes into a street. Torches were already breaking up the gloom where gallants swaggered to some rendezvous amid a swarm of their retainers. The city's voice had altered from the day din to the night roar; it suggested carnival, although there was no merrymaking in the streets; whoever had no bodyguard slunk swiftly through the shadows. Bellowing voices on the stone blocks under yellow lamps announced attractions within walls; the miserable eating-houses and the wine-shops did a thronging trade; but the streets were a danger zone, dagger-infested, along which the prosperous strode in the midst of armed slaves and whoever else ventured went swiftly from shelter to shelter. Dawn never broke but saw the slaves of the *municipium* pick up dead bodies in the street.

"To your house," Tros commanded, as if giving orders from his own poop, and Zeuxis led the way, his five slaves, fussily important, doing their utmost to make the party look too dangerous to interfere with.

But Zeuxis was in no mood to dispute the right of way with any Roman gallant and his gladiators. At the sight of any group of men approaching he turned instantly down side-streets. He preferred to risk a scuffle with the unattached ruffians who made a living by taking one side or the other in the riots that the politicians staged whenever a court decision or a ruling of the senate upset calculations. Such men seldom attacked any one unless paid to do it. Gladiators who attended gallants on their way to dissolute amusement flattered their owners' vanity by bullying any group they met less numerous or pugnacious than their own.

So they were a long time reaching the bridge that crossed the Tiber, and had splashed into many a pool of filth besides unconsciously assuming the rather furtive air that strategy of that sort imposes on pedestrians. The five slaves altogether lost their arrogance. In the glare of the lanterns at the guard-house at the bridge-foot, where the stinking empty fish-boxes were piled and the boat-men slept like corpses on the long ramp leading to the quay, they made no deep impression on the guards of the *municipium*.

"Halt there! Stand aside and wait!"

A gruff ex-legionary, leaning on a spear and leering with the easy insolence acquired in six campaigns, made a gesture that brought six more spearmen into line behind him, barring the narrow approach to the bridge. Over beyond the river there was torchlight. There came a trumpet call. It was answered by shouts from guards stationed at intervals along the parapet in impenetrable darkness. Lights on the bridge were forbidden.

Then another trumpet call. Presently a stream of torchlight flowed on to the bridge, its glare reflected is the water. Fire laws, or any other laws, are subtly honoured when the famous disobey them.

"Who comes? Pompey!" said the spearman, grinning into Tros's face. "Better get out of the way, my friend!"

His insolence was tempered by familiarity. He seemed to recognize in Tros an old campaigner like himself. Though Tros stood still, he made no effort to enforce the order, merely moving his head sidewise, curiously, to observe him with a better slant of light. The wooden bridge began to thunder to the tramp of men all breaking step.

"Let us stand back in the shadow!" Zeuxis whispered and set the example, followed by his slaves, but Tros remained facing the spearman and Orwic, arms folded, stood with him.

"Are you one of Pompey's veterans by any chance?" the spearman asked. "Take my advice, friend. This is a poor place and a poor time to approach him."

"He expects me," Tros answered and the spearman stared at him with new appreciation.

"You are either over-bold or more important than you look with that small following," he said. "We will see. We will see. I have seen strange happenings in my day."

Tros turned to Orwic and spoke quietly in Gaulish:

"When the lictors order us to stand aside, keep place abreast of me."

A horse's head—a phantom in the torchlight—tossed above the lictors' fasces. Dimly, behind them, more horses appeared, and streams of men on foot, like shadows, with the torchlight shining here and there on armour or an ornament; but there was silence except the groaning of the bridge's timbers and the echoing tramp of feet. There was a sense of mystery—or portent.

Suddenly the man in front of Tros threw up his spear and swung the men behind him into line, facing the roadway. They stood rigidly, like statues, as the lictors, two lines of four in single file, advanced with all the dignity attainable by human symbols of authority in motion. Stately, measured, neither slow nor fast but like the passing of the hours into eternity, they strode toward Tros, and he was no such fool as to attempt to let the two files pass on either hand. Though Rome was rotten at the core, that very fact increased insistence on respect for the tokens of her magistracy. To have dared to stand ground would have meant, more likely than an interview with Pompey, a cudgelling and then a ducking in the Tiber. He shouted before they reached him.

"Pompeius Magnus, hail!"

His voice was like a captain's on his poop—resounding, sudden, vibrant with assurance. There was something of a gong note in it.

"I am Tros of Samothrace!"

"Halt!" said a bored voice and a dozen men repeated the command. There was a rush of footmen to surround the leader's horse, then silence so tense that the swirling of the river past the bridge-piles struck on the ear like music.

Torches moved, swaying confusedly. Pompey, his cloak thrown back so that torchlight gleamed on the gold inlay of his breastplate, leaned forward on his horse, shielding his eyes with his right hand. "Who did the man say he is?"

"I am Tros of Samothrace."

"I believe I remember him. Let him approach."

Two lictors lined up, one on either side of Tros; two more opposed themselves to Orwic and prevented him from following. Tros was marched to about half a spear's length from Pompey's stirrup, where the lictors signed to him to stand still and a dozen faces peered at him.

"Is this an omen, Tros?" asked Pompey in a pleasant, cultured voice suggestive of half humorous contempt for his surroundings. "I remember you. I gave your father leave to use all Roman ports. I trust he has not misused that privilege."

"He is dead," said Tros. "I have word for your private ear."

"All Rome has that!" said Pompey. "I am pestered with communications. However, I will hear you. What is it?"

"Secret as well as urgent. Name place and hour and let me speak with you alone. I seek nothing for myself."

"Rare individual! Comites," said Pompey, laughing in the patronizing way of men who have been flattered until all comment becomes condescension, "here is a man who has sufficient. He asks nothing! Envy him! So many of us have too much!"

He stared at Tros, signing to some of the slaves to move the torches so that he could better read his face. His own was pouched under the eyes but rather handsome in a florid, heavy, thick-set way. His eyes glittered. The lips curled proudly, and he sat his horse easily, gracefully, with rather portly dignity. He looked as if success had softened him without his being aware of it, but there were no signs of debauch.

"You may follow," he said, "and I will hear you when I have time."

But Tros had cooled his heels once too often in the anterooms of Alexandria, where Ptolemy's eunuchs pocketed the fees of applicants, kept them waiting and dismissed them without audience, to be pigeon-holed as easily as that. His sureness that the gods were all around him made him no cringing supplicant.

"You may listen or not, as you please, Pompeius Magnus. I have crossed two seas to speak with you. Name me an hour and a place, or I will find another who will listen."

Pompey legged his horse to hide astonishment. In all Rome there was only Cato who had dared to affront him since Crassus went away. A handsome youngster strode into the torchlight and stood swaggering in front of Tros.

"Do you know to whom you speak?" he demanded.

"Please, Flavius! Stand aside!" said Pompey, reining his horse toward Tros again. "This may prove interesting. Tros, do you know where the temple of Vesta stands? Approach me there, after the morning ceremony. Forward!"

The two lictors hustled Tros aside. The bridge began to tremble as the march resumed and Pompey passed on into darkness, torchlight gleaming on the shield and helmet carried for him by a slave in close attendance.

"You are mad!" remarked Zeuxis, striding gallantly enough out of the shadow when the last of the long cortege had streamed by and a roar in the narrow city streets announced that Pompey, recognized already, was receiving an ovation. "If you go to the temple of Vesta Pompey will offer you employment, for the sake of obtaining your Northmen and Britons, about whom Nepos certainly will tell him before midnight. And if you refuse, he will seize your men for the arena. He will throw you into prison if you make the least fuss; he will simply say you are the enemy of Rome. You are as mad as Cato himself! You should have won his favour while you had the opportunity."

"You will do well if you earn mine!" Tros retorted, visibly annoyed. "Lead on." Zeuxis fell into stride beside him but there was no more talk until they came to Zeuxis' house. Relationship of host and guest was obviously superficial now. Neither man trusted the other. Even Orwic, who could understand no word of Greek or Latin, realized that Zeuxis' house had turned into a place of danger rather than a refuge.

Virgo Vestalis Maxima

*How I wonder at the credulous who think their impu-
dence endows them with all knowledge! So vast is their
credulity that if they hear of something that they understand not, they declare it is not. Such is their credulity
that they believe their senses. But they disbelieve in spirit,
though they see death all around them and not even their
ignorance pretends to know what breathed the life into that
which dies when the breath is withdrawn.*

—From the Log of Tros of Samothrace

Tros wished now he had come to Rome without his men—
even without Orwic. He would have been safer without them. He
could easily have hired two dozen Romans to act as bodyguard;
he might even have bought gladiators; there were second-hand
ones, maimed, that could be bought cheap. But all those possibili-
ties had occurred to him before he left his ship, outside Tarentum
Harbour, and his real reason for bringing both Northmen and
Britons remained as important as ever; they were hostages.

However much he trusted Sigurdsen, he knew he could better trust him not to sail away and turn to piracy so long as
eight of his nearest relatives and a dozen other countrymen were
ashore and counting on him to keep tryst. The Britons on the
ship were not particularly loyal to Orwic; they might not hesitate to leave him languishing on foreign soil; but the Northmen
were as loyal to one another as even Tros himself could be to any
man who served him honestly.

But that consideration made it all the more essential to save the men he had with him. If they should lose their lives in a fair fight, that might strengthen the bond between him and their relatives on board the ship, it being Northman aspiration to die fighting; but to lose them like a dunder-headed yokel choused out of his wares would be an insult and a breach of trust for which no Northman would forgive him any more than he, Tros, could forgive himself.

He could see through Zeuxis' subtlety. He suspected the Greek had all along known that the praetor's men were nowhere near his house. Zeuxis might have staged that panic in order to introduce Nepos, who, he probably felt sure, would try to get Tros's Northmen for the school of gladiators. Should Tros's men be seized on some pretext, it would be a typical Greek trick to ask for pearls with which to purchase their release. And no bag of pearls would be deep enough. He saw through Zeuxis.

That being so, he surprised him. He preferred, if destiny intended he should lose his men, to do the thing himself, and blame himself, rather than enrich a treacherous acquaintance—and the more so when suspicion was corroborated by the Northmen after he reached Zeuxis' house.

He went straight to the Northmen's quarters. There were lodged in a barn between the cow-byre and the long, low, crowded sheds in which the Greek's slaves lived. When he aroused them from sleep they reported there had been no difficulties such as Zeuxis' slave had spoken of. They had not feared for Tros. They hardly knew he was away. Some slave-women who knew Gaulish had made love to them and tried to persuade them to get drunk. But they had kept their promise and behaved themselves, suspecting trickery. Besides, they had not known when Tros might need their services, so they had slept whenever visitors would let them. Between times they had mended foot-gear, persuading the Britons to do the same thing, to keep the Britons out of mischief.

There was nothing to be done with the weapons or baggage but to leave them all in Zeuxis' charge. Tros did not dare to enter Rome with armed men at his back. Not even Pompey would have let his followers wear more than daggers openly, when they were once inside the city walls, unless the senate should expressly grant permission—not that Pompey cared a copper as for what the senate thought, but to have done so would have been tantamount to a declaration that he had assumed the sole dictatorship—which would have brought Caesar hurrying from Gaul to wrest it from him.

So Tros told the Northmen to hide daggers in their tunics and make bundles of their other weapons to be left wherever Zeuxis cared to stow them. He disarmed the Britons altogether, since he could not depend on them to keep their heads in an emergency. Then, telling each man to equip himself with a flask and haversack, he bribed Zeuxis' steward heavily to serve out rations for a day or two. Experience had taught him that the Northmen's zeal depended on their stomachs much more than was the case with men from southern lands. Well fed, he would have dared to lead them against twice their tale of Roman legionaries; hungry, they would run away from ghosts.

Then he went to his room and dressed himself in his gorgeous oriental cloak and Grecian tunic, presently joining Zeuxis at the supper-table, where they were waited on by girls—descendants of the decadents who ruined Greece. It was the steward, whispering, who broke the news to Zeuxis that Tros's men were ready for a night-march.

"You desert me?" Zeuxis asked, with viperish resentment in his voice. But he was not so startled that he did not gesture to a slave girl to pay Tros more intimate attention. "Surely you will sleep here? You can leave at dawn and be at the shrine of Vesta before Pompey reaches it."

"If I should wait, I would have more to beg of Pompey than I care to crave from any man," Tros answered. "Guard my baggage, Zeuxis, and remember—I have promised you nine pearls on a condition. If I fail, or if you fail me, though I had to throw a thousand pearls into the Tiber I would take care you should get none! I perceive your friendship is a purchasable merchandise. I bid high, and I paid you half down when we struck the bargain."

Zeuxis' lustrously immoral eyes were looking at Tros's cloak. As plainly as if speech had said it, he was wondering where so great a weight of pearls was hidden. The lust that jewels have the power to arouse in some men, and some women, burned behind the Greek's eyes. The smile that stole over his face was like a mask deliberately chosen—thoughtfully adjusted—changed a time or two until he thought it fitted.

"Drink, noble guest!" he said, and signed to a Syrian slave to fill the cups. "This night has gone to both our heads. We talk like madmen rather than two sons of Hellas. Samothrace is stepson to Eleusis—drink! I pledge you brotherhood. May wise Athene's owls bear midnight wisdom to you. Drink!"

But Tros set down the silver cup untasted. Though he doubted that his host would poison him, he knew the Syrian slaves' infernal skill and read the greed in Zeuxis' eyes.

"Pallas Athene, judge then! I will drink with you again, friend Zeuxis, when I have accomplished my purpose. Though the goddess deserted Hellas, may her wisdom govern us! And now your drooping eyelids welcome sleep, so I will act the good guest and not stand in Morpheus' way. Sleep soundly, and may all Olympus bless you for your hospitality."

He took his leave magnificently, as if Zeuxis were a king, bestowing largess on the servants and avoiding any conversation that could give the Greek a hint of his intentions. He refused the offer of a guide; such a man would merely be a spy for Zeuxis. He laughed as he strode toward Rome at the head of his men, for a slave went by on horseback, full pelt; and although he did not recognize the man, he was as sure as that the moon was rising on his right hand, that the Greek had sent a messenger to Pompey, or else Nepos, which amounted to the same thing. Pompey would learn of the pearls before dawn or, if not Pompey, one of Pompey's personal lieutenants, which might be even more dangerous.

He had one advantage. Wind and sea observe no hour-glass; he who has stood watch, and reefed, and gone aloft in midnight gales has lost the greater part of that inertia that dulls the wits of superstitious men in darkness. Tros could take advantage of the night and steal a march on treachery; and he thought he could count on his men to obey him though the shadows seemed to hint at unseen horror—though the Via Appia was lined with tombs and gloomy cypresses all haunted by the spectres of the dead, and wind sighed through the trees like ghost-worlds whispering.

"I am afraid," said Orwic, striding beside Tros. "We Britons have an extra sense that warns us of things we can't see. My grandmother had the gift remarkably, and I inherit it. I wish I had a sword. This dagger isn't much use."

"Play the prince!" Tros answered gruffly. "Any fool can be afraid at night."

Himself, he had only one dread, one pertinent regret. He feared for Conops, who could hide himself in Ostia and watch for the arrival of the ship without the least risk of detection, if only Zeuxis had not known about it. He gritted his teeth as he condemned himself for not having sent Conops straight to Ostia before he ever entered Zeuxis' house. More to encourage himself than for Orwic's benefit, he broke out in explosive sentences:

"A man can't think of everything. The gods must do their part. We should be gods, not men, if we could foresee all. It would be impudence to take the full responsibility for what will happen. Are the gods dead—dumb—ignorant? And shall a god not recognize emergency?"

"Suppose we pray," suggested Orwic.

"Like a lot of lousy beggars. Rot me any gods who listen to such whining! Shall the gods descend and smirch themselves amid our swinery, or shall we rise and breathe their wisdom?"

Orwic shuddered. Celt-like, it disturbed him to assume familiarity with unseen agencies. Drunk or sober, he could swear with any lover of swift action, taking half the names of Britain's gods in vain, but when it came to thinking of the gods as powers to be reckoned with he thrilled with reverence. He could, and he invariably did, scorn druids in the abstract. In the presence of a druid he was insolent to hide his feelings. And when—as Tros invariably did—he felt himself within the orbit of the gods he was more fearful of them than encouraged—whereas Tros regarded gods as friends, who laughed at men's absurdities, despised their cowardice and took delight only in bravery, honesty, willingness, zeal.

"I think I hear the gods," said Orwic; for the trees were whispering. An owl swooped by on noiseless wings. The shadows moved in moonlight. "What if the gods are warning us to turn back? What can thirty of us do in Rome to hinder Caesar? We have been having bad luck since the boat upset us in Tarentum Harbour. We were robbed in the inns on the road, and we were cheated by stage-contractors—eaten by the bedbugs—sickened by the bad food and the worse wine. Then Zeuxis' house, and treachery if ever I sensed it with every nerve of my skin! Cato—and what good did that do? He simply arrested that woman, which will turn her into our malignant enemy! Now we march into Rome without weapons, to see Pompey, who—"

Tros silenced him with an oath.

"Take all my men then! Go to Ostia! Wait there! I will do better alone, without such croaking in my ears!"

"No," Orwic answered. "By the blood of Lud of Lunden, I will not desert you. You are a man, Tros. I would rather die with you than run away and live. But I am not confident, nevertheless. I think this is a desperate affair."

"It is the gods' affair," Tros answered. "Nothing that the gods approve is desperate."

The Northmen, meanwhile, swung along the road with the determined step of well-fed venturers whose faith was in their leader. Two circumstances gave them confidence—that Tros was wearing his embroidered cloak implied that he anticipated welcome from important personages; and that they had left their weapons in Zeuxis' barn convinced them trouble was unlikely. They were thrilled by the thought of exploring Rome—the fabulous city of which they had heard tales by the winter firelight in their northern homes; and they began to sing a marching song, the Britons taking courage of example, humming the tune with them. And when men sing on the march their leader

71

grows aware of spiritual thrills not easy to explain, but comforting. That singing did more to restore Orwic's nerve than all Tros's argument, and Tros grew silent because pride in his men smothered lesser emotions.

By the great stone gate, the Porta Capena, the guards of the *municipium* stared sleepily, but they were no more than police. The city was defended on her frontiers—far-flung. Mistress of all Italy and half the world, Rome recognized no need to shut her gates; they stood wide, rusting on their hinges like the Gates of Janus at the Forum that were never closed unless the whole Republic was at peace, as had happened in no man's memory. Tros led in through the gate unchallenged and at that hour of the night there were no parties of young gallants and their gladiators to dispute the right of way. Rare guards, patrolling two by two, raised lanterns as they passed, by way of a salute. More rarely, a belated pair of citizens, escorting each other homeward from a rich man's table, hurried down a side-street to avoid them. Now and then a voice cried from a roof or from an upper window in praise of Pompey; coming in the wake of the ovation Pompey had received. Tros benefited by it; men supposed he was bringing in the rearguard of Pompey's followers. Notoriously Pompey never entered Rome with any show of military power; it was like him to divide his following and bring the last lot in at midnight. There were even some who caught sight of the gold embroidery on Tros's cloak as he passed a lantern flickering before a rich man's house and mistook him for Pompey himself; but, since it was to no man's profit to inquire too closely into Pompey's doings in the night, those flurries of excitement died as suddenly as they were born.

But in the Forum there were guards who dared not sleep, since they protected jewellers and money-changers and the officers of bankers who bought and sold drafts on the ends of the earth. Nine-tenths of Rome's own business was done by draft, men trading in each other's debts until the interwoven maze of liabilities became too complicated to unravel and the slave was lucky who could say who rightly owned him. Where the round shrine of the Flame of Vesta stood—Rome's serenest building, in which the Vestal Virgins tended the undying fire and no unhallowed eye; beheld the seven symbols hidden there, on which Rome's destiny depended—there were lictors and a lictor's guard.

Another lictor and his guard stood over by the Atrium, where the Vestals lived in splendid dignity; and yet another lictor stood watch by the Regia, headquarters of the one man in the world who had authority to choose and to appoint, and even to condemn to living burial, if they should break their vow of chastity, the six most sacred personages whom Rome the more revered the more her own unchastity increased.

By daylight, when the Forum roared under a roasting sun, there was no understanding Rome's invincibility. But in the night below the frowning shadow of great Jupiter's Etruscan fane that loomed over the Capitol, when only lanterns and the lonely guards disturbed the solitude, and moonlight shone on rows of statues of the men who had drenched Rome in blood, or had defended her against Epirus, against Carthage, against Spartacus—of men who had returned from laying Rome's heel on the necks of Hispania and Greece and Asia—of stern men who had made her laws and stalwarts who had broken them but never dreamed of Rome as less than their triumphant mother—understanding swept over a man, and even Tros stood still in admiration, hating while he wondered.

Orwic stood spellbound. The Northmen gazed and hardly breathed. Awe stirred imagination and they thought they saw the images of gods who governed Rome. To them the stillness was alive with awful entities.

A bell rang—one note, silver and serene, in harmony with moonlight and the marble. Silently, as if a grave gave up its dead, the shrouded figure of a woman came out of the Vestals' palace. Instantly, as if he stepped out of another world, a lictor took his place in front of her and led toward the shrine of Vesta. Slaves, more dignified and gentle looking than free women, followed. Every guard within the Forum precincts came to statuesque attention and Tros raised his right hand, bowing.

The procession passed and vanished into shadow in the porch of Vesta's shrine. Tros signalled to his men to form up; silently they lined the route between the palace and the shrine, ten paces back from it. Tros growled in Orwic's ear:

"I told you the gods guided us! I did not know the hour the Vestals changed the watch."

He stood alone in front of all his men, a fine, heroic figure with the leaner, lither looking Briton half a pace behind him. On his right, in line with Orwic, the grim, bearded giant who served as deputy lieutenant of the Northmen, in place of Sigurdsen who had to bring the ship to Ostia, stood breathing like a grampus.

Then again, the one note on the silver bell. The lictor strode out of the shadow and the same procession wended its way back toward the palace, only that the Vestal Virgin this time was an older woman, statelier, who walked more heavily. Folds of her pallium, ample and studiedly hung, the arrangement of pallium over her head to resemble a hood, the repose of her shoulders and rhythm of movement united to make her resemble an image of womanly dignity conjured to life. Not the lictor himself, with his consciousness of centuries-old symbolism, more than echoed her expression of sublime, accepted and unquestionable honour. She was majesty itself—aloof, alone, so higher than the law that she looked neither to the right nor left, lest some one in the law's toils should be able to claim recognition and be set free. None, even on the way to execution, could behold a Vestal Virgin's face and be denied his liberty.

As she approached, Tros bent his right knee, raising his right hand, his head bowed. Orwic, uninstructed, copied him. The Northmen and the Britons knelt like shadows thrown by moonlight on the paving-stones, as Tros's voice broke the silence.

"*Virgo vestalis maxima!*"

Lover of all pageantry, and scornful of all life that was not drama, he omitted no vibration from his voice that might add to the scene's solemnity. It rang with reverence, but was a challenge, none the less. No less obsequious, more dignity-conceding summons to attention ever reached a Vestal Virgin's ears! It was the voice of strength adjuring strength—of purpose that evoked authority!

The Vestal faced him, pausing, and the lictor seemed in doubt exactly what to do; he lowered his fasces, the edge of the axe toward Tros, who made a gesture, raising both hands upward and then, standing upright, spoke exactly seven syllables in a language neither Orwic, nor the lictor, nor the Vestal's servants understood. But the Vestal drew aside the pallium that half-concealed her face—not speaking—pale and as severe as chastity, her middle-aged patrician features hard as marble in the moon's rays.

"In the Name I may not utter, audience!"

She nodded, saying something to the lictor, and passed on. The lictor signed to Tros to follow at a decent distance and three women, hooded like the three Fates, arm-in-arm, lingered a little to make certain of the interval, their glances over-shoulder not suggesting any invitation to draw nearer. Tros signed to his men to follow. Not a sanctuary in the sense that criminals might find a refuge there, the portico before the Vestal's palace was a place where waiting, unarmed men were hardly likely to be challenged.

At the palace door he was kept waiting so interminably that his men grew restless. Orwic whispered that another night was wasted. But the lictor came at last through a painted, carved door opening on silent hinges. The lictor beckoned. Orwic followed Tros.

They stepped on marble into a dim magnificence. An atrium adorned with columns and the statues of dead Vestals faded into gloom, so that the walls were hardly seen. Gold glinted on the cornices. There was a glimpse of marble stairs. Dark tapestries receded into shadow. There were two chairs, ebony and ivory, beneath a canopy between two pillars; and a rug was spread before the chairs that Pompey looted from the bed-chamber of Mithridates' queen—a thing of gorgeous silences, in which the feet sank deep.

The lictor turned his back toward the door, his fasces raised. A bell, whose note was like the drip of water in a silver basin, rang once and a curtain moved. In dim light from the lanterns near the canopy two Vestals—she to whom Tros had spoken and another, twenty years her junior—each followed by her women, entered and the women rearranged the folds of their white pallia as they were seated.

"You may approach now," said the lictor.

The chief Vestal murmured, hardly opening her lips. Slave-women moved into shadow. The surrounding gloom became alive with eyes and figures almost motionless but it was possible to speak low-voiced and be unheard by any but the Vestals. Tros and Orwic marched up to the carpet, bowed with their right hands raised, and stood erect, waiting until the chief of the Vestals spoke.

"Your name?" she asked.

Her tone implied authority that none had challenged. Equally, no pride obscured her calm intelligence; she looked like one at peace within herself, because she understood and was assured of peace whatever happened. There was candour in her eyes that might turn cruel, but no weakness and not too much mercy. She was the patrician, consciously above the law and none the less steel-fettered by a higher law of duty.

"I am Tros of Samothrace."

"You have appealed in the unutterable Name. It is forbidden to seek favours for yourself in that Name. Nor am I initiated in the mysteries that you invoke, save in so far as I must recognize all branches of the Tree. For whom do you seek benevolence?"

Tros, taking Orwic's hand, presented him, the younger man not lacking dignity; his inborn aristocracy impelled him to behave as if the Vestal, of whose virtues he was ignorant, was no less than an empress. He conveyed the unmistakable suggestion that respect paid by himself was something that the very gods might envy—and the Vestal smiled.

"Orwic, a prince of Britain," Tros announced. "Regrettably he knows no Latin."

In his heart he laughed to think that Orwic knew no Latin. He could plead the Britons' cause more artfully than any Briton could, and run less risk of noosing his own neck.

"You seek benevolence for him? Is he accused of crime? Is he a fugitive from justice?"

The Vestal's voice was tinged with iron now. She held her power to set aside the law—no cheap thing, not a force to be invoked for ordinary reasons. Conscious of responsibility as well as privilege, doubtless, too, she understood the value of not interfering often; privileges, strengthened by their rare use, grow intolerable and are lopped off when they cease to be a nine days' wonder—which is something that the privileged too seldom bear in mind.

"Virgo vestalis maxima, we plead for Britain! Caesar plans invasion against people who have done no injury to Rome. The Roman law permits him to declare war and to make peace as he chooses, and the Roman senate is as powerless as I am to prevent him. We appeal to you, who are above the Roman law—"

"Caesar is Pontifex Maximus!" the Vestal interrupted. "I will hear no calumnies."

But Tros knew that. He knew that Caesar was the only man on earth who even nominally had authority to discipline the Vestals, and he guessed that was the key to Caesar's plans. Though theoretically uncontaminated by political intrigue, the Vestals' influence was much the subtlest force in Rome; it easily might be the factor that should tip the scales in Caesar's favour, more particularly since his influence depended on the plebes, whose favour he had always courted. Not even Marius, nor Sulla at the height of the proscriptions when the garden of his private villa was a torture-yard and headless corpses strewed the paths, had dared to refuse clemency to any one the Vestals indicated. It was not in the arena only that their thumbs turned upward could avert the very blood-lust of the crowd, though only there, when a man lay bleeding on the sand, was their interference open. It was never challenged, because not abused; they never interfered to save a sentenced criminal. The crowd, that enjoyed butchery ten times as much because it took place in the presence of the Vestals, had an extra thrill whenever the six Virgins autocratically spared a victim. As far-sighted as he was ambitious, Caesar had chosen the office of Pontifex Maximus as his first step toward malting himself master of the whole republic, and there had been many an apparent stroke of luck since then that might have been explained as something far more calculable if the Vestals had not been past-mistresses of silence. Tros's last thought would be to try to turn them against Caesar.

"I have come to assist Caesar," he said, swallowing. Resentment against destiny half-choked him. "Virgo beatissima, my father was a prince of Samothrace. He foretold, with his last breath, when his spirit stood between two worlds and he could see into the future and the past, that I, his son, should turn away from enmity of Caesar and befriend him. This I do, not gladly, but with goodwill, since I know no other way of saving Britain, and a friendship may not be forgotten for the sake of enmity. The Britons are my friends. So I will yield my enmity and be of use to Caesar, though three times to his face I have repudiated him."

The Vestal nodded. Though aloofness limits men and women in the field of action, it enlarges their ability to see deep into character.

"How shall you save Britain and be Caesar's friend?" she asked.

"Virgo vestalis maxima, can Rome survive, if Caesar fails?" Tros answered. "He will meet with resistance in the Isle of Britain that will tax his strength and give the Gauls encouragement to rise behind him. What then? Are the patricians strong enough, or well enough united to keep Rome from anarchy, if Caesar meets disaster? Can Pompey hold the factions that would fly at one another's throats if Caesar's standards fell?"

"What if Caesar should prevail in Britain?" asked the Vestal.

"Virgo beatissima, if all Rome's legions should invade that wooded isle, in five years they could not boast they had conquered it! There is a race of men who have defeated Caesar once. There is a king who will oppose him while the last man breathes."

"Yet Mithridates fell. Is Gaul free?"

"Wait yet for the news of Crassus!" Tros retorted. "Roman arms are not invincible. Let only Crassus meet defeat, and Caesar fail to conquer Britain—who then shall preserve Rome from the people's tribunes and the mobs? Pompey? The patrician who holds his nose because the rabble's stench offends him? Pompey, who has twice let pass an opportunity to seize the reins? Pompey, who refuses the dictatorship because he knows his popularity would melt like butter in the sun? Pompey, whom the tribunes hate because he lords it over them, and keeps postponing the elections to upset their plans? Will tribunes, and the mobs they lead, serve Pompey—or rebel? And if the people's tribunes should successfully rebel, how long then—"

The Vestal stopped him with a gesture, frowning. It was not compatible with dignity to lend ear to a stranger's views of what demagogues might do to Rome's most sacred institutions.

"For a stranger you are possessed by a strange interest for Rome," she said ironically.

"Rome is not my city, but I know her weakness and her strength," said Tros. "I would rather save Rome than see Britain ravished by the legions to whom Caesar has been promising the plunder."

"Caesar is not straw blown by the wind," she answered. "Nor is he a slave to be beckoned—"

Tros slipped a hand under his cloak.

"Nor a hireling to be bought," she added, sure she understood that gesture. "He is not like Cato, who prefers the lesser of two evils; Caesar seizes on the greater evil as the keenest weapon. Nor does he resemble Cicero, whom gratitude or grudge can turn into a purblind hypocrite. Caesar is not Antonius, whom the mob's praise renders drunk. Nor is he a fool like Sulla, using power for revenge; he makes friends of his enemies if they will yield to him. There is no man in the world like Caesar. Who shall tame his pride?"

"But one may foster it," said Tros, and put his hand under his

79

cloak again. When he drew it forth there rested on his palm a heavy leather bag, not large but tightly filled and tied around the neck with gold wire.

"Why," he asked, "does Caesar say he goes to Britain? What bid has he made to justify himself?"

The Vestal almost smiled.

"He has told all Rome that he will bring back pearls," she answered, "for a breastplate for the Venus Genetrix."

"These pearls," said Tros, "are plenty for that purpose—I am told they are superior to those that Pompey brought from Asia and put on exhibition in a temple, but did not give. They were entrusted to me by those who ponder over Britain's destiny. I am to use them as I see fit, in the cause of Britain. Virgo beatissima, I crave leave to deposit them in your charge, as a trust, for Caesar's use, to be employed by him to make the breastplate for the goddess, to be known as his gift, if—and only if—he turns back from invading Britain!"

Not one moment did the Vestal hesitate.

"You ask what I may not refuse," she answered. "Whosoever obtains audience may leave whatever sacred things he pleases in my charge. But had I known what you intended you would not have been received! I am not Caesar's monitor; nor have I any means of reaching him. If it were known in Rome that—"

She glanced sharply at the younger Vestal—then at the lictor over by the door—then swiftly into the shadows where her women stood, all eyes—but they were out of earshot.

"Were it known that I send messengers to Caesar," she said, lowering her voice, "all Rome would say the Vestal Virgins are no longer higher than intrigue. And Caesar's ways are too well known. No woman corresponds with Caesar and remains above suspicion."

"Virgo beatissima, send me!" said Tros. "I have a ship—my own swift, splendid ship, well manned. By the unutterable Name, I swear that rather than betray you to the Romans I will taste death sooner than my destiny intends, and every man of mine shall taste it with me! I fulfil a friendship, than which no more

80

godlike course is open to a man in this life. And I hold that he who trims his sails to catch the gods' wind, wrecks his soul if he breaks faith! If you think Caesar can save Rome from anarchy, send me to save him from invading Britain, where he will only squander strength and wreak a havoc, while Rome dies, mad and masterless!"

"I can not protect you. I can not acknowledge you—except to Caesar," said the Vestal.

"Let the gods protect me! Let the gods acknowledge me!" Tros answered. "If I will do my duty they will do theirs."

For a while the Vestal pondered that, chin resting on her hand, her elbow on the chair-arm.

"Caesar's pride will be well satisfied," she said at last. "If he could make believe he had brought pearls from Britain for the Venus Genetrix—he might assert they are a tribute from the Britons—that would glut his craving for renown, at least a little while. He is a madman with a god's ability, a man's lust to appear generous, and a fool's ignorance of where to stop and when to turn. He might have been a god. He is a devil. But he can save Rome, being ruthless, and because, although he panders to the mob, he will deceive them, saving Rome's heart, seeming to supplant her head. Rome may live because of Caesar and in spite of him."

"I am not Rome's advocate, but I will serve Rome for the sake of Britain," Tros exclaimed. He held the bag of pearls out in his right hand, kneeling. "Virgo beatissima, so send me now to Caesar with your word."

The Vestal took the bag of pearls into her lap and Tros stood up. Not even in a climax of emotion did it suit his nature to stay long on bent knee. Even reverence had limits.

The Vestal beckoned and a woman came; she whispered and the woman brought a golden bowl, engraved with figures of the Muses, that had once adorned a temple before Sulla raped the shrines of Hellas. When the woman had retired into the shadows she undid the golden thread and poured the pearls into the bowl, the other Vestal leaning to admire them, not exclaiming and not opening her lips—but her nostrils and her throat moved suddenly, as if she caught her breath. Tros had not enlarged beyond the bounds of truth. Not even Rome that plundered Ephesus had seen such treasure in one heap. Those pearls, under the lamp light, were like tears shed by a conquered people's gods.

"Draw nearer," said the Vestal, and again Tros knelt, that she might whisper in his ear. She said one word, then laid her finger on his lips.

"That word," she said, "will be sufficient proof to Caesar that you come from me. He will believe your lips. But if you use it falsely, then I know of no death and of no curse that were not bliss as compared to what your destiny will hold! There are degrees of shame below the reach of thought. And there are depths of misery where worms that crawl in corruption appear godlike in comparison to him who dies so deep! Not Tantalus, who told the secrets of the gods, knows suffering so dreadful, as shall he who violates that confidence!"

"I keep faith, not from fear," Tros answered, rising stubbornly. "What word shall I take to Caesar?"

"Bid him look toward Rome! Bid him waste no energy, but keep his hands on Gaul, that when the hour strikes he may leave Gaul tranquil at his back."

Tros bowed. Her attitude appeared to signify the interview was over, but he had a task yet—and he needed for it greater daring than he had yet summoned from the storehouse of his faith in the invincibility of promises performed. He had assured Helene he would do her no harm if she trusted him; his own interpretation of that promise was a thousand times more generous than any she was likely to assume. Mistaken he had been in letting Zeuxis guide him to her house, and he had made a worse mistake confiding in her; but none of that was her fault. He would set right the results of that—and yet if he proposed to save her from the praetor's torturers he must summon enough brazen impudence to plead, before a woman whose authority depended on her chastity, for mercy for an alien whose insolent contempt of chastity was typical of what was steadily destroying Rome!

He made abrupt, curt work of it:

"If Caesar is to save Rome, let him use all agencies," he said. "There is a woman in the clutches of the praetor's men, whom Caesar had employed to ferret information. Helene, the daughter of Theseus of Alexandria—"

"That immodest rake—!"

"Is Caesar an immaculate?"

"Caesar is Pontifex Maximus. For Rome, and for the sake of institutions older than the city, I let myself see only Caesar's virtue. For that woman I will not offend against the public decency by turning up my thumb!"

"Virgo beatissima, let Pompey carry that blame!" Tros retorted. "He has violated modesty so often that one more offence will hardly spoil his record! I am told he comes—"

"At dawn," she said, "to offer sacrifices for his wife's recovery."

"Virgo vestalis maxima, one word from you will be enough. If Caesar's daughter—Pompey's wife—dies, who then shall keep Pompey from defying Caesar? Will the mob not rend Rome unless Caesar can prevail over the patrician factions, into whose hands Pompey will deliver Rome's fate? And shall Caesar be allowed to fail because, forsooth, unquestioned chastity was timid and too careful of itself to whisper in behalf of Caesar's spy?"

"You overstep your privilege," the Vestal answered frowning. "I will mention her to Pompey. I will keep these pearls in trust, for Caesar's gift to Venus Genetrix, provided he draws back from Britain. But remember—I can not protect you or acknowledge you. Farewell."

She rose, inclining her head slightly in reply to Tros's salute, her dark eyes curiously scanning Orwic, whose expression suggested a schoolboy's when a lesson-period was over.

"This way!" said the lictor loudly. "This way! More to the right!"

Tros and Orwic backed, until the silent door shut slowly in their faces and they turned, expecting to be greeted by the Northmen.

They were gone! The portico was empty. Silence, silver moonlight and a Forum peopled only by the statues and the watchful guards, who leaned against the closed shop-windows.

Silently a lictor, followed by a file of four men in the Vestals' livery, emerged out of the shadows and stood guard before the Vestals' door.

"Move on!" he ordered arrogantly. "This is no place for loiterers!"

The Praetor's Dungeon

*I have seen more lands than many men have heard of,
and more dungeons than most men believe there are. Ever I
visit dungeons, because their keepers are seldom as cruel as
their masters who commit the victims to living death in the
name of justice. Many a man, for a coin or two to ease a
jailor's avarice, has died on parchment. Many a corpse has
pulled an oar on my ship—aye, and pulled well, no better, it
may be, but at least no worse for freedom and work.*

*If I see a city's dungeons, thereafter that city's rulers are
an open book. The worse the dungeon, the more surely the
city's rulers are unfit to clean it; justice is for sale in that
city, and its dungeons are a likeness of its rulers' hearts.*

—FROM THE LOG OF TROS OF SAMOTHRACE

Tros's first impulse was to rush around corners and hunt for
his men. Orwic's bewilderment brought out his reserves of level-
headedness.

"If they are near, we shall soon know it," he said, shrugging
off the tremor he felt creeping up his spine. "If they are far, then
only wits, not feet, can find them."

He strode up to the nearest watchman, who lounged
against a shop-front entertaining himself by plaiting a wrist-
thong for the vicious looking bill-hook of a weapon that
he carried. The free man, an Etruscan, merely grinned when
questioned, spat, and called Tros "Pretty Hercules"—then
asked whether the gods had use for money on Olympus. Tros

produced a coin. The Etruscan spun it in the air. As he caught it back-handed and spun it again he answered Tros's question by putting another:

"Will they seat you in among the equites? Or are you an ambassador? The senate sometimes entertains ambassadors in very good seats, but the compliment fools nobody. Ambassadors in Rome pay richly for whatever courtesy they get. Me? I am paid to guard this goldsmith's. Is there no more money in Olympus? Have our Roman armies stripped that treasury, too?"

Tros showed him another coin and let the moonlight glint on it.

"Which way did my men go?" he asked. "Who took them?"

"How should I know they were your men? Who else should know it, either? I should say they were suspicious characters and that's what the praetor's man thought, evidently."

Fifty guards could not have arrested his Northmen without a clamour that would have wakened Rome. There had been trickery, not violence. He showed the coin again.

"The praetor's man may have thought there was a bribe let to pick up, but he could not make those wooden-headed fellows understand him. What were they doing, lurking in the Vestals' portico? He had a right to order them away. But it is forbidden to make noises there at night, so he tried arguing, instead of sending his runner to turn out the guard. But I daresay he would have had to turn out the guard all the same—for they were dumb fools—if a fellow who looked like a Greek hadn't turned up and told them to follow him. They went like goats after a piping boy. Ss-s-s-t! Haven't you forgotten something? Gold, eh? Hercules, I thank you! If I weren't afraid to lose my sinecure, employment being none too plentiful for free men nowadays, I might advise you to go hunting for your men not far from Pompey's school of gladiators. Things being as they are, I don't dare to give advice; the owner of this place I'm paid to watch is one of Pompey's clients. What breed of barbarian is that one?"

He pointed to Orwic, who stood like a statue, moon behind him, peering into gloom along the Via Sacra.

"I would give a month's pay to see you and him in the arena! You should wield a club, like Hercules, or take the coestus. He looks like a retiarius—as agile as a leopard—look at him! See how he supples his loins when he moves!"

"Would you know the Greek again who led my men away?" Tros asked him.

"Maybe. But I also know on which side of the street the sun shines. Even in the senate there is only Cato who tells all he knows. Perhaps he likes to have stones thrown at him! For myself, a little bread and wine and olives, with a ticket for the circus now and then, seems better than wagging the tongue and what comes of it. But I have seen that Greek in company with Zeuxis, who is one of the contractors who—but I am not a woman. My peculiarity is silence as to matters that are no concern of mine."

The news that Zeuxis had a hand in the betrayal of his men made Tros draw on instantly his full protective armour of dissimulation. He hid his consternation—swallowed it—suppressed it—grinned—put his wits to work. He knew the Greek mind. He could outplay Zeuxis!

It was no use going to him; direct means would be met with plausible obscurity—countered with guile. He must be indirect, and swift.

"You have relieved my mind, my friend," he said to the Etruscan. "Now I know where I can find my men, and that is worth another coin or two—here—pocket these. For a moment I feared my men had met such a fate as that woman Helene's, whom the praetor dragged out of her house! What happened to her? Was she thrown into the Tullianum?"

"Hardly!" The Etruscan laughed. "She is worth too much to be let rot in that hole. Not even Cato would do that with her. Cato is economical. That Tullianum is a pest-house; there's a dark hole where they lower them and let them perish of disease or hunger. I have seen it; I was sent in with a message for Septimus Varro, who was the custodian until they caught him substituting corpses for the prisoners whose friends had money and were free with it. Varro was crucified; so money isn't everything, after all; but I never heard that the men who bribed him suffered. If you asked me, I should say that some of Cato's men will disobey him and take as good care of Helene as they think her fashionable friends will pay for. Cato might have her scourged—he's a stern men, Cato is—but that won't happen until tomorrow or the next day, when he tries her case in public. Meanwhile, she'll be lodged under the praetor's office; you can see the front wall of the cells from here, but where she'll be is 'round behind; they'd be afraid to keep her where her friends might rescue her."

"She'll be guarded closely."

"Not a doubt of it. But praetor's cells are not the Tullianum. Any one with money in his hand can see a prisoner on one excuse or other—that is, if the torturers aren't busy with them; now and then they torture some one all night long to save the magistrate's time next morning, but you can generally hear the outcry when they're doing that. You see, they can't take evidence from slaves unless they're tortured first, and any one who's not a Roman citizen is liable to have his testimony questioned with a hot iron. That's a good law; it makes citizenship valued—not that citizens aren't liars, but they've a right to be privileged over mere colonials and slaves and aliens. If everybody was allowed to tell lies in the law-courts how could justice be administered?"

Tros walked away, but the Etruscan went on talking to the night. Orwic stepped forth like a shadow from among the statues in the Forum and followed Tros, who led toward the praetor's office. There were no lictors on the portico, they being personal attendants on the magistrate; in place of them a guardian as grim as Cato, without Cato's dignity, yawned while he watched three underlings throw dice beside a lantern.

"Halt!" he ordered, as Tros started up the steps. "No visitors. The praetor will be here soon after sunrise."

"I have urgent business," said Tros.

"Who cares? Have you a permit? Jupiter! Am I to be disturbed all night long by the gallants who buzz for that woman Helene like flies after fruit? Get hence!"

But already Tros stood on the portico. The guards ceased throwing dice to stare at him and reached into the shadow for their weapons, but none showed any eagerness to be the first to try to throw him down the steps. Their chief, a fat man with a double chin and strange, old-fashioned keys hung from a big ring fastened to the girth on his big belly, puffed his cheeks out and exploded, tilting back his stool on one leg:

"Jupiter! What now? Did you hear me tell you to be gone? By sulphury Cocytus—"

"I have heard," Tros answered. "You have yet to hear. Come yonder and speak alone with me."

He strode along the portico and waited, leaving Orwic standing near the upper step. Inquisitive, astonished, curious—inclined to continue asserting his official consequence, but growing cautious now that he could see the gold embroidery on Tros's cloak—he with the two-fold chin said something to his men about observing Orwic and, arranging his own cloak over his great belly, shuffled toward Tros, his slippers rutching on the stone.

"It is no use, master. I have turned away two-score of gallants, though they offered me enough coin to have bought the next election! There are definite orders. The praetor has—"

Tros interrupted

"Cackler! I have come from Pompey, who intends to set the woman free. Have you not heard that Pompey entered Rome?"

"By Venus, who did not hear? He and his men made noise enough! But what has that to do with me?"

"If you wish Pompey's favour you will let me in and let me speak to her."

"Nay, master! Nay, nay! It is all my place is worth! If Pompey wants to override the praetor's orders, let him come himself! I mean no disrespect for Pompey. Bacchus knows, I drank to him but two hours since. I wish him the dictatorship. But Gemini! What sort of guardian does he think I am, that he should send a stranger to me—and no writing—not a signet—nothing? Tell me your name. Who are you? Offer me a proof that you are Pompey's messenger."

Tros could invent a tale more suddenly than any Parthian could wing an arrow on its way. His amber eyes, glowing in moonlight, looked like pools of honesty; his bravery of bearing and his air of power in restraint aroused conviction. It was next thing to impossible to guess that he was lying. Even that familiar of courthouse perjury and criminal intrigue believed him.

"Pompey was in great haste," Tros said, speaking swiftly. "As an act of generosity to Caesar, he intends to set that woman free because he knows she has been doing Caesar's errands. He will make no scandal. Therefore, he will first see Cato in the morning. Meanwhile, he dreads that the woman, in fear, may reveal such information as she has, and to prevent that he has sent me to assure her she shall go free. There was neither time to write a permit, nor would that have been discreet; such messages are best conveyed by word of mouth. He told me, though, that I should find you are a man of excellent discretion who would have no scruples about doing him this favour when the matter is explained. I am to tell you, you may look to him for favourable notice."

"Did he tell you my name?" asked the keeper of the keys, a shadow of suspicion dimming credulity.

"No. Neither he, nor any of his friends remembered it. He called his secretary, but the secretary had forgotten, too. A nobleman like Pompey has so many interests, it would be strange if he could name you off-hand."

"He is likely to forget this service just as easily," the other grumbled.

"Aye, he might," said Tros. "Great men are not fastidious rememberers! But that is my responsibility; you may depend on me to keep you in his mind. Lead on; I have to make haste; I must report to Pompey before daylight."

Doubtfully shaking his keys—although he did not any longer doubt Tros's story—the man led the way into the praetor's office, down a dimly lighted stairway and along a passage stifling with dampness and the smell of dungeons.

"Look you!" he said, turning suddenly where a guttering

candle threw distorted shadows on an ancient wall. "Is this a trick? We lost two prisoners a week ago through people passing poison in to them. They dread the torture and their friends dread revelations! You're not meaning to slip her a dagger? No phials—nothing of that sort? Cato would have me scourged if I should lose one as likely to tell other folks' secrets as she is. Well—you can't go in. You'll have to speak to her through the grating, and mind you, I'll watch. I want to see both your hands the whole time."

Tros clasped his hands behind him. The custodian led toward a heavy oaken door and hammered on it with his keys. The thump and jingle brought a dozen answers from the nearby cells, including one that cried out from the dark for water:

"I will tell all! Only give me a drink and I will tell all I know!"

"Time for that in the morning!" said the jailer. "Silence!"

He shook the keys again and slapped Helene's cell door with his flat palm.

"Mistress!" he whispered hoarsely, "wake up! Here's a visitor—and as you love your life, don't let a soul know I admitted him! Understand now—if you get me in trouble over this—"

"Who is it?"

Fingers appeared through the grating and a nose was pressed against it.

"Keep those hands down! You may talk to him, but if I see a thing passed in there'll be trouble! Now," he said, signing to Tros. "Be quick and keep your voice low. There are three-score ears, all listening."

Tros stepped up to the grating, keeping his hands clasped behind his back where the custodian could watch them in the candle-light.

"Water! Water! I'll be dead if you don't let me drink! I'm dying now!" a voice croaked from the darkness.

"Silence!" roared the jailer, "or I'll let you know what thirst is! Shall I fetch salt?"

That threat was enough. The passage ceiling ceased to echo

to the cries. There fell the silence of a tomb, irregularly broken by the clank of fetters and the dripping of some water set where the man in agony of thirst could hear it.

"Who are you? I can't see you," said Helene's voice.

"Tros of Samothrace."

"You! You! I have friends who will—"

"Sh-sh-sh-sh! I received word that Cato had ordered you seized. I have worked to release you, and I know now I can manage it."

"How? Who?"

"Never mind. Cato is determined to have you scourged as an example, and the more your friends try to dissuade him the more determined he will be."

"By Isis! It is I who will prevent that! I have death-drops hidden. Even Romans don't flog corpses!"

"Sh-sh-sh-sh! There are greater ones in Rome than Cato. I have influence. By noon tomorrow you shall go free. But remember—you will owe your liberty to me and you will have to recompense me."

"How? They will have looted all my property! The rascal who owns my house will have put his bailiffs in already. They have chained my slaves. It will take me months to recover, even if I don't catch plague in this pest-hole! The worst is that Caesar is sure to hear of it. He'll say I'm an incompetent and never trust me any more. I'm ruined!"

"No," said Tros, "but you might easily be ruined if you failed to keep in my good graces! I will make your peace with Caesar, if you—"

"You? You are Caesar's enemy!"

"Not I. Now listen. It is Pompey who will order your release, but he will do it proudly and against his will. Don't trust him, but pretend to trust him. When they let you out, go straight to the house of Zeuxis and pretend to Zeuxis that you don't know it was he who betrayed both of us."

"He? Zeuxis? What has he done?"

"Nothing that can not be undone. I will tell you when we

meet at Zeuxis' house. He wants my pearls. He thought I had entrusted some of them to you—"

"The Greek dog!"

"Watch him! Aid me to make use of him and I will stand by you as long as you deserve my confidence."

The custodian rattled his keys.

"Make haste!" he urged. "There's no knowing when they'll bring in prisoners. It's all my place is worth to have you seen down here!"

"Are we agreed?" Tros asked, his face against the bars, for he was curious to see what clothing they had left her and whether she was locked into a less filthy dungeon than the others. Suddenly Helene pressed her lips between the bars and kissed him.

"Aye! Agreed!" she said, and laughed. "I am no imbecile, Tros of Samothrace! You need me, or you would never have stirred a finger to release me. You shall have me!"

"Come!" exclaimed the jailer. "Come now! You have been here long enough to tell the story of the fall of Troy!"

He took Tros by the arm and tugged at him. As Tros turned, scowling at the prospect of intrigue with any kind of woman, he could hear Helene's voice, half-mocking but vibrating with excitement, as she whispered:

"It was Tros who founded Troy! Argive Helen owes a recompense to Tros! I think his gods have set this table for a feast of the affections! Go and lay an offering on Venus' altar, with a gift from me beside it"

Pompeius Magnus

I am not of their number who deny the virtue or the greatness of a man because he lacks a touch or two of modesty and honesty. I make allowances for the poison of his flatterers, whose filthy lies would rot a man of iron. But what he has done is not my measure. What is he doing? What will he do? I have seen men so proud of their record that they view the future through a veil of vanity on which the past is painted. Their future discovers such men trying to relive the echoes of the deeds they once did.

—From the Log of Tros of Samothrace

Dawn found Tros and Orwic striding gloomily along the Via Sacra, turning and returning until they knew by heart the statues and the very cracks between the flagstones. Dust was stirred into their nostrils by the city slaves, who appeared in an army to sprinkle and sweep, their overseers watchful to pounce on coins or jewellery. One slave was flogged until he lay half stunned for trying to secrete a coin he picked out of a gutter.

Very shortly after dawn, demolishment resumed where Caesar's agents had bought up the ancient buildings, and the usual cursing and thrashing attended the first speeding up of sleepy slaves, dog-weary from the day before. Draft animals were better treated, having cost more money; there was scarcity of horses, and the price of meat was higher than when Spartacus had raided the Campagna, but since Pompey drove the pirates from the seas there had been no interruption in the streams of slaves that found their way to market, so a slave of the labouring sort cost very little. It was reckoned economical to work a man to death and buy another in his place.

The hurried sweeping done, on temple porticos and at an altar in the middle of the Forum, shaven-headed priests went through a ritual of invocation. There appeared to be a competition between temples to see which could hurry fastest through the service, for the wind had risen and the clouds of dust made the increasing heat unbearable. Dust gritted in the teeth and filled the nostrils; it was underfoot again in grey drifts almost as soon as the sweeper gangs had vanished.

Shops were opened, and the yawning shop-assistants sunned themselves, greeting their neighbours and cursing the builders who obliged them to clean shop so constantly. There was a sudden roar of voices and a fire-brigade, all clad in leather and brass helmets, streamed across the Forum carrying their ladders, ropes, poles and leather buckets—hundreds of buckets all nested together, for use by any slave or citizen they could impress into the service. Their united shout was like a war-cry:

"Crassus! Crassus!"

In his absence Crassus' agents were neglecting no chance to make money for their master; they preserved Rome from the flames, but he was richer by each fire they extinguished, though they forced the passers-by to form the bucket gangs and drove the neighbours' slaves into the hottest smoke.

And Pompey not yet. It was two hours after dawn before he came, on a big bay horse, magnificent in golden armour, attended by a host of friends and followed by a roaring crowd that choked the Via Sacra, thundering his praises. There was no name too good; imperator was the mildest; half the crowd was calling him dictator, he occasionally making modest efforts to take the crowd at its word. He shook his head repeatedly.

No armed men followed him. There were a dozen men on horseback and at least three times as many walking, all wearing the deep blue-bordered toga of the equites and each man followed by his personal attendants. Pompey's own slaves were innumerable. It was their task to keep the crowd from swarming in on the procession, and their method varied from remonstrance to the use of heavy cudgels.

In among the horsemen behind Pompey was a litter borne by slaves and loaded heavily with gifts; between the folds of linen that protected them from dust the glint of gold shone now and then; it was not Pompey's way to ask a favour of the gods without enriching their establishments with plunder from the fanes of other gods less fortunate.

The crowd swarmed in among the statues, yelling, and a company of Pompey's slaves ran in among them, handing out free tickets for the races and the ensuing combats between gladi-ators in the Circus Maximus. Speculators bought up the tickets promptly. Tros and Orwic each received a ticket as they worked their way into the crowd toward the semicircle formed by Pom-pey's friends and attendants facing the shrine of Vesta. It was only by dint of struggling that they came within two paces of a horse's heels.

Pompey, in the middle of the semicircle, swung down from his horse and strode with all a Roman's dignity toward the en-trance of the shrine, his white cloak that he wore against the dust revealing as it fluttered in the wind flashes of his golden corselet. The slave-borne litter followed him. In the porch be-fore the shrine the slaves knelt, waiting until the Vestals' women came, white robed and wearing rosaries, to bear the gifts within. At each gift that they took up from the litter all the women bowed to Pompey, he saluting with his right hand raised. He was a splendid figure. He stood like a god in armour—which was two-thirds of the secret of his influence; the mob roared satisfac-tion at the very way he walked.

When the gifts were gone he strode into the shrine alone, as if he were the sun-god come to visit the undying fire. As imper-ator, triumvir and priest, his eyes were hallowed and his person sacrosanct. He never doubted it. No shrine was closed to him— although the very Roman brothels gasped when it was known that in Jerusalem he had invaded the Jews' inner shrine to look, as it was said, into the face of Jahveh. Pompey, but not many Romans other than the ritually ordained priests—and they but seldom, at appointed times—might see the sacred fire and the historic image of archaic Pallas, brought by Aeneas from burning Troy; but there was scepticism on the faces of his friends, and there were dry jests on their lips. Tros heard some conversation:

"Gemini! If Julia dies in spite of all this, he'll regret those costly gifts!"

"What odds? The Vestals will find some suitable explanation. Even Vestal Virgins die, you know."

A shrew-faced man, between the two who had just spoken, laughed.

"The point is, Pompey has paid handsomely for something. Wait and see. If he should win the Vestals' influence—"

"Phagh! All he can expect from them is 'thumbs up' if his fancy gladiator gets the worst of it. The Vestals serve their pontifex. I told him only last week, he must find some way of weakening the Vestals if he hopes to outbid Caesar for the mob's vote. Bury one of them alive at the Porta Collina—you can prove a case against any one by torturing a dozen slaves—and—"

"Sh-sh-sh-sh!"

"What frightens you? Convict one of unchastity, and for a year to come the sweet unsensuous crowd would talk about abolishing religion! That would cost Caesar his grip on the plebes. It's the plebes who—"

"Who would have you crucified if they could hear you talking! Have you placed your bets yet on the races? Which team do you favour?"

"I don't know yet. I usually bet on white, but I have heard Helene the Alexandrian has a team of Cappadocians that she will enter, and they say she has adopted red—the gods know why! You'd think a woman of her laxity would choose the virgin's colour! I have heard, too, that she wished to drive the four-horse team but was forbidden. If I knew who is to take her place I might bet on those Cappadocians—I've seen them—gorgeous beasts! And besides, I consulted the auguries—"

"Hah! And were informed, no doubt, that red might win unless the white should have the best of it! Who wouldn't be an augur! They make money either way—no need to bet! I'll wager you weren't warned that the praetor's men would seize Helene yesterday! There's a rumour that Cato means to have her scourged and driven out of Rome."

"Jupiter omnipotens! Is Cato crazy?"

"Probably. He'll do it, if he's sure it would annoy some political enemy. He likes to be pelted with stones and vegetables. It makes him feel honest. And he thinks nobody will dare to kill him."

"He'll discover his mistake if he scourges Helene! If he threw her to the beasts the mob might stand for it, because they'd have the spectacle. But scourge her? I think not. If he did that, who-ever killed Cato could be sure of the mob's verdict."

"It wouldn't surprise me to know that Cato would enjoy death if it came to him in that way! The man isn't in his right mind. Did you hear how he gave his wife to young Hortensius? They say Alilia, his new wife, can't endure him; he goes bare-footed through the streets and thinks she ought to do the same! I've heard—Venus! Look at Pompey's face! Has he been trying to seduce a Vestal? Somebody has slapped him!"

Pompey was looking indignant. He was flushed. He tried to hide embarrassment by adjusting his cloak as he strode from the shrine, but he only succeeded in looking too proud to share his annoyance with any one else. His very gesture, as he drew the cloak around him, was a service of warning to friends not to question him. His lips were shut tight.

Tros tugged the nearest Roman's cloak.

"I have urgent business with Pompey. He expects me. Make way."

"Jupiter, what insolence! Stand back!"

"If I should have to shout to him," said Tros, "you might re-gret it. I am Tros of Samothrace."

"Oh. He who stopped him at the bridge last night? Save yourself trouble then. Pompey has changed his mind; your news, whatever it is, has ceased to interest him. Stand back!"

It was no use courting dagger-blades, and from the rear the crowd was roaring a new tumult, drowning speech. Though Tros had shouted at the limit of his lungs there was no chance that Pompey's ears would pick out one voice from the din. The crowd had swarmed up on the statues. There were men on the backs of other men—all yelling, and the pressure from the rear to catch sight of Pompey as he mounted his horse was prodigious. Dust was mixed with the sweat on men's faces. Tros could hardly breathe.

However, Orwic was beside him, smiling, masking his emotions.

"Stiffen yourself! Seize my foot!"

Tros sprang on Orwic's shoulders, balancing himself by setting one foot on a man's head, sparing his victim a swift smile that excused the liberty. Then Pompey could not help but see him; he was gorgeous in his cloak—a black-haired, handsome figure, like a gold-embroidered god, miraculously raised above a sea of faces.

Pompey hesitated. Tros—salt-sea-taught to use his helm between the waves—made up his mind for him. He sprang, as if thrown by the roars of the mob, and came down like a wedge between two of the horses that blocked the way. They reared and shied away from him and through the opened gap between their shoulders, quicker than a horseman could have drawn a dagger, Tros strode up to where the slaves held Pompey's horse. Still Pompey hesitated, frowning.

So they met on level flagstones, eye to eye. Pompey lacked the great advantage of the night before, when he could talk down proudly from his horse and Tros must look up like a poor petitioner. True, if Pompey had made but a sign, there would have been a dozen daggers buried in Tros's back before he could have turned; but Pompey was a lot too proud to trifle with that sort of cowardice; he threw his hand up to restrain his men and faced Tros with a curling lip.

"Mercury! You reach your goal!" he said, eyeing him steadily. Then he lowered his voice, so that not even the slaves who held his horse could overhear. "So you are Caesar's man! You come here plotting against Caesar—and yet serve him? I have heard you bearded Cato. Cato himself said it! Fool! The very whispers of the senate reach my ears! And now what? I am told that I must not harm Tros of Samothrace! I come to read the embers for an augury—my wife is ill—I seek foreknowledge of her destiny—and I am told I must give no offence to Tros of Samothrace! Have you the ear, then, of the Vestals? Are you Caesar's spy?"

Tros answered without betraying that he recognized the danger he was in:

"Pompeius Magnus, if the Vestals so admonished you regarding me, shall I believe they were the first to speak of me? Or did a spy report my movements? Did the man who stole my men say how it happened they stood leaderless? Then you—deliberating whether it were safe to throw my men into the arena—wondering what influence I might have—doubting your spy's word, possibly—inquired about me of the Vestals. Is it not so?"

"Meddler! What do you in Rome?" demanded Pompey.

"Triumvir, I turn my back on Rome the instant you return my men to me!"

"It seems to me that Tros of Samothrace may harm himself," said Pompey. "Men armed with daggers in Rome in the night are not immune from interference because Tros of Samothrace pretends he owns them! Are they citizens? Are you a citizen? Are you a peregrine? Are you a citizen of any state allied to Rome or even recognized by the senate and the Roman people? Have you any rights in Rome whatever—of person or property? And, if those men are truly yours, may you possess them under the Roman law? If not yours, are they free—and if so by what right? If they are not free, then who is their master?"

It appeared to Tros that the triumvir was lashing himself into a rage deliberately—possibly to justify a course of conduct not in keeping with his dignity, whatever law might have to say about it. Pompey's eyes—full, lustrous and intelligent—eyes normally suggesting rather tolerant autocracy, betrayed unsteadiness. He was expecting something—bullying and threatening in hope of forcing information without actually asking for it.

"It appears to me," he said, "that Cato has arrested the wrong malefactor. He should set Helene free and question your activities!" Tros held his tongue.

"It was not of your men you wished to speak when you accosted me at the bridge last night," said Pompey.

There was still that look of speculation in his eyes—almost of irresolution. He seemed to be giving Tros an opportunity to volunteer some information that he needed. Pompey, potential autocrat of two-thirds of the world, had far too many sources of information to make it safe to trifle with him—too many irons in the fire for any visitor in Rome to touch the right one at a guess without more luck than any reasonable man could look for.

"You have sent a man to Ostia," said Pompey suddenly. "How did you enter Italy? By land or sea?" Then, as Tros still held his tongue, "I am told you landed at Tarentum. Your ship will come to Ostia?"

That prodded Tros on his Achilles' heel! That ship was to her master and designer as a woman is to most men. Tros lied desperately—instantly.

"That ship is Caesar's! I have authority from Caesar to use all Roman ports."

He drew out from his cloak the parchment Caesar had been forced to sign in Gades—unrolled it—flourished it—thrust it under Pompey's eyes, pointing to the seal—the beautifully modelled figure of Caesar, naked, in the guise of Hermes. Pompey did not even glance at what was written; the proud sullenness of his eyes increased.

"Caesar's protection? You had nothing you wished to say? No message?"

"I demand my men."

"Let Caesar attend to it!" said Pompey. "Let me see that parchment."

He held out his hand but Tros thrust the parchment back under his cloak. There was nothing on it stating that the ship was Caesar's; to the contrary, it definitely named Tros as the owner, merely authorizing him to enter and to clear from Roman ports for purposes of commerce. There were doubtless flaws in it that any legal mind could drive a wedge through instantly; it was even doubtful whether Pompey would need lawyers; since the war against the pirates his authority with shipping had been almost absolute.

Tros's back was cold; he sensed a climax now with the same nerves that always warned him of a coming storm at sea. But Pompey was an expert at deferring climax:

"That is all then," he said, turning to his horse, and at his gesture three intimates strode from the ranks. They pretended to help him to mount, but insolently shouldered Tros out of the way, turning their backs to him. Two horsemen beckoned, making a narrow gap in the ranks, sneering as Tros went by. The very crowd, still yelling Pompey's praises, knew he had been rebuffed; a thousand eyes had seen him flourishing the parchment. It was usual to try to thrust petitions into great men's hands, and though such documents were usually tossed to secretaries who ignored them, it was customary to accept them formally unless the individual petitioned wished to snub the applicant.

So the crowd mocked. When he made his way to Orwic's side and they began to force a way together through the throng some humorist made fun of the moustache that drooped on either side of Orwic's mouth. Then Tros's gold forehead-band came in for comment. In another minute he was forced to doff his cloak and fold it to prevent its being torn off. Some men thought he was a Parthian, come craving relief from Crassus' legions; they yelled at him "Crassus! Crassus!" until those who could not see believed the fire brigade was coming and divided down the midst.

So, down that rift, sweating and indignant, Tros and Orwic bolted into the comparative seclusion of the side-streets, where they turned at last into a fly-blown cook-shop and, discovering a table in an alcove at the rear, ate food concocted from the meat bought from temple priests—whose incomes were increased enormously by selling the fat carcasses donated by the pious for the satisfying of the gods.

"I wager we are eating Great Jove's heifer!" Tros remarked. "Be that an omen! Fragments from Olympus' table fortify us! If the gods of earth and sky are not asleep they—Orwic—has it ever dawned on your imagination that the gods ought to be grateful to us men for giving them an opportunity to use their virtue?"

"Nothing dawns on me at all," said Orwic. "It appears to me we have a lost cause. We are two lone men in Rome, and all Rome seems to be our enemy."

"No, for there are honest men in Rome," Tros answered. "I have made an enemy of Pompey. He is irritated because I went over his head to the Vestals. Arrogant aristocrat! He will hardly dare to disobey them openly, but neither will he swallow what he thinks is an indignity. A man in Pompey's shoes needs only to nod and there are fifty men at once to do whatever work he thinks too dirty for his own white hands. Indeed, I tell you, Orwic, a whole host of gods has reason to be grateful to us for an opportunity. Let them act godlike!"

The Carceres and
Nepos, the Lanista

Weigh well thy motives, trusting destiny to weigh thy deeds. I have heard this—it was Caesar said it—that a captain should mother his men because he may need them later and they will die more bravely for a captain who has showed them loving-kindness as well as strength. But I think otherwise. I say a captain who has not loving-kindness for his men is unfit to be died for. If he understand not that they need him, and be not ready to die with them, in an hour of worst need he shall learn that he knew not what leadership is.

—From the Log of Tros of Samothrace

Tros's attitude was brave, but in his heart was nothing to support it. He was on the deepest bottom of despair. The need of keeping up appearances for Orwic's sake alone prevented him from giving way. He was a man who lived by energy; the exercise of will invoked new powers of imagination. But now that there seemed no concrete thing to do, his very will dried up.

Thrusting the unfinished food aside he rallied himself by summing up the facts, inviting Orwic to discover a solution. He slew flies with a spoon, arranging them in geometrical designs on the cook-shop table—one design for each fact, involutions indicating intricacy; then, thumbing off the gravy from his plate, he tried to work the calculus by smearing all the facts together into one plan.

"Zeuxis—who doesn't know yet that I know his treachery. That one's Zeuxis. He believes I'm carrying a thousand pearls under my cloak. Zeuxis, or else Nepos—very likely both of them—sent word to one of Pompey's agents that my men would make good gladiators. Probably the agent acted on his own responsibility, consulting Pompey afterwards—perfectly simple—sent one of Zeuxis' servants, whom they'd recognize, to tell my Northmen—in Gaulish, which they'd understand sufficiently to get his meaning that I'd come out of the Vestals' palace through a back door, or by an underground passage or some such story. They supposed I'd sent for them—and walked straight into an ambush.

"Helene—presently at liberty and dangerous. There's Helene—that one. Has her eyes on me—anticipates a drama of affection, and the least she'll do will be to stir the jealousy of half-a-dozen dagger-digging sons of equites! Caesar's spy. Probably knows enough to blackmail any one in Rome except Cato. Very likely she can help by an appeal to Caesar's agents, of whom Memmius, a candidate for consul, is the foremost in the public eye. Call that one Memmius—a very doubtful quantity—a politician; anything that he does will be paid for through the nose by some one. All those other flies near Memmius are politicians, each with his palm itching for a bribe—which each of them would pocket and forget!

"The senate. Those flies are the senate—not sitting—too hot for them, more ways than one, and the Forum too noisy, not counting the danger of riots. Villas in the country are more dignified. Only a small committee of the senate holding meetings behind locked doors in the temple of Castor and Pollux. There's the committee—probably inaccessible, but said to be plotting against Pompey, whom they hate nearly as much as they hate Caesar and with equal cause.

"Cato—praetor and a member of the senatorial committee. If we could see the committee Cato would be there, and he's the only man in Rome who dares to challenge Pompey openly; but the rest of them hate Cato because he rebukes them for corruption. Cato intends to enforce the law as long as he's praetor and he'll be venomously angry because Pompey has compelled him to release Helene.

"I have made one mistake after another, Orwic! I believe two-thirds of Pompey's enmity this morning is accounted for by his having been told by the Vestals to procure Helene's liberty. He can't refuse. Their influence is much too artfully directed. They could turn all Rome against him. Probably he hates the thought of having to ask a favour of Cato, who will certainly hold out for terms. Cato can't be bribed, but he's a politician, always looking for the lesser evil; he would compromise, but like an undefeated swordsman.

"Pompey—he's that big fly—half out of his wits with worry. A good soldier and a rotten politician, drunk with renown—no doubt wishing he had not encouraged Crassus to go to Asia, since now he must stand alone against Caesar. More than likely Pompey is encouraging Caesar to invade Britain, hoping he may meet defeat. Pompey has a notion that by keeping my men he can force some information out of me, and if I could guess what he wants to know I might out-manoeuvre him; otherwise he will have them killed in the arena. He loathes the mob, and de-spises butchery, but he knows his influence is waning, so he will do almost anything for popularity. Spectacles—spectacles—doles of corn—anything; they say his agents scour the earth for wild beasts for the arena. Zeuxis undoubtedly told him of the pearls I brought from Britain. Pompey thinks too highly of himself to try to steal them, but he wouldn't hesitate to let Cato take them in the name of the Roman law. He very likely traded you and me to Cato for Helene! Now do you see what an error I made? Do you begin to understand the danger?

"Conops—nothing simpler than to catch Conops. Zeuxis has betrayed him. What then? My ship comes to Ostia and Sig-urdsen drops anchor in the Tiber-mouth. Pompey has author-ity to order out as many triremes as he wishes; there are always two or three available. They'll either blockade Sigurdsen or force him to run if he's lucky. If they do blockade him, he will soon run short of food and water."

"Run for it!" said Orwic. "You must leave your men in Pompey's hands and hurry to Ostia."

"I will die first!" Tros answered, shaking the oaken table. "I expect my men to die for me. Shall I do less for them? Nay! What is duty for the man is obligation for the master! As the head rots, so the fish stinks! Orwic—"

Suddenly his amber eyes appeared to stare at an horizon. Parted lips showed set teeth and his fingers gripped the table edge.

"No cause is lost while there remains a weapon and a man to use it! I might go to Cicero. He corresponds with Caesar. He has influence, and he is Cato's friend; but Cicero is in Pompeii, which is far off, and they say he is worried with debts and doubt. If Zeuxis told the truth—he often tells it when it costs him nothing—Cicero is planning to defend Rabirius for Caesar's sake; if he will plead that rascal's cause before the judges he should not balk at protecting us!"

"Make haste then. Let us go to Cicero," said Orwic.

"No. He is a lawyer. I dread the law's delay. Nor will I cool my heels at the temple of Castor and Pollux until some senator comes out from the committee room to find out whether I will bribe him heavily enough to make it worth his while to promise what he never will perform! Nor do I dare to return to Cato; Pompey will have told him I am Caesar's man, and I was with him only yesterday attempting to persuade him to turn on Caesar! He will think Caesar sent me to tempt him, meaning to denounce him if he fell into the trap—intriguing against Roman arms!

"No. Cato has probably undertaken to condemn my men to the arena, and will do the same for you and me if we attract his notice! That is just the sort of trick that Pompey would turn on the honest old fool—persuade him that my men are criminals, encourage him to have them butchered; then, supposing that the men are really Caesar's, letting Caesar know Cato is to blame for it, thus aggravating, he will think, the hatred Caesar has for Cato. Do you see it? Pompey would get credit from the mob for showing eight-and-thirty victims of a new sort in the amphitheatre. Cato would get the blame. And Caesar, so Pompey would think, by trying to avenge the insult, would drive Cato to join Pompey's party. Quite a number of important people might follow Cato when the crisis comes. Rome's politics are like hot quicksilver."

"You appear to me to know too much," said Orwic. "In my own land I have found the politics bewildering, and they are simpler. How can you, who are not a Roman, pick the right thread and pursue it through the snarl?"

Tros paused.

"Men are born with certain qualities," he said, re-estimating Orwic—reappraising him; and there returned into his eyes that far-horizon look. "For instance, you were born with an ability to manage horses, which is something I could never do."

He mulled that over in his mind a minute. Then:

"Because I know ships and I understand the sea, it is a mean ship that will not sail faster under my hand than another's. Is it so with horses? Will a good horse, or a good team gallop for you faster than for me?"

"Undoubtedly," said Orwic. "What has that to do with it?"

"This—that I think the gods expect each of us to play his own part. There is a part that the Vestal Virgins play best, and there are other parts for you, and me, and for Helene—and even Zeuxis. It is not alone the great ones of the earth who—Let us leave this place! I saw a man who might be an informer hurry out and look too shrewdly at us as he passed the door."

He doffed his forehead-band and folded up his cloak, but even so he was too masterful a figure to escape the notice of the crowd. Men followed him and Orwic through the winding streets, accosting them in any fragment of a foreign tongue they knew. Thieves tried to rob them; half a dozen times Tros had to use his fist to save his cloak, until at last he struck one slippery Sicilian and sent him sprawling in the kennel.

Instantly a cry went up that a barbarian had struck a Roman citizen! Three narrow lanes disgorged a swarm of loiterers whose life, endured in vermin-ridden tenements, was never raised out of its shabbiness except to see men slain splendidly in the arena.

Rome's mob could rise as swiftly as the reeking dust, amuse itself a minute with a man's life, laugh, and disappear as casually as the knackers of the slaughter-yards returning home to dinner.

Orwic drew his dagger and the two stood back-to-back, Tros making no haste to display his weapon; through the corner of his mouth he growled:

"Don't stab unless you must! Stand firm, look gallant and expect some favour from the gods!"

Then:

"Citizens!" he roared, attempting to adopt the vulgar idiom that politicians used when cozening the crowd for votes. "One rattle of the dice yet! Hold!"

"Aye! Hold hard!" said a voice he recognized, and the Etruscan—he who was night-watchman for the goldsmith's in the Forum—elbowed his way forward, grinning. The whole crowd knew him; he appeared to have authority of some kind; they obeyed the motion of his hand and half a dozen men leaned back against the swarm behind them, vehemently resisting the efforts of others to get to the front.

"Porsenna! Let us hear Porsenna!"

The Etruscan smiled with the familiar, ingratiating, confident good humour of a popular comedian, long used to waiting for the crowd to quiet down before he loosed his jests. But when the yelling had died down enough for one voice to be audible, he wasted no time on amusing them. He threatened.

"It will be a good show in the Circus Maximus, but perhaps you would rather riot now than get free tickets; I am on my way to get the tickets. What will Pompey's secretary say, if I should have to tell him you have injured two of the best performers? How many tickets then for the people in my streets? Home with you!"

He gazed about him, memorizing faces, or pretending to, and if he had been a praetor he could hardly have received more prompt obedience. With jests, and here and there a grumble, they implored him to remember them and melted away up side-streets, not more than a dozen lingering in doorways to assuage their curiosity. Porsenna grinned at Tros.

"A good thing for you that the man who shares a bed with me is sick this morning! I had nowhere to sleep. And besides, it is true, this is the day I must distribute tickets. I get no pay for it, but people who want tickets have a way of keeping on the easy side of me, which makes life tolerable. We Etruscans love our bellies, and I assure you there isn't a house in all these streets where I can't get a good meal for the asking—that is to say, if they have anything, which isn't always. But there's always somewhere to turn for food or drink; I've noticed it never happens that they all starve on the same day. But have you found your men? No? Well, I'll find them for you. Only you must bear in mind I'm only a night-watchman and distributor of tickets, so you mustn't expect me to do more than show you where they are. I wouldn't have helped you just now if you hadn't given me a lot of money last night. You're a rich man and a stranger, and it always pays to go to a little trouble for folk who have generous tendencies. We Etruscans have a name for being sharp customers, but that's not true; we merely like the soft jobs and the good things and exert ourselves to get them. Let us come this way. Does it seem to you you owe me anything for that little service I did you just now?"

"Show me my men and I'll pay you handsomely," Tros answered.

The Etruscan led on through a maze of streets until they reached the valley below the Palatine, where an enormous wooden structure nearly filled the space between surrounding houses. The high walls were covered with electioneering notices in coloured paint, and there was a constant pandemonium from cages, underground, where most of the wild animals were kept in darkness until needed for the public execution of Rome's criminals. There was a stench from an enormous heap of mixed manure that slaves were carrying away in baskets to be dumped outside the city, and the air was full of dust, besides, from heaps of rubbish being showered into carts.

There was a great gate at the end that faced the river Tiber, suitably adorned with horses' heads, weapons, shields and crudely fashioned lions, but the public entrances were all along both sides, and at the farther end were stables built of stone, beneath which were the cells in which most of the prisoners were kept who had been sentenced and awaited death in the arena. In the open space at the end there were spearmen, but not many and they did not seem to expect to be called upon for action, merely staring with indifference at Tros and Orwic as Porsenna led them toward a wooden office at the rear, where there was a small crowd of men, not one of whom seemed satisfied.

"They grumble, they grumble, they grumble!" Porsenna remarked. "But if there were enough tickets for every one in Rome, what profit would there be in being a distributor? Would anybody think it worth his while to curry favour with us? Some folk don't know an advantage when they see it. Watch them struggle for the allotments! Good sweat and excitement gone to waste! If there is one thing in all Rome that is honestly apportioned it's the circus tickets, region by region. There are so many for each important politician—so many for the giver of the games—and the rest are divided equally to us distributors. Now watch me."

He thrust two fingers in his mouth and whistled, then threw up his hand to catch the attention of a man at the office window. The man recognized him, nodded and tossed a bundle of tickets on to a shelf.

"There. That's the way to manage it. Now I can get mine when the crowding's over. All that costs me is two tickets; and since I'll know where they are I can do a favour to some one in one of my streets by telling him where he can buy them. Now come this way."

Farther to the rear, behind the stables, in between two rows of racing chariots that stood with poles up-ended, was a stone arch with a barred iron gate providing access to steps made of enormous blocks of stone that led down steeply into gloom. A fetid prison-smell came through the opening, and at a corner, where the steps turned, there was one lamp flickering. A spearman, with a great key at his waist, stood by the gate and sullenly ignored the pleas of half-a-dozen women, one of whom, on her knees, had torn her clothing and was beating her naked breasts.

He recognized Porsenna instantly and drove his spear-butt at the woman to get her out of the way. "No!" he said. "No! Get away from here! If you want to see your husband, get a permit from the praetor's office. Otherwise, get sentenced, too, to the arena; then they'll let you die with him! You wish to visit the dungeons?" he asked, grinning at Porsenna. "You and two friends? I would let you pass in free."

Tros took the hint and dropped two coins into Porsenna's palm, who cleverly hid one and gave the other to the spearman. The gate opened on oiled hinges and a wave of filthy air came through the opening as Tros and Orwic followed the Etruscan down the steps.

And now noise blended with the smell. Infernal mutterings suggestive of the restlessness of disembodied phantoms filled the atmosphere; the sound, the Stygian gloom and the disgusting stench were all one. On a stone floor in the midst of the great square columns that supported a low roof three men played at dice by candle-light and half a dozen others watched them. All wore daggers; there were spears beside them, leaned against the wall; each man had as well a heavy iron club with a short hook and a sharp spike at the end. The dice intensely interested them; they scarcely looked up—snapping fingers and adjuring Venus to reward them for the sacrifices they intended to bestow on her.

The murmuring came through heavy wooden doors, in each of which there was a bronze grille at about the level of a man's face from the floor. All the doors were made fast by bars that fitted into sockets in the oaken posts. There appeared to be a perfect maze of cells, with narrow, almost pitch-dark corridors between them; and at the far end of the vault there was another set of stairs, of solid masonry, that evidently led to the arena or to some enclosure at one end of it. There was a charcoal brazier not far from where the men played dice and two clubs, similar to those the men had fastened to their wrists by thongs, were thrust into red-hot coal. A slave was blowing on it, and the red glow shone reflected in his face.

The slave spoke and one of the men removed a hot club from the fire, wrapping a wet cloth and then a leather guard around the handle. Two who had been watching the dice followed him. A fourth man lifted out a bar that locked a cell door, and the three went in, he who held the iron going last. The fourth man shut the door again, not locking it, and went back to the dice.

There was a great commotion in the cell—blows, oaths, scuffling, a screech—then one long yell of agony that seemed unending, as if the victim never drew a breath. The dice-players took no notice.

When the yell died to a sobbing groan the three came out again and one of them tossed the hot club to the slave who watched the char coal brazier. The fourth man left the dice and went and set the bar in place. It was his voice that made Tros's blood run cold; he recognized it instantly. It was Nepos!

"Did you injure him?" asked Nepos.

"Not much. Just burned his fingers enough to teach him not to try any more digging. That's the third time he's tried to escape."

Nepos returned to watch the dice. The men resembled phantoms in the gloom; the candle-light broke up the shadows, distorting forms and faces, but the voice of Nepos was unmistakable.

"Who comes?" he asked, shading his eyes as he glanced at the three who were standing with backs to the entrance-steps, a puzzling light behind them.

"Porsenna—and two visitors," said the Etruscan.

"Visitors? Have they a permit? Who—what have they come for?"

"This nobleman has lost his men. I tell him he will find them here, though much good that will do him!"

"Who is he?"

Nepos approached. He appeared to be not the same man who had entertained Tros in his house. His ferocity, all on the surface now, had changed the very outline of his face—or so it seemed.

"Tros?" he said. "Tros of Samothrace? Who sent you here? That rascal Zeuxis?"

"I have come to find my men," Tros answered.

"Out! Get out of here!" said Nepos, flourishing his club at the Etruscan. Something in his tone of voice attracted the attention of the dice-players. They all came crowding behind Nepos.

"Well, I warned you I couldn't do more than show you where your men are," Porsenna remarked amiably. "You have heard him. He says I must go."

He turned toward the stairs. Tros, fingering his dagger, made as if to follow him but Nepos gestured to the others, who immediately cut off Tros's retreat and one man let Porsenna feel the point of his iron club as an inducement to go swiftly.

"You shall see your men," said Nepos. "Come."

He beckoned. If he was afraid of Tros he gave no sign of it although his keen eyes must have seen Tros's right hand at his dagger. Orwic drew his own short weapon and whispered to Tros excitedly:

"Don't follow him! Let's fight our way out!"

"No," said Tros, "let's find the Northmen."

He preferred to follow Nepos rather than be torn with iron hooks and clubbed. He took his hand off his dagger and touched Orwic's arm to reassure the younger man. Together they strode behind Nepos down a narrow corridor that stank of ordure and wet straw. There were cell doors right and left, and at the end, below a candle on a bracket, a peculiarly narrow opening protected by an iron grille—so narrow that if the grille were swung clear on its heavy hinges only one man at a time could possibly have passed.

"Do they know your voice?" asked Nepos over-shoulder, his voice rumbling along the tunnel.

"Sven! Jorgen! Skram! Olaf!" Tros shouted.

There was instant pandemonium. A deep-sea roar of voices burst out through the grille:

"Tros! Tros! Ho, master! Lord Tros! Come and rescue us!"

The prisoners in two score cells all added to the Babel, clamouring for mercy; they supposed some great official had come looking for a lost retainer and on the spur of the moment every man invented reasons why he should be set free. Nepos struck his iron club against the grille and threatened to send for hot irons, but the Northmen did not understand him and their chorus roared louder than ever. An arm protruded through the grille and Nepos struck it, arousing a curse that sounded like a taut rope bursting suddenly.

"Silence!" Tros thundered, again and again; but not even his voice quieted them.

"Master, we sicken! We die, Lord Tros! Release us! Let us out!"

But it suddenly occurred to them that if he spoke they could not hear, and there was no sound then except their breathing as they crowded at the grille. Tros let his wrath loose:

"This is what I get for trusting you!" he growled in Gaulish. "Fine men! Follow the first lousy Greek who lies to you! Hopeless fools! Now I must buy you back like a job-lot of left-over slaves!"

He glanced at Nepos who was standing in between him and the grille.

"Whom should I speak to about freeing them?" he asked in Latin. Nepos grinned sourly and turned a thumb down.

"They're due to die in the arena. If you like good advice, I'd say to you: leave Rome in a hurry!"

Tros held his breath. He thought of madness—of plunging his dagger into Nepos, loosing his Northmen and fighting the way out.

"It's too late to befriend them now," said Nepos. "This is the gate to the land of death."

Something in the tone of his voice reminded Tros that Nepos was a man of strangely mixed peculiarities and loyalties.

"What I have, won't help," he said. "I have this tessera." He drew up a broken disk of engraved ivory that hung on a cord around his neck, beneath his shirt. It was approximately half of an ancient ornament, irregularly broken off, its ragged edge enclosed in a thin casing of gold to preserve it. "My father exchanged tessera with Zeuxis' father—"

"Eh?" exclaimed Nepos. "What? Here, let me have a look at that. Has that Greek tricked me into sacrilege? If he and you are hospites—"

He gestured with his arm along the passage and pushed Tros in front of him.

"Go back there where it is lighter. I must know the truth of this."

They returned to the echoing half-light where the slave still blew at the brazier, the men with iron clubs retreating backward and then standing near to protect Nepos. But that grizzled veteran seemed totally indifferent to danger. He kept muttering:

"Jupiter hospitalis!"

Tros slipped off the cord over his neck and gave the tessera into his hand. Nepos pulled off with his teeth the gold band that protected the jagged edge and held the piece of ivory toward the candlelight.

"That might be genuine," he muttered. Then, sharp eyes on Tros: "Do you swear to me that Zeuxis has the other half of this?"

"Not I," Tros answered. "I am from Samothrace and therefore take no oath at random. But I swear to you—"

"By Jupiter hospitalis?"

"Aye, by Jupiter hospitalis, that my father and Zeuxis' father exchanged tessera, of which that is the one that I inherited."

"And has Zeuxis never given notice of repudiation?"

"Never. To the contrary, he welcomed me with such effusion that we never spoke of tessera at all. There was no need. I arrived at his house without sending him warning and he welcomed me with open arms."

"The Greek dog!" muttered Nepos. "Are the Greeks not bound by oath of hospitality? Great Jupiter! In Sulla's time a thousand Romans risked proscription for the sake of that oath! I myself—But are you sure the Greek knew? You say your father and his father exchanged tessera, but did Zeuxis know of it?"

"He did. Nine years ago in Alexandria he claimed my father's hospitality, on board my father's ship, when Ptolemy's men were after him for having said too much to the wrong listener. My father hid him in the hold between barrels of onions, and that was where I first met Zeuxis. It was I who took food to him, lest the crew should learn his whereabouts and drop a hint to Ptolemy's men."

Nepos began breathing through his nose, his windy grey eyes glinting in the candle-light. He stood with clenched fists on his hips considering, not Tros apparently, but the atrocity that had been done to his own person.

"Even if the Greek was ignorant, the oath was binding until publicly annulled," he muttered.

"Zeuxis is a Roman citizen," said Tros.

"Aye, that he is! These Greeks who become Romans need a lesson. They accept Rome's credit and deny her claims! They grow rich and they—this is too much, Tros—"

He shook his finger under Tros's nose, as if Tros had been a party to the sacrilege.

"You, too, are an alien and may not understand Rome's principles. I tell you, I have seen men sent to this place, to be torn by animals, for crimes that were glorious deeds compared to this atrocity! I would prefer to see a Vestal Virgin immured living! An offence against hospitium!—If Cato knew of it—"

"Send word to him," said Tros.

"No. That would do you no good. Cato is—what is it he calls himself?—not a philosopher—a logician—that's it, a logician. He would order Zeuxis crucified, but he would not let your men go. He would say, let each man die for his own offence."

"Offence?" said Tros. "I haven't heard of one. Who charged them? Who tried them? Who passed sentence?"

Nepos stared at him, incredulous. He appeared to think Tros bereft of his senses.

"Your men," he said, "were caught red-handed lurking in the portal of the Vestals. They are not entitled to a hearing. An offence against the Vestals is beyond the law's arm, even as they are above it. They may not be mentioned in a court of law. No law can touch them. They may not be haled as witnesses. How then shall a magistrate try such a case? Besides, your barbarians are not Roman citizens, nor subjects of any kingdom that Rome recognizes—are they? Pompey himself ordered the lot of them into the arena! My friend, they're your men no longer. They must die."

Nepos began drumming on his teeth with horny finger-nails.

Tros spoke:

"Then I die with them. They are my men."

Nepos blinked at him. "You would make a splendid specta-cle," he said. "Do you fight well?"

"It remains to be seen," Tros answered. "But they will fight better with me than without me."

"Have you broken tessera together?"

"Nay, we broke bread. We have built and sailed a ship together."

"You should have been born a Roman," said Nepos. "Once in a hundred years or so we breed a few of your sort. Well, I can do you the favour. You may die with your men if you see fit. You shall go in there with weapons. I can arrange that."

"You will earn my good-will, Nepos."

"Well, I like that better than your ill will. It will suit me; I shall get the credit for a fine spectacle. And who knows? If you have the Vestals' favour you may be safe in the arena. They may turn their thumbs up when the time comes. I can send you against Glaucus. He shall run you through the thigh. One can depend on Glaucus; many a time I have used him to preserve a man's life, but it never worked unless the Vestals had a hand in it."

He went on scratching at his chin. The wretches in the cells around him made noises like caged animals, all sounds unit-ing into one drab, melancholy moan. There was a conversation going on between cells in the polyglot thieves' jargon that cre-ates itself wherever criminals are thrown together—droning, wholly without emphasis, resembling an echo of what hap-pened last week. Its effect on Tros and Orwic was as if death clutched at them, but Nepos and his men seemed not to notice it—not even when a man in agony from their inflicted burns yelled imprecations.

"There is no place here to make you comfortable," Nepos said at last. "Are all oaths sacred to you?"

"Any of my making."

Nepos, scratching at his chin, nodded and nodded: "Swear you will be here!"

"If my men are here, here I will be," Tros answered.

"And that barbarian?" He glanced at Orwic.

"He was the first against Caesar's legions on the shore of Britain. Yes, I answer for him."

"Very well. Here, take your tessera and keep it. Trust me to deal with Zeuxis. There is no worse sin than violation of hospitium. You swear now—no trickery—you will be back here?"

"I agree," said Tros. "But what of my men? Can't you treat them better? They will sicken in that cage."

"Aye, they shall have good treatment. They shall be better fed. There is a shortage of strong barbarians to make a showing against the King of Numidia's black spearmen. They tell me your men fight with axes, which would immensely please the populace. As for Zeuxis—"

"If there's a law in Rome, my men shall go free yet!" Tros interrupted.

"Take my advice," said Nepos. "Let the law alone! If you apply to any magistrate he will inform himself as to Pompey's wishes and then condemn them legally on any trumped-up charge. As it is, they are not condemned. If the Vestals should bid them go free none could quarrel with it, could they? or with me either."

"Money," said Tros, "would buy Rome. Tell me whom to see about it."

"Nay, nay, why buy promises that no one could keep even if he dreamed of doing it! Whom would you buy—Pompeius Magnus? Rich—proud—I suppose he bears you private enmity, but that is not my business. Whom else? The Vestals? You can't buy them. You might petition them. You will have to do that secretly and very craftily. As for Zeuxis—if that scoundrel isn't crucified within the month for sacrilege against Jupiter hospitalis, then my name isn't Nepos!"

But Tros's wits were working—furiously. It would not give him the slightest satisfaction to see Zeuxis crucified. Revenge on such a rascal was beneath his dignity. But if the man who had betrayed him could be made to undo the disaster at his own expense.

"Whatever Zeuxis did, I hold his tessera," said Tros, "and I am bound by oath to treat him as a hospes until he or I repudiate the bond before witnesses. And it is I who should accuse him, not you, Nepos. I prefer to give him opportunity to purge his sacrilege."

"Impossible!" said Nepos. "There is no way of condoning that offence. It is against God; it is against Rome; it is against citizenship. Zeuxis—"

"Is my hospes," Tros interrupted. "I implore you to refrain from interfering with him until I have my way first."

Nepos demurred: "If you were a Roman that might satisfy the gods, but you are not a Roman. Jupiter hospitalis looks to us Romans to uphold his dignity. However, I concede this—if you can find a way of punishing that scoundrel, do it. I will give you time before I inform Cato and have him crucified. Meanwhile, no warning him! If he escapes, I will hold you answerable! He who overlooks such sacrileges as that knave has committed is as guilty as if he had done it himself! I will set informers on the watch to make sure Zeuxis does not escape to foreign parts."

"So do," Tros answered. "That will serve me. Let me speak to my men. Can you put them elsewhere? That dungeon they are in stinks like an opened grave."

"I will move them to the upper cells," said Nepos, "if you will guarantee their good behaviour."

Tros strode back to the grille, where he was greeted by another chorus of lament.

"Silence!" he commanded. "Who shall have patience with faithless fools who run after the first Greek that lies to them? Dogs! I have had to beg a better cell for you; and now I go to buy you from whoever sells such trapped rats! Let me hear of one instance of misbehaviour between now and then, and I will leave the lot of you to rot here! Do you understand that? You are to obey this honourable Nepos absolutely until I come, and if he tells me of one disobedience these walls shall be the last your eyes will ever see!" He turned his back, indignant that he should have to speak so cruelly to decent men, then followed Nepos to the steps, and to the upper iron gate, and daylight—where the stable smell was like the breath of roses after the abominable fetor of the dungeon.

As he walked off, he smiled wanly at the thought of how thoroughly cowed he had left his men, and for a moment he felt guilty of having been too harsh.

Tros Forms an Odyssyian Plan

In a world so full of rubbish that even rich men's wastrels
find amusement, the most worthless trash of all is revenge.
Justice knows not vengeance, or it is not justice. But I see no
unwisdom in putting a spiteful fool to work to spite himself
into a net, if so be that should suit my purpose.

—FROM THE LOG OF TROS OF SAMOTHRACE

Tros made his way to Zeuxis' house in no haste, although
Orwic was impatient. It was essential to take time to instruct
Orwic thoroughly.

"Romans," he said, "have certain virtues, of which loyalty to
certain customs is the greatest. They respect the Vestal Virgins
and the law of hospitality. Whoever offends against those ancient
institutions puts himself outside the pale and they regard him almost as no longer human. That is why Nepos turned on Zeuxis
and befriended us. That is also why Pompey turned so suddenly
against me. I have made one mistake after another, Orwic. If I
had said nothing to the Vestals about Helene, Pompey very likely
would have let my men go; more than likely one of his lieutenants seized them at Zeuxis' suggestion and Pompey knew nothing about it until afterward.

"It is not quite like Pompey to do such under-handed
work. But then the Vestals told him not to interfere with
me, and they also asked him to procure Helene's liberty. He
jumped to the conclusion, I suppose, that Caesar, the pontifex
maximus, is trying to make use of the Vestals, and when I

showed him Caesar's seal that made him sure of it. No doubt he had already heard of Caesar's swoop on Gades, which is in Pompey's province. He is beginning to feel nervous about Caesar. I ought to have known he would resent having the Vestals drawn into politics. He probably made up his mind to have you and me thrown into the arena along with my men, to teach the Vestals a lesson. If Caesar cared to take that up, Pompey could make a public issue of it and accuse Caesar of tampering with Rome's most sacred institution. Now do you understand?"

"No, I don't!" said Orwic.

"Very well, then leave it to a man who does! Observe whether we are being followed, and hold your tongue while I think!"

But thought comes wrapped up in obscurity when men are irritated, and whichever way Tros switched his speculation difficulties seemed insuperable. He supposed Conops would be in the dungeons presently and he would have no means of learning when his ship arrived at Ostia nor any way of warning Sigurdsen to put to sea again and try some other port.

"There is nothing for it," he said finally, "but to try to use Helene's wits and Zeuxis' knavery! I have some money left, and fifty pearls, not counting the big ones I hid on the ship. Let us see what the gods can make of that material!"

"But what of me?" suggested Orwic. "I can out-ride any Roman! Get me a horse and let me find the way to Ostia. I can out-swim any Roman, too! Let me watch for the ship and swim out and warn Sigurdsen."

Tros turned sarcastic:

"You who can speak neither Greek nor Latin! It would be easier for you to find one bug in a dunghill than Conops in Ostia! Nay, Orwic, we stand at death's gate. Let us gut death together, if we can't scheme a way out."

The lean, impertinent-eyed eunuch at the gate announced that Zeuxis was away from home.

"Then he will find me here when he returns," said Tros. "Admit me!"

"I have no such orders from my master," said the eunuch.

"Shall he find a dead slave at the gate?" Tros asked, his right hand on his dagger, so the eunuch changed his mood to an obsequious, sly suavity and Tros strode in.

And on the porch Helene greeted him, all laughter. She was dressed in pale blue silk from Alexandria, with roses in her hair and gilded sandals.

"I am washed clean—come and smell me! It took three women' three hours to make me know there were no longer any vermin in my hair! Tros—Tros of Samothrace—"

"Have you seen Zeuxis?" he interrupted.

"Yes. He went to my house to take inventory and discover how much the public custodians stole—also to turn out the landlord's bailiffs. Zeuxis says it was you who betrayed me to Cato; but he pretends that he is sorry to hear that your men are in the carceres, and he also pretends to be worried about your fate. He proposes to restore my popularity by getting my Cappadocians entered in the quadriga race, but all the Thracian drivers who amount to anything are bought up—and besides, one can't trust them, because owners who have backed their chariots to win bribe even an honest man out of his senses."

She led into the courtyard by the fountain, where she lay luxuriously on a divan and ordered Zeuxis' slaves about as if she were the mistress of his household. Wine was brought.

"Already some of my friends talk of stabbing Cato in the Forum," she remarked. "They talk too loud, the hot-heads! I am here because I daren't go home for fear they may compromise me in some foolishness. I would rather have to love old Cato than be crucified for listening to plots against him! Drink to me, Tros of Samothrace! Drink to the light in my eyes—I am told it resembles starlight on the Nile!"

Tros gulped wine, coughing to disguise embarrassment, so nervous that he could not even make believe to like her company. Her morals were no least concern of his; he knew his own strength. But he dreaded feminine intrigue as some men loathe the presence of a cat; it was indefinable but no less an obsession—almost superstition—probably heredity, due to his father's austere striving to prepare himself for the higher Samothracian Mysteries.

Helene studied him and laughed.

"Lord Tros," she said, "I like you better than the best in Rome! You challenge me! Are you a Stoic? I will wreck your stoicism! Come, drink to me—and smile a little while you do it—because I will certainly do you a great service. I perceive you are not to be won by being beaten but by being helped to succeed."

"Pearls you shall have," Tros answered, and she nodded, her eyes smouldering.

"Beware of me!" she said. "I am a great gambler. I play fair. I risk all on a throw. I would wreck Rome for the sake of what my heart is set on—aye, Rome and Alexandria, Caesar and Pompey—and you and me! Now craftily—here is Zeuxis!"

Naturally, Zeuxis was not taken by surprise; the eunuch at the gate had warned him. He affected to be pleased—ran forward to embrace Tros—let his jaw drop with an exclamation of astoundment when Tros held him off.

"I heard you had been seized. I have rushed here and there endeavouring to find friends who could help you. I—Tros, I—"

Tros drew out the tessera and held it under Zeuxis' nose.

"Now—no lies! Zeuxis, I can call eight witnesses to prove that your father and my father took oath of hospitium. There is Xenophon the banker for one, and there are doubtless temple priests who will remember it. If you have burned your tessera or lost it, that is no affair of mine. The oath holds—father to son, father to son—and you have broken faith. No lies, I said! Don't make the matter worse!"

"You never claimed hospitium," said Zeuxis, stammering.

"I had no need. The oath holds whether talked about or not. Two hospites have no need to repeat their obligations to each other, more especially when you, whose life my father saved for the oath's sake, received me open-handedly. You said your house was mine. You bade me enter and possess it. Should I then have pinned you, like a lawyer, to the details of your obligation?"

"Tros, what does this mean? I have done you no wrong," Zeuxis stammered, glancing at Helene, and his eyes were shrewdly speculative although fear blanched his cheeks.

Helene, dangerous for very love of danger and in love with Tros and with intrigue and with amusement, nodded, reassuring him. He jumped to the conclusion she was loyal to himself.

"I have done you no wrong," he repeated, meeting Tros's gaze. "Who has lied to you?"

Conceiving that Helene was his friend, he let his mind slip sidewise like mercury to another possibility, but Tros now understood the man he had to deal with and interpreted the changed look in his eyes.

"Neither poison nor dagger nor any other kind of treachery will help you any longer, Zeuxis. You have shot your bolt! Nor will it help to have me waylaid and returned into the prison, where my men lie at the risk of plague. Your infamy is known! If I die, that will not absolve you. Mark this—masticate it—let it become all your consciousness and govern you. You have but two alternatives, death or my mercy!"

"You threaten me?" Zeuxis stuttered. Fear had robbed him of his wits at last; he was trembling.

"Aye, Zeuxis! And a threat from me binds me as inescapably as any other promise! You are watched, so you can not escape abroad. The Roman who knows of your crime against Jupiter hospitalis itches to make an example of you, but I begged the chance for you to make amends. I have not yet repudiated my share of the vow, although you broke yours. I will still protect you, if you turn about—now—smartly—and undo your sacrilege by helping me, as you have harmed me hitherto, with all your zeal and cunning! I will even lie for you in that event; I will deny that my misfortune was your doing."

Zeuxis' face changed colour. Pride, resentment, fear all fought for the control of him, but fear prevailed—fear and perhaps a grain of gratitude.

"Tros, you are very generous. It is true that I lost the tessera and it escaped my mind; but you exaggerate the wrong I did, which was an indiscretion, not deliberate treachery. I took a slave into my confidence, who went and sold your men to Licius Severus, Pompey's master-of-the-horse, and it was too late then for me to—"

"Lie me no more lies!" Tros interrupted. "You intended to divide my pearls with Licius Severus! I will make him party to the sacrilege and have your slave's testimony taken on the rack if there is any doubt in your mind as to my earnestness! I know the law. An offence against hospitium is treason against Rome; so your slaves can be tortured against you—and you also! But I blame myself a little, Zeuxis; I should not have tempted you by telling you of all those pearls—which are in a safe place now, where neither you nor any other rogue can get them."

That last argument, like a knife that cuts two ways, instantly converted Zeuxis. Where the fear of punishment alone had undermined his will but left him infinitely capable of treachery, information that the pearls were out of reach removed all motive for infidelity. He wept and kneeling, clasping Tros's knees, begged him for forgiveness.

"Tros—honoured hospes—I am dying of the shame this day has brought on me! Accept my—"

But Helene knew no sentimental qualms, nor had the slightest patience with them.

"Tros!" she exclaimed, rising. "What have you done with the pearls?"

She poised a wine-cup as if taking aim. She pointed one hand at Tros's eyes. Her own eyes glared. "Are you a pauper? Is your wealth gone?" She was much more beautiful in that guise than when trying to seduce. Beautiful—unlovely! Artificiality was stripped off. Her nature was more naked than her body had been when she fought the gladiator. She was a human cobra— honestly venomous—openly baffled and angry and revengeful.

"Tros!" she said. "Have you deceived me?"

"Aye," he answered. "It appears I made you think I fear you!"

He seized her wrist. She sprang at him, but he jerked her arm and twisted it behind her back until she bit her lips in agony—then lifted her by arm and leg and threw her sprawling in a corner, where she caught the curtain to break her fall and tore it from its rod.

"Bring me a whip!" he commanded. "Swiftly, Zeuxis! Did you hear me say a whip? This slave shall learn—"

But there was no need for the whip. The word "slave" whipped her better than the strongest arm could have. She was a slave pretending to be free. No doubt the hold that Caesar, or more likely Cesar's secret agent, had over her was just that fact, that she was slave-born. In an instant she could be thrown down from whatever pinnacle she might attain. Society protected itself ruthlessly against its victims. The slave found taking liberties with freedom could be sure of nothing less than scourging—would be lucky if not crucified—lashed to a gibbet, that is, and mocked by other slaves as death came slowly of thirst and flies and gangrene.

Helene grovelled. She was too much of an artist in emotion to waste blandishments on Tros in that mood, and her slave-birth carried with it, as almost always, the peculiar slave-consciousness that crisis could bring to the surface, however deeply it was buried or however artfully concealed. The free man's scorn of slaves was not totally unjustified; tradition of the centuries, heredity, education, had instilled into the slave-born a subconsciousness of slavish spirit that mere manumission rarely overcame. It was not without inherent justice that the slave set free was still the former master's client and in many ways still bound to him, as well as denied many of the rights pertaining to a free-born citizen. Society had bred the slave and brutalized him, but it understood the problem. The slave wars that had nearly ruined Rome had served to unite all free and freed men into one close corporation, ready to endure extremities of any kind in preference to imposition by its subject human beings. If discovered, it would not have helped Helene that her owner was of high estate and her abettor in the crime against society; not even Caesar could have saved her then.

She laid her hands on Tros's feet, abject in submission on the floor in front of him. Her silence was a stronger plea than any words she might have spoken; she was pleading not alone for Tros's silence but for his protection, too, from Zeuxis who had heard the word "slave," who understood, and was incapable of not exploiting the discovery unless Tros should prevent.

"Get up!" Tros ordered. She obeyed, with all the cobra-venom gone—a piece of merchandise, worth nothing if denounced. Not Pompey, with his power to impose his will on four-fifths of the senate, could have saved her if the truth were known. For the moment she was too submissive to imagine the alternative that she had threatened through the grating of the praetor's cell; she did not feel sufficiently her own to kill herself.

That mood, Tros understood, would not last long. Her elasticity would set her scheming presently. Unless he guided the reaction she would turn more desperately dangerous than she had been. He supplied the necessary ray of hope:

"I go to Caesar soon," he said. "I have obtained a lien on Caesar's influence. Obey me wholly—without flinching—and I will not only give you the pearls I promised, but I will also demand that Caesar shall manumit you."

"Caesar doesn't own me," she said dismally. "I am only rented to him by Rabirius."

"Good. Caesar shall instruct Rabirius, who is in fear of an impeachment and will bid high for Caesar's influence with the judges. Meanwhile—" he turned on Zeuxis—"Silence! Spare that woman as I spare you! As the gods are all about us, I will ruin you if you betray her!" Then he swung around again and faced Helene. "Fail me in one batting of an eyelid and you shall see what happens to the slave caught posing as a free-born woman!"

He began to pace the floor as if it were his own poop, striding the length of the room and back again, to judge, under lowered eyelids, when he turned, the speed and the extent of Zeuxis' and Helene's recovery—intending they should not recover too far before he yoked them, as it were, and set them working. He had handled far too many mutinies at sea to let much time lapse between victory and imposition of a task.

"My men lie rotting in the dungeons," he said suddenly. "My ship makes Ostia, and my man Conops very likely has been picked up by the praetor's men or by some of Pompey's followers. I need help. Where shall I find it?"

"I have influence with Nepos," Zeuxis began, and paused. The smile on Tros's face was sardonic; there was something enigmatic in the way he stood with folded arms. "Nepos might—"

"Let us talk about today, not yesterday!" said Tros, "and of what you will do, not what Nepos might do. What is this about the races and the team of Cappadocians? Are you so situated you can enter that team?"

"Easily," said Zeuxis.

"In Helene's name?"

"Yes, under red or white, but she has no charioteer except the Sicilian who keeps the horses exercised—a freed man—a good trainer, but sure to lose his head when an opponent crowds him to the spina and the spectators begin yelling. He would also certainly be bribed to lose the race."

"What if a charioteer is found?" Tros asked.

"Who knows? If I knew the man I would bet on the Cappadocians. Otherwise I would bet just as heavily against them."

"Here is the man," said Tros. He laid a hand on Orwic's shoulder. "This is the best horseman from a land where chariot driving is the measure of a man's worth. I have seen Prince Orwic drive unbroken horses. He has magic in his hands, or in his voice, or else he owns an extra sense akin to seamanship, that says 'yes' and can make the horses say it when the gods themselves appear to say 'no'! Let him see those Cappadocians, and rig them in a chariot, and feel their helm a time or two. Let him con the course and memorize the landmarks. Then there is utterly no doubt who wins, if those four Cappadocians can run!"

It took an hour to stir enthusiasm. Zeuxis and Helene were both crushed; he had to coax them back to confidence. Zeuxis could think of a thousand doubts as to the value of the plan, and of its outcome even if successful. It was all discussed in front of Orwic, who ignorant of Greek or Latin—and they talked both—did not understand one word of it.

"Most charioteers are slaves," said Zeuxis. "Some are freed men, and the rest are of the type of gladiators—that is to say, regarded with contempt. But your friend Orwic is a prince. What will he say when he learns that the mob, which roars itself hoarse for the winner and heaps flowers on him, nevertheless thinks a charioteer no better than a gladiator—meaner, that is, than itself?"

"Who cares what a mob thinks? No task can lower a man," Tros answered. "It is men who lower their profession. If the Lord Orwic were an upstart or a mere inheritor of titles he might flinch from such a stigma, but I brought no flinchers when I picked my crew! If he had thought whatever he might do for Britain possibly could be beneath his dignity, believe me, he would be in Britain now, not sharing my adventures! Orwic!" he said suddenly, "how long is it since you made sacrifice to any god whatever?"

Orwic rose out of a chair and yawned, then shrugged his shoulders.

"Long enough for all the gods to have forgotten me," he answered.

"Are you willing to make sacrifice?"

"Aye, to your necessity. Some gain might come of that. But you have taught me not to whimper to the gods. I do nothing by halves, Tros. I have come to expect the gods to serve me, not I them."

"They will serve you best clean-shaven," Tros observed, "because the praetor's men are very likely looking for a prince with a moustache! The gods might prefer the Gaulish costume to the Roman, when the praetor's men are looking for a Briton in a Roman tunic! It is easiest to coax the gods by doing what one does best."

"I can hunt, ride, fight and drive a chariot," said Orwic, "nothing else. I am one of those unfortunates born out of time—as useless as a pig's tail. Two or three hundred years ago I might have amounted to something."

"Go and let Zeuxis' barber shave you. We will see what you can do," said Tros. Then to Helene, "Go and give your thanks to Pompey. Overwhelm him with your gratitude for having freed you from the praetor, and beg leave to reward him for his generosity by entering your Cappadocians in his name, to be driven by a Gaulish charioteer named—named—let us see, Ignotus."

Ignotus

I was born among wisemen. My father was a Prince of Wisdom. In Alexandria I attended the schools of philosophy, by nature nonetheless observant of the uses to which wisdom may be put, and never fond of thinking without doing. Unused wisdom is a vinegary wine that rots its barrel. There is no end of wisdom, but a swift end for him who forgets that wisdom flows, it is not stagnant. Speaking for myself, I have never found a set of circumstances that a little wisdom could not unravel; no error that a little wisdom could not remedy. But wisdom is not in book or bag. It is a stream, and down-stream it is foul with yesterday's mistakes. Let a than look toward its source, and dip thence; he shall not lack inspiration.

—FROM THE LOG OF TROS OF SAMOTHRACE

The Circus Maximus re-echoed to the shouts of charioteers schooling their teams at the turns, and to the hum of the voices of extravagantly well-dressed loungers gathered in groups near the gate where the chariots entered, or sprawling on the seats reserved for equites, to watch the practice gallops and lay bets or learn the latest rumours about who had bribed which charioteer.

There was a new bay-coloured team of Cappadocians yoked to a chariot embossed with Pompey's monogram and driven by a young, athletic looking man in Gaulish costume who drove them at a walk around the course so many times that the observers presently lost interest. Then, suddenly, he launched the team into a frenzied gallop, reining in again before he reached the turn.

"Did you see that? All four on their toes at once—as sudden as a javelin! That man will bear watching!" said a dissolute-faced youngster, leaning on his elbows over the barrier near the box reserved for patrons of the games.

"Better watch Helene," his companion suggested. "That is her team. The charioteer is probably her slave, and she's as crooked as Rabirius, who is said to have adopted her in Alexandria because she knew too much about his goings on! Have you heard the latest? Cato had her arrested, and Pompey interfered! Some say Pompey did it to oblige Rabirius as a desperate effort to keep on friendly terms with Caesar. And by the way, there's news this morning: Caesar has invaded Britain. Caesar's agent is backing Rabirius, whom Cato wants to prosecute for extortion in Alexandria; and now everybody is wondering what concessions Pompey had to make to Cato to get Helene out of his clutches."

"Oh, didn't you hear?" said the other, with the air of a man who always knew the news. "My steward was told by the barber who shaves Cato's secretary, that Pompey had to agree to leave Nepos in charge of the dungeons. There was talk, you know, of one of Pompey's veterans getting that job. They say Julia has sentimental prejudices and wanted a venial rascal in there who would substitute a corpse for any prisoner whom she thought unjustly condemned. But the doctor who physics Lavinia's slaves was told by one of Pompey's doctor's slaves that Julia is dying, so I daresay Pompey didn't think it worthwhile arguing. Old Cato is a Roman if there ever was one."

"Nonsense! He's a bundle of old-fashioned prejudices, with as much sense as a last year's statue on a dust-heap!"

"Never mind. He enforces the law. When a criminal has been condemned he dies in the arena. No more slaves or substitutes while Nepos is in charge and Cato shuffles off to the slums to talk with him half the night! I have old-fashioned notions. I rather admire Cato, although I admit, I would not like to entertain him in my house; he would probably arrive bare-footed, bring in the lictor with him, and discuss morality. Watch that team now!"

The Cappadocians at last were being sent around the course at full speed, he who drove them displaying none of the histrionics generally practiced by charioteers to excite the crowd. He did not shake the reins or shout; he did not fan the horses with his whip; he stood as rigidly erect as possible, allowing for knees bent to absorb motion as the chariot bumped behind the stretched out team; but any judge of speed—and there were scores of them looking on—knew instantly that this was faster than any chariot had moved that morning. There was magic in the driver's hands, that loosed four horses in one spasm, as it were, of concentrated force.

"Who is he? Look at that! Jupiter omnipo—"

There were ten teams practicing. Most of the charioteers were taking short spurts at the turns to teach their horses how to cut in when another chariot was forced outward by its own momentum at the curve. As Orwic whirled at top speed around the far end of the spina two other charioteers deliberately swung into his path, pretending not to see him!

"Gemini!"

He dodged between them as a hare slips in between the hounds, made time to lash one charioteer across the face with the butt end of his whip and, striking the other's wheel with his own hub, spilled him, hardly seeming to have lost speed, turning to laugh at the man sprawling among struggling horses.

"That's the team I bet on! The man knows his business! Mark you—that was no accident. Those are slow teams turned out purposely to injure him. Some one with a big bet is afraid of him. He shall carry my money."

"Aye—to Hades, if you're such an idiot! If they think he stands a chance of winning—the better he is, the worse for him! If they can't wreck him in the practice gallops he'll be dead before the day comes, or else some one will poison his horses or saw through the chariot axle! When did a man ever win who wasn't so well known that nobody dared to play foul? Probably Helene is in need of money, in which case the exhibition is simply an invitation to bribe her to withdraw the team or else to guarantee to lose the race!"

Meanwhile, Tros was wasting no time watching Orwic, who, well warned, was living with the horses day and night with two hired Gaulish gladiators to protect him. Though Helene had entered the team under Pompey's name, that was in some ways a disadvantage' because Pompey himself had returned to his villa to be with his ailing wife and had left all arrangements for the coming games in the hands of one of his lieutenants. There were fourteen races to be run before the third day of the games, when butchery of prisoners and combats between gladiators would begin, so Pompey's worried manager was best not approached; if asked to protect Helene's charioteer he would probably have done exactly the opposite, to avoid the risk of losing friendships among influential equites, who would object to losing money through an unknown charioteer's surprise victory. There was as much corruption in the races as politics, and there was also jealousy from Pompey's own great racing stable to consider.

But Tros had to depend not only on Orwic's victory, but on the acclamations of the crowd. He had to make Orwic popular, while he himself kept out of sight for fear of being recognized by any one who might report him to the praetor. Nepos had refused to intervene with Cato, saying he could not afford to lose the praetor's friendship; more, when Tros went to him with fruit and vegetables for his men, he said: "Are you a turn-coat after all that bold boast?"

"Get away from Rome then, now, before it's too late. Your men must tread the sand unless orders come from Cato or the senate. You have three more days, so stir yourself! I have told Cato you are in the carceres—which is near enough to the truth; I hold your promise. Cato says you have been plotting against Rome, besides intriguing with the Vestals. If Cato catches you, he'll only send you to me. There's nothing I can do, unless you want yourself run through the thigh. You might appeal then to the Vestals. They might dare to protect you; but if they should look away I would have to order out the masks and hooks. I would prefer to fight it out if I were you."

So Tros kept Zeuxis and Helene hard at work manipulating Rome's news-avid underworld. They sent their slaves into the city to inform whoever had a ticket for the games that it was safe to bet on Helene's Cappadocians and the charioteer Ignotus. Rumour having spread that Caesar had already attacked Britain, advantage was taken of that to excite superstition. It was whispered, as a deadly secret—which naturally spread like wild-fire—that Ignotus was a Gaul and had been sent by Caesar to foreshadow his own success in Britain by winning a victor's laurel in the Circus Maximus.

The mob loved Caesar and his everlasting triumphs over foreigners, whose property poured into Rome, so there were only enough doubters to keep the odds against Helene's Cappadocians comparatively tempting. The Jews, Greeks and Armenians, who openly conducted lawless betting dens under the eyes of bribed officials, did a thriving business.

Three of Zeuxis' slaves were sent to Ostia to try to find out what had become of Conops, failing which they were to watch for Tros's ship and send word by runner. But the first message they sent back was to the effect that Conops had vanished as if earth had swallowed him and that there was no sign of the ship, although two triremes, with full crews on board, were anchored near the harbour-mouth and seemed to be expecting action.

Tros made one desperate effort to reach the Vestals and appeal for their protection. But Pompey had begun to pave the way for a public protest against the Vestals' alleged intriguing in behalf of Caesar. Their palace was heavily guarded. Even when the Vestals went to change the watch over the undying flame they walked between two lines of armed men, who turned their backs toward them and faced the other way. Tros did not dare to draw attention to himself.

So he had to pin his whole faith to the wildest plan ever a desperate man invented! Orwic must be the victor in the last quadriga race on the third day, when the crowd would already be mad with excitement. Orwic must win money for the crowd as well as foretell Caesar's coming triumph. That was something that the gods and Orwic must contrive between them. Then, the races over, Orwic must join Tros in the carceres and sally forth the next day into the arena, while the crowd still loved him, and so make Tros and his Northmen popular. Whether they should have to fight Numidians or beasts, Orwic must appear to be the leader; Tros himself would simply guard the young man's back and rally the Northmen when they needed it. Then, when the foes were beaten—as they must be!—Tros, acting as interpreter for Orwic, would appeal to the spectators—to the Vestals—even to Pompey himself as the patron of the games! The odds were half a million to one against the plan's success—and yet no other plan was possible.

There was nothing to count on but the mob's emotion, absolutely unpredictable, although the Roman mob was sometimes generous toward prisoners who showed good sport. The Vestals, if the mob were not enthusiastic, might not dare to give the signal to let Tros and his companions go free. Possibly Pompey had conveyed a hint to them. But if they did dare, nobody would question the decision afterward—not even Pompey himself.

And meanwhile, not a sign from Conops—not a hint of where the ship might be. She might be wrecked. Or Sigurdsen might have flinched from the risk of putting into Ostia and, turning pirate, might have set forth on a mad cruise of his own. And Caesar already invading Britain. Probably Caesar was short of men because of the lack of shipping and the dire necessity to hold Gaul with numberless garrisons all ready for emergency. But even now Caswallon and his Britons might be fighting desperately for their Lunden Town. He could almost hear Fflur saying: "Tros will defeat Caesar. Never doubt him!"

And last, not least, Helene added to the climax of perplexities.

When he told her his plan and she understood he had nothing to depend on but the very doubtful generosity of the spectators, she recovered self-possession. The cobra-venom in her took a new lease of existence.

"Tros," she said, "Lord Tros, you are no judge of women, but to judge men shrewdly is my one gift. I find you admirable. You can thrill me as no man ever did, and you can make me flinch without a blow, which is a rapturous sensation now I come to think of it. And I adore a man who is so faithful that the very Roman headsman trusts him! Nevertheless, I think you are the least wise man I ever saw!"

"Rot me your opinion!" Tros exploded. "Save your own skin by obedience."

"Lord Tros," she answered, smiling, "I believe I know a better way than all this trusting to your gods, and to the crowd. I don't believe in any gods, not having seen them, but I know the Romans; I have seen them sobbing at the death of elephants and howling in the next breath for the death-blow to a brave man, simply for the lust to see a man die! A good gamble is exciting, and the game has most zest when the stakes are highest. But why give too long odds, when there is a better chance, and more to win, in an equally exciting game?"

"What treachery do you brew now?" Tros wondered, staring at her.

"None. Tros, I love you! I would rather die with you in the arena than betray you or see you lose."

"Tros," and there was anger in her eyes now, "do not doubt me. I will gamble with you to the end, and I will do my utmost to prepare the crowd to set you free by acclamation. But remember—if you go free, that will be in part my doing. I will have a claim on you."

"True. I will remember it," said Tros. "Pearls you shall have, and your freedom when I reach Caesar."

"If you leave Rome, I come too!" she retorted. "Do you think my heart is anything to trifle with? And it is easier to shake off war's scars than—"

She perceived she had not even penetrated through his thoughts of fifty other matters that obsessed him.

"Conops," he said, looking absent-minded, "may have fallen foul of drink and women. He is a faithful little rascal, but the wine shops on the harbour-front of Ostia—"

Helene laughed—abruptly—bitterly. "Tros, do you think I am not worth more to you than any longshore sailor?"

"Deep-sea sailor," he corrected.

She ignored the interruption.

"I have said, I love you. I have never loved until I saw you—never!"

"Tchutt! That reminds me," said Tros, "I must take care of Zeuxis."

"It is I not Zeuxis who will cause the crowd to free you," she retorted. "I am spending all my money. I am even begging the favour of Lucius Petronius—that dog!—if he will use his influence among the equites. And do you think I will let you leave me to Petronius? You shall take me with you, or you shall never leave Italy!"

But Tros was thinking of Caswallon and the Trinobantes, probably retreating before Caesar's doggedly advancing legions. He could almost see Caswallon's kind face and the eyes of Fflur. Almost he could hear Fflur speak:

"The Lord Tros will never desert us. Somehow he will find a way to worry Caesar's rear. Tros never would forget a friendship."

Slowly the far-away look in his eyes relaxed, and the frown melted. As he threw off that mood, he laid his hand abruptly on Helene's shoulder—not particularly gently, noticing the strength of her young muscles, smiling at the thought that she should waste affection on him.

"Woman," he said, cheerfully, "if you prefer to ruin me, arrange for me to die in the arena! Now I go to give my men encouragement. If you love me, as you say, then watch for my man Conops. If he comes contrive to let him reach me. And one other thing—attend to it that Zeuxis sends into the carceres those weapons that my men left in bundles in his charge."

"I am yours," she answered. "I will serve you. But remember—I am yours as much as any of your men and you shall not desert me! Tros, I have warned you! Did you hear me? Did you understand?"

Conops

In Alexandria there are slaves who teach philosophy, and they are good teachers. From a slave I learned the trick of calculus by which I built the ship I visioned, whereas all he saw was calculus. It is true, I have found my freedom is slavery to the daily need to enlarge it, lest it grow less and ensnare me into love of thinking but not doing. But I find my slavery is less humiliating than that other.

Nevertheless, there are men whose virtue lacks direction. Such men need a master, to whom they yield obedience in exchange for stanch exaction of the best they can do. Not being God, I know not why this is, but I observe it. I myself would willingly obey a man who could exact from me more than I give to the men who obey my commands.

—From the Log of Tros of Samothrace

In cellars, dens and storerooms under the tiers of wooden seats, in the dungeons, and in the big, stone-walled enclosures at either end of the Circus Maximus pandemonium reigned for many days before a public spectacle. In nothing had the Romans carried organization to such a pitch as in the management of public games, so discipline prevailed in spite of frantic haste and privileged interference. The actual control was in the hands of experts, many of whom were foreigners, and each of whom knew the last detail of his own particular responsibility.

The giver of the games—he who paid the bill—was only nominally in authority; he left all details to subordinates, of whom the greater number were, like Nepos, permanently employed by the city and responsible to elected officials. They resented the officious interference of the patron's own men, whose ambition naturally was to produce a spectacle more magnificent and thrilling than any one that had preceded it, the whole purpose of the spectacle—originally a religious rite—being to increase the patron's fame.

Pompey lacked—and his lieutenants knew he lacked—a true grip on the popular imagination. His tastes were literary and artistic. He loathed the brutal exhibitions that had become the crowd's first test of a man's fitness to hold public office. Although his agents scoured the earth for animals and gladiators, though his school of gladiators was the best in Rome, and though his racing-stable was superbly managed, beyond ordering his treasurer to pay the bills he gave scant personal attention to any of those interests, preferring his country estate and his library, both lavishly adorned with plunder that he brought home from his conquests in the East.

Pompey was a man whose natural ability was undermined by vanity and by contempt for details. It pleased him to believe that, in his own phrase, he could stamp his foot and raise an army—to accomplish any purpose. Temperamentally he was lazy, vain and opportunist; politically he was autocratic but averse to civil violence except in so far as it was necessary to enforce his own convenience; his own lieutenants were as arrogant and violent as any men in Rome, but he upheld them. Theoretically he was opposed to looting, but he had enriched himself by that means; in speech and writing he condemned corruption, but his own front garden at election time was set with tables, at which his corps of secretaries handed out the money for the votes. His magnanimity was frequently spectacular and very often genuine, particularly if it ministered to pride; but he could shut his eyes to things he did not want to know, with almost ox-like indifference—in which respect he was so far inferior to Caesar that there was no comparing the two, politically. Caesar ignored nothing. Pompey, equally an opportunist, blazed out of retirement, exercised his genius until he wearied of it, and withdrew again.

Naturally, his character had bred a corresponding attitude of mind in his lieutenants, who irritated Caesar at every opportunity and looked to Pompey to control the consequences. It was well known, even to outsiders, that the only bond of peace between the two men was the fact that Caesar's daughter Julia was Pompey's wife and that Pompey was extremely fond of her. Caesar depended on Julia to preserve at least the outward appearance of friendship, although it was a moot question whether she deliberately fed Caesar's ambition or was simply eager to contrive peace.

Now, although the doctors held out hopes of Julia's recovery, they only deceived Pompey who, as usual, believed what it pleased him to believe and shut his eyes to an alternative. None who had seen her recently had any doubt that Julia was dying; and none doubted that when Julia was dead the open breach with Caesar must inevitably follow. Pompey's closest friends, in fact, were eager for the issue; it was clear to them that Caesar's influence was gaining and delay increased his chances of success. The time to split the breach wide open was while Caesar's hands were full in Gaul and Britain.

So the men who took over the Circus Maximus in Pompey's interest determined that the crowd should recognize him as the greatest entertainer who had ever squandered his munificence on Rome. They would make Caesar's entertainments, recklessly extravagant though these were, fade from the public memory. They nearly drove the staff of regular attendants mad with their interference and Nepos, for instance, cursed the very name of Pompey. The dens and cages under the high tiers of seats, and the cellars below those, were so packed with roaring animals, and the stench from them was so atrocious, that it was even doubted whether horses would be manageable during the three days chariot-racing that were to precede the slaughter.

The dungeons were so thronged that no excuse was needed for confining Tros's men in wooden cells above the level of the ground. Nepos even used the Northmen to help spread the loads of coarse sand brought in by countless carts from the sandpits near the Via Appia and many another prisoner toiled in fetters, hoping that goodwill might cause him to be spared some last indignity. The risk of fire was so great that the whole of Crassus' fire-brigade and all the sailormen ashore in Ostia were summoned to stand watch, with the result that two whole crowded streets of Rome were gutted by the fires which raged with no one to extinguish them. All Rome talked of nothing but the coming games.

Nepos, who never went home now but spent day and night attending to his prisoners and rearranging groups for this and that atrocious butchery, made quite a confidant of Tros, invited him to share his hurried meals and grumbled to him about every countermanded order and new interference with his plans.

"Why can't they leave it to men who have done this kind of thing all their lives? Take your men, for instance. First, I was to send them in to fight Numidians. That would have been good; but, some fool thought it would be better to send them against Roman gladiators, who would finish them off and then slaughter the blacks—which would have been a sort of compliment to the ever-victorious Roman legions.

"Well, that wouldn't have been so bad, although it would have cost like Canna in expensive gladiators. But some other idiot remembered your men are criminals and not entitled to a fair chance. One man said I shouldn't give them weapons. I had Hercules' own labour to convince that stupid fool—he's one of Pompey's favourites and probably the man who agreed with Zeuxis to put you in trouble for sake of your pearls.—Did you have pearls? Did the wrong man get them from you? This job looks to me like spite."

"I have fifty, and a little money," Tros said, looking keenly at him.

"Well, you can't buy me! If you get out of this you will need all—but I don't believe that's possible. If it's a case of masks and hooks that cloak of yours shall hang on my wall. I will keep an eye on the men who drag you to the spoliarium. That fool argued that you and your men are criminals and should be torn by beasts; he tried to bribe me to have you trapped somehow and used on the bulls that Caesar sent here recently. When he sees you in the arena he'll be surprised. He'll expect me to claim that bribe. Maybe I will! Luckily for you Caesar's agents wouldn't let us have the bulls; Caesar expects to use them for his own show later on. I insisted you're not regular criminals, not having been committed by a judge, and somebody might hold me liable if I should send you in unable to protect yourselves. Then they thought of a new notion—not a bad one either. Your men are to have the weapons they're used to and fight lions; then Numidians; then, if they survive that, Roman gladiators. And now listen; I'm an old hand at this business. Since you're going in with them they'll have a leader, and that makes a big difference.

"The longer you last the better the crowd will like you, unless they suspect you of stalling. On the other hand, you'll have to use caution. If you're too cautious the overseers will order out the whips and hot irons to inspire you. You must take a very careful middle course. If you overcome the Numidians too easily the populace will lust to see the tables turned on you and you'll get no mercy when the gladiators lay you on the sand. But if you lose a few men to the lions, and some more to the Numidians, and then fight well against the gladiators, they'll take pity on you from the benches. What do you say? Shall I promise a few pearls to Glaucus—he fights with the sword and buckler and has never been touched once—he's in his prime—unbeatable. For half a dozen pearls he would run you through the thigh. And Glaucus is a decent fellow—good-natured—gallant—knows how to throw an attitude, and smile, with his foot on a man's body, that persuades the crowd to spare his victim nearly every time."

Tros nodded.

"Mind you, I can't guarantee the populace," said Nepos. "But if your man, Orwic, wins his race, and joins you, and plays leader against beasts and men; and if you fight capably, I think they will wave their handkerchiefs. If the applause is loud enough the Vestals are almost sure to add their verdict, and whether they order you released or not I can pretend I understood that. I should say you have a fifty to one chance, which is more than most men have who go in under my auspices!"

Tros thanked him.

"Don't offer me money!" said Nepos. "I'm old and don't need it. I'm devoted to justice, like Cato. I like to see the enemies of Rome die, but I prefer to give an honest man a chance. And by the way, remember about the lions. They'll be half-starved, two to every one of you, and each will get a touch of hot iron as he comes out of the trap. Nine men out of ten get killed by striking at them too soon. Coax them, if you can, to spring. Then duck—don't spring aside—and rip them up from under. The worst are those that don't spring but lurk and then come running at you. Then what you chiefly need is luck, but the best plan is to run at them—meet them midway; sometimes then they flinch. Flinching costs life, man or beast; and mark you—never try to avoid them! Meet them head on. They can claw you sidewise quicker than a knife-stab."

Tros went to instruct his men and met less trouble than he feared. It thrilled the Northmen that their leader had preferred to share their fate, though they had walked into a trap like fools. Their own tradition, that a death in battle was a passport to the halls of everlasting revelry, was no half-hearted superstition; they regarded life as an exordium to death. They would have gloomed if left alone; with Tros to lead them they were jubilant.

Tros borrowed a harp and set the skald to singing legends of Valhalla, until the Northmen roared the old familiar refrains and even the homesick Britons joined in, experts at a tune, although the vowel sounds they made instead of words were meaningless. So Nepos sent them wine, because their chanting cheered the other prisoners and it was half his battle to get men into the arena looking like men and not carcasses already three parts dead. The hot iron and the whip could work a semblance of rebellious indifference, but song, so rarely heard within those walls, made men again of tortured rift-raft, who were lucky—as Nepos tactfully assured them—not to have been crucified at crossroads with their entrails showing through the wounds made by the scourge.

There was wine for all the prisoners the last three nights, because Tros persuaded Nepos to permit it and himself defrayed the cost, but the effect of that was largely offset by precautions against suicide; men fettered hand and foot watched by slaves with heated irons are not easily encouraged. There were cries from a few caught opening a vein against a fetter's roughed edge or attempting to strangle each other. They were whipped for it, burned, then lashed to the pillars to keep them from try-ing again. The roaring of the beasts—beginning to be starved now—made night horrible, and there had been a grim rehearsal in the afternoon that left its impress on the prisoners' minds. The picture was ineradicable—of the empty seats, where presently free Romans and their wives and daughters would lean gasping, lips parted, to gloat at the carnage.

Nine elephants, tortured to make them dangerous, were trumpeting their indignation. Wolves, that were to tear their next meal from the throats of unarmed men, howled in mel-ancholy chorus. Bulls bellowed; and a great rhinoceros—a rar-ity Rabirius had begged from Ptolemy the Piper—pounded his cage with a noise like a splintering ship. One whole cage full of leopards got loose in the night and wrought havoc be-fore they were cornered with torches and netted. The torches set fire to the planks of the seats overhead, and when that was extinguished the carpenters came to rebuild, so that morning might find the arena undamaged—new-painted—agleam in the sun.

It was under the din of the hammers, through the min-gled stink and clamour of the beasts, that Tros heard a voice he thought he recognized. At first he mocked himself, believing he was dreaming. There were no lights, saving where the bra-ziers glowed and where a guard or two moved phantom-like in gloom, occasionally pausing to insert a lamp between the bars and make sure that no prisoner should cheat the appetite of Rome by smothering himself. A shadow seemed to move within the shadow that lay slanting at the bars of Tros's cage—Nepos had assigned him to the cage-of-honour, reserved for women as a rule, where a breath of air could enter through the bars whenever any one passed through the wooden door into the unroofed arena. But Tros thought he had imagined that. He even looked away, not liking that imagination should deceive him; it suggested that the horror of the situation had begun to undermine his self-control.

But the voice spoke louder:

"Master! This is Conops! I am come from Ostia! I have three boats below the fish-wharf on the Tiber! Sigurdsen picked up a breeze off Corsica and now stands off and on before the harbour mouth, where two great triremes lie at anchor."

"How is it I had no word from you before this?" Tros demanded.

"Master, when I got to Ostia I knew that was no place for me! There were women and wine—no sight of Sigurdsen—I couldn't have resisted. So I stole a sail-boat and took with me a one-eyed slave, who called me brother. He wanted to escape to Corsica, where there are outlaws in the mountains, so he helped me to steal provisions from the stores behind the sheds where the imported slaves are quarantined, and we put to sea by night. I knew Sigurdsen would keep clear of the coast of Italy for fear of triremes. And I knew the pilot was a duffer who would want to sight land frequently. There was also food and water to consider; Sigurdsen would have to make some port of call before he dared put into Ostia with the chance of being chased away before he could re-provision; and besides, he would know you might want to put to sea at once, so he would fill the corn-bins and the water-butts at least. I picked him up the fourth day—saw his purple sails against the skyline.

"There was not much mutiny aboard. Such as it was soon quieted when I climbed over the rail. I gave them news of you. I said the Roman senate had proclaimed you admiral! But master, master, what is this! What—"

"Swiftly with your tale!" Tros ordered.

"I returned with the ship, and when we sighted Ostia we had to put that Roman pilot in the fore-peak. He was up to mischief, trying to lay us on a sandbank where the trireme men could come and pick us clean in the name of salvage. We had brought along Bagoas, the slave. We shaved his head and I rubbed some stain on him, but he understood that the disguise wouldn't help him if he didn't act right. He was so afraid of being recognized and flogged to death for escaping that I had hard work to get him ashore.

"I was for hurrying to Rome. But the first Roman I met after I reached shore stopped me and asked whether I was Conops. I couldn't even talk Greek, naturally. I was from the western coast of Gaul and none too handy with any kind of speech, but quick-footed; and it was dark, so that was the last I saw of him. It seemed proper then to peel an eye before I cast off, so I sent Bagoas to a wine-shop to discover what was being said—you know the wine shop near the rope-walk, where the big fat Jewess sells charms against scurvy and all the freed men go to learn the shipping news? I didn't give Bagoas enough money to get drunk, and pretty soon he overheard a loud-mouthed man who was looking for two lost gladiators. He was from Rome that hour. I had the news of you as soon as One-Eye had swallowed his quartarius."

"One-Eye wanted to be rid of me then, so I warned him I'd sell him to informers if he didn't stand by, and I promised him a billet on the ship if he behaved himself. He was a stoker in the baths before he ran, so anything looked good to him. I sent him back to Sigurdsen that night with orders to send our longboat and a dozen Northmen with a week's provisions. They were to row straight up-Tiber—there's no tide worth mentioning, and the stream isn't too swift, not for one of our boat's crews. They were to wait for me where the barges lie anchored below the brick-kilns on the south side of the river. Then I hired two more boats—good ones—money down; and there was big fish, tons of it, all waiting to be boated up to Rome as soon as ever the slave-gangs came down stream. But something had delayed the slave-gangs and the fish was liable to rot, so I made a bargain to boat that fish to Rome at half price, they to load it and the merchant to give me a pass in writing in the name of Nicephorus of Crete. That made me right with any one who might ask questions. Then I ran up-river to the brick-kilns and fetched the Northmen; and what between rowing and towing, and they not knowing any human language so they couldn't answer questions, we made Rome all right; and the man who paid me for delivering the fish agreed to give me a cargo of empty oil-jars if I'd cut the price and wait a week."

"I stipulated he should give my men a shed to sleep in, down there by the Tiber, and what with hinting I might do a bit of smuggling for him, and my not seeming to know the price of freightage on the Tiber, we struck up quite a friendship and the crew are as safe as weevils in a loaf of bread. They're supposed to be Belgae, taken captive by Caesar and sold in Gaul. I told him I'd left the papers for them with a Roman in Ostia who lent me money on that security; so he won't try any tricks; they'll be there when we want them.

"Then I went to Zeuxis' house, and found Helene talking with him. Something's up. They're hatching something. But she said where you are, so I brought Bagoas and came here to apply for a job to rig the awnings over the spectators' seats. That let me into the arena and the rest was easy. One of the guards here thinks I'm a slave belonging to the blacksmith who was fetched in a hurry to repair the hinges on the dungeon gate—the one that opens into the arena. That's his sledge you hear."

"But now, master, what next? I'm only a seafaring man, and I've probably overlooked a lot of things, but you just say the word and I'll do my best for you, by Heracles. I've left Bagoas out in the arena, where he's chewing onions and waiting for the dawn to go on rigging. We can easily escape into the street. What then? I'm at the rope's end. There are three boats waiting, and a good crew. We can row downstream like Hermes—in-a-hurry—but how get you out of here?"

Tros reached an arm between the bars and gripped his shoulder.

"Little man," he said; and then, for a few heart-beats there was nothing he could say at all.

"Go you back to Sigurdsen," he ordered. "Bid him stand by in the offing five more days. Then, if I come not, divide the ship between you—he to be captain, you lieutenant, sharing profits equally. But I believe that I will come before the five days. Go you back to Sigurdsen and take Bagoas."

"Nay, I will not!" Conops answered. "I will stay here. You have been my master since I taught you how to splice a rope-end and—"

"You shall obey me!" Tros retorted. "Go you and tell Sigurdsen I come in five days. Say nothing more to him—unless I come not—only bid him watch those triremes in the port of Ostia and show them his heels if they put to sea. But on the fourth day, or the fifth day after you reach Sigurdsen, if you should see our three boats putting out, stand in then with all three oar-banks manned and all sail ready to be shaken down. Stand by to pluck us out from right under the triremes' noses if you must."

"But, master—"

"Mutiny? In this pass? You are the man I have always trusted, Conops. Do as I bid you!"

"Master, if we never meet again—"

"By Heracles, if I could get out I would break your head for such dog's whimpering! Obey! Step lively! Shall the gods come to the aid of men who drown good bravery with tears like pork in brine? Of what use is a sentimental lingerer by cell-doors? Do you think this is a brothel, that you dawdle in it? Off with you! Almighty Zeus! Have I neglected discipline, that my own man should flout me and defy me when I bid him—"

"Nay, not Neptune would defy you in that mood, master. Farewell!"

"Farewell, Conops. And expect me on the fifth day after you

reach Sigurdsen—or sooner! Keep two good men at the mast-head. Grease all blocks and reeve new running gear wherever needed. Serve out grease to all the rowers and don't let them waste it on the oar-ports; watch them rub it on the leathers. If I find one speck of dirt above-deck or below there will be Zeus's own reckoning to pay!"

Circus Maximus

I know the virtue of a fight. Who knows it better than I?
For I have fought against beasts and men, the elements, mu-
tinous crews, treachery, and my own ill-humour. If wisdom,
aye, or cunning, aye, or a moderate measure of yielding what
is mine, can not preserve me from a fight then let my enemy
look to his guard. Peace, bought at the price of cowardice,
is too dear. I love a fight that I have done my utmost to
avoid—aye, it may be not all my utmost. I am human.

But I rate an animal more highly than the man who
gluts his eyes on cruelty, feeding his own foulness with the
sight of boughten slaughter. The fish, that slay only what
they need, are less contemptible.

—FROM THE LOG OF TROS OF SAMOTHRACE

As the fungus grows on dunghills and the burned stump sends up shoots before it dies, life took a three day lease of hopeless men, and there were strange events within the dungeons while the chariot-racing lasted. No stone walls could shut out the blare of trumpets, the thunder of wheels and hoofs and the roar of the throng. Not a criminal down in the dark but knew the names of all the charioteers, and there was actually betting between cell and cell, men wagering their miserable pittances of bread, the doles of water or the questionable privilege of being last through the gate when the time came to face the arena. Last men usually got a taste of red-hot iron.

Dungeon-keepers, thronging at the gate to watch the racing, had to take turns hurrying below to name the winner of each missus, as a seven-round race was called; and there were twenty on the first day, twenty on the second. If a dungeon-keeper carried the news tardily there was a clamour that set Nepos in a frenzy for his reputation; and it generally sent him to Tros in the end because he had formed a strange attachment to him and it calmed the old man's overwrought nerves to talk frankly. His sinews stood like taut cords from the mental tension he was under.

"I grow old, Tros, but I never lose the fascination of these last hours. I have seen so many die that you would think I should feel indifferent. I tell you, curiosity grips me harder now than when I first had charge of the slaves who lop the heads off prisoners of war after a triumph. When I trained the gladiators, it was always the same fascination—where do they go when they die? What do they think when their heads are cut off? Why is it that excitement seizes them when the time draws near? Races—that is only an excuse. If there were silence out there on the sand, they would find some other reason to act foolishly. Tros, I have seen men who have been tortured until hardly any flesh remained on arms and legs, laugh gaily on the last night—men so racked that they had to be carried in and staked in the arena for the beasts to maul. Why? What is it that so takes hold of them and makes them reckless of whip or anything?"

"So many men, so many points of view," said Tros.

"Aye, maybe. But one death for all of them, whatever caused it! You are probably about to die. What thoughts are calming you so that you sit and clean your belt, whereas I fret myself? Ho! Brutus! Take an iron down there and use it freely unless they stop that clamouring—The races, Tros, excite me not at all and I can watch men being tortured—aye, and women, without even curiosity. But when it comes to death I must confess that interests me. Tell me, of what are you thinking?"

"Of the destiny that governs us," Tros answered. "I have seen death, too, and I have not yet met the man who must not die.

But I believe it is impossible to kill a man until his time comes. And I think that if the gods have use for any one they pluck him out of any danger. But they have no use for men who pray to them and waste good time and energy on whining. I am waiting for the gods to show me half an opportunity."

"But I was talking about death," objected Nepos. "In the next three days eight hundred men, including gladiators, are to die where now the chariots are racing. What think you of death?"

"It is like tomorrow. I will face it when it comes," Tros answered. "In the meantime I would like to meet the miscreant who made this belt. He fashioned it too narrow and forgot that sea-air calls for double tanning of the leather. I would let him feel the belt a time or two and learn his trade; some never learn until it dawns on them that being flogged hurts!"

"Have you no fear?" Nepos asked. "I have seen men so in the grip of fear that they could not feel."

"I am familiar with fear," Tros answered. "It has also grown familiar with me and has abandoned many of its tricks as useless. Now I am afraid of one thing only—that the Britons may believe I have deserted them. There is a king in Britain, and a woman by the name of Fflur, his wife, who love me, and I love them. It would be a miserable destiny to die and leave them thinking I had never even run a risk to protect them from Caesar."

"But if you went free, could you do that? How?" asked Nepos.

Tros's leonine eyes observed him for a moment. He was instantly alert for signals that the gods might give.

"If I should swear to you that I am telling naked truth, would you believe me and not ask questions?" he demanded.

Nepos nodded.

"I have heard strange truth from many a man in this place under a seal of secrecy. No law obliges me to tell what I learn here. Whoever comes into the carceres, the law has done with; he is a dead man and his secrets die too. But if you speak of the Vestal Virgins I will not listen, because—"

"I will not speak of them," said Tros. "But I will say this—if the gods, or you, or any one can get me out of here alive—and I will not go, mind you, without the men who call me master!—I can call off Caesar."

"How?"

"By turning him toward Rome! That is naked truth, on my oath by the shrines of Samothrace."

"You have a message for him from—you mean, that if you reach him—"

"He will take his eyes off Britain and make Rome his goal. He will believe the time has come to try out destiny!" said Tros.

The Roman throng in the arena roared like mad beasts—shrieked, yelled, clamoured—as a four-horse chariot went down under another's wheels. The tumult swallowed up the roaring of the beasts and there were warning trumpet blasts to stop stamping that might wreck the rows of seats. Expectancy silenced the dungeons, until suddenly they burst into a tumult because nobody reported what had caused the uproar. At a nod from Nepos half a dozen men went into the arena, armed with hooks and ropes, to drag away dead horses and a mangled man.

"Their first taste of blood!" said Nepos. "This time tomorrow you will hear them offering money to the charioteers to smash their opponents' wheels! There's little chance for any novice such as your man."

"So?" said Tros.

"No chance at all. They'll roll him in the sand before he goes around the spina once. However, I have always thought Pompeius Magnus was a danger to Rome. He has none of the true bronze in him that Caesar has. Caesar can be cruel; he has virtue; he is not afraid of anything and he isn't lazy. Cato is wrong about Caesar, as I have told him half a hundred times. And so you think the gods make use of you and me? I doubt it. That is not a Roman way of thinking of the gods. However, each to his own theory—and death to us all in the end! Well, Tros, keep up your courage. I would like to see Julius Caesar come to discipline this city! And if Pompey accused you of intriguing with—Who should know better than They what will happen? Well, keep up your courage. It's against the rules for any one to beg their favour or to hand them a petition, and it's death, mind you, to insult them, but listen now! There's no law against, for instance—"

Nepos hesitated. He was actually trembling. Vestal Virgins were a power so intensely reverenced that even in the carceres their name was sacrosanct. Not only were they unapproachable, but all the reverence of Rome for her traditions and her old grim gods had centred—rallied, as it were—around the persons of the Vestals. They alone were without blemish and without reproach.

"Not even Pompey dares to put a spite on them!" said Nepos. "But do they know you are in here? I'll bet they don't. Who told them? You can't have told them. They will know for the first time when they see you march out of the dungeon gate. Well—there is no law against my changing the arrangements. Listen—when I send you in to face the lions, march you straight to Pompey's box and there salute him. That is something only gladiators are supposed to do. Then turn toward the Vestals in the box beside him on his right hand and salute them. Maybe then they'll recognize you. Who knows? The attendants are supposed to loose the lions instantly when you appear but I will bid them wait while you march once around the arena and let the populace observe how gallantly you bear yourselves. When you have slain the lions, make no appeal but await the Numidians close to the Vestals' box. And the same when the Numidians are beaten and the gladiators come. Then, if the Vestals choose to spare you, they will have the verdict of the populace and Pompey himself will have to bow to it."

Within the dungeon recklessness increased as time wore on. The night after the second day of racing a rebellion broke out and nearly ended in escape. A score of men pounced on the guard who entered their dark hole to feed them, robbed him of his hooked club, slew him, seized the hot irons from the braziers and stormed the stairway leading to the upper cells. Extra guards were summoned from the outside and for an hour there was infernal war by torchlight until all the men who had escaped were roped and four guards, suffering from ghastly wounds inflicted by a hooked club, had been carried out. All the while the fighting lasted Nepos' voice kept threatening drastic penalties to any guard who "spoiled" a man, as he expressed it; they were needed whole for the arena, able to stand up and die excitingly, so it was the guards, that night, who suffered.

"Nevertheless," said Nepos, "they shall wish they had refrained from that attempt. That batch was destined for the elephants, who slay swiftly. Now they shall be torn by dogs, and they shall enter the arena first."

His honour was offended by the outbreak and he even put an extra chain and lock on Tros's cell door.

"Not that I doubt your good-will, but a madness seizes men at times and they act like leopards," he explained. "I have known prisoners to break the bars and kill the other prisoners who would not join them."

But he let Tros out of his cell next day to watch the racing through a small hole in the dungeon wall. He fettered his wrists behind his back and chained him to a ring-bolt in the stone floor, as he explained it, to prevent the guards from telling tales about him; but the truth was, Nepos was himself half mad with nervousness, as fascinated by the prospect of the butchery to come as were the citizens who packed the seats in the arena.

They were yelling now for blood. It did not satisfy them that the charioteers showed almost superhuman skill in swinging four-horse teams around the curves at each end of the course; they urged the men to break each other's wheels, to cut in and break horses' legs, to beat each other with their whips. They howled and whistled when a man won easily. And when the next teams lined up for the start, instead of waiting breathless for the starter to give the signal from his box they yelled advice to the contestants to play foul and hurled abuse to the officials whose duty it was to compel the charioteers to line up properly along the oblique starting-line which was arranged to compensate the outside chariot for the wider circle it must make at the farther end.

The spina down the centre, adorned with flagpoles and dolphins, was as crowded with spectators as were the surrounding tiers of seats. The mob roared loudest when a group who leaned over the spina, clinging to one another, fell and were crushed under chariot-wheels; their bodies tripped a four-horse team and the resulting crashing carnage produced roars of satisfaction that aroused the lions and indignant elephants—so that it was impossible to get the horses started for the next race until attendants seized their heads and some of them were kicked and crushed under the wheels.

It was mid-afternoon before Orwic's turn came, and the din that greeted him from the upper seats was evidence enough that Zeuxis and Helene had neglected nothing that could stir the popular imagination. He was dressed like any other charioteer, in Roman tunic, with a red badge to distinguish him, and came out first of four teams through the archway, in a chariot bearing Pompey's monogram. That meant that he had drawn the inside berth, and the betting odds changed in his favour rapidly, as the mob's voice indicated, breaking into short staccato barks.

There was a breathless silence as the four teams moved up to the line, each charioteer reining and urging his horses to get them on their toes—then suddenly an uproar like a vast explosion as the chariot next to Orwic's swerved in to lock wheels and pin him up against the spina—a trick often played on novices to spoil their chance before the race began. But the uproar broke into a tumuli of astonished laughter at the neatness with which the unknown man shot clear of the entanglement and, wheeling, struck the offending veteran across the face. The crowd applauded him until the frantic horses nearly broke out of control, and the more they plunged and fought the men who tried to hold their heads, the more the spectators thundered, stamping their feet until attendants armed with staves belaboured them to save the wooden floors.

Then laughter; for the race was a procession of three chariots pursuing Orwic's, weaving in and out, manoeuvring to wreck each other at the turns, but never coming within lengths of the bay team driven by the Briton, who could hug corners with his horses belly-to-the-earth because he had been taught from infancy to do the same thing with scythe-armed chariots on either hand. The unknown man was in his element. In contrast to the furious histrionics of the others he was quiet, almost motionless. Excepting at the corners, which he took on one wheel like a sail-boat in a squall, he stood erect, his only gesture a salute to Pompey's box and to the Vestals as he whirled by.

Men threw money at him; women, flowers when the race was over. Crowned with a wreath of myrtle leaves he was sent once around the course at a slow gallop to acknowledge the applause and Pompey, ignorant of who he was, threw his own wreath down to him. The significance of that could hardly have escaped even a Northman. Orwic reined in to receive the wreath from an attendant, and as Pompey gave his seat to a substitute to preside over the last three races and turned to leave the box he waved his hand in acknowledgment of Orwic's courteous salute. The last three races were run in a half filled Circus; the noisiest spectators had won money at exhilarating odds, and had gone home to exult about it and to rest in preparation for the much more thrilling entertainment to begin tomorrow.

It was night when Orwic came, spluttering and gasping at the prison stench and pinching at Tros's muscles through the bars. "A man rots swiftly in a dungeon," he remarked, then laughed, a little reassured because Tros gripped him with a sudden strength that hurt.

"Tros, twenty men have tried to buy me from Helene! I was mobbed out there behind the stables! If it weren't that I'm supposed to be Helene's slave I never could have got here. I'd be drunker than a sailor! She pretended I was in danger from the other charioteers—and that was true, they'd kill me if they had a chance."

"She had her own slaves spirit me away and one of Zeuxis' fellows brought me here after dark. Good Lud of Lunden, what a land of stinks! Helene is now spreading rumours that one of Pompey's men has had me thrown into the arena because she refused to sell me, and that he had bribed the peregrine praetor, whatever that is, to refuse to interfere. It was difficult for me to understand, because the interpreter she had to use knew only a little Gaulish, but I gathered she is working up a great reception for us. What are we supposed to do? Fight lions? Men, too? Romans? I will gladly take a long chance for the sake of gutting half a dozen Romans! How are the men? And have the weapons come? Oh, by the way; Helene said this, or so I understood her; mind you, she is using an interpreter:

"'If you deny me, you shall lose your ship. If you accept me, you have only to fight gallantly and you shall sail away.'

"It sounded like a threat, Tros, but she is working day and night to save you. So is Zeuxis. I understood Zeuxis to say that Conops turned up and joined you in the carceres. What happened to him?"

Nepos came and with a nod of recognition let Orwic into Tros's cell. He was too busy for conversation, but he grinned and jerked his thumb up to encourage Tros. His face looked like a demon's in the lantern light, with tortured, nervous eyes that lacked sleep. Tros and Orwic talked until silence fell, then slept. That night the only men within the carceres who did not sleep were the suspicious guards, who prodded prisoners at intervals through cell bars to assure themselves that none had cheated the arena.

The Link Breaks

*No wise man fights. Wisdom solves all riddles, and a
fight proves nothing except which of a number of fools can
hit the harder blow. To be compelled to fight is a confession
of stupidity or worse, and very likely worse.*

*But few are wise. Unwisdom traps us in the nets of
savagery, from which fear finds no way of escape. Then
the luckier fool may win, unless the lesser fool remembers,
even in the tumult of the fighting, Wisdom that has no
fight to win.*

*The fool says the fight shall settle something; it shall be
the end of this or that. Let the lesser fool remember there
is no end of folly, but there is a beginning of Wisdom. Let
him storm the gates of Wisdom toward a new beginning.
Then, though that gate be death, that he assaulted it as a
Beginning shall have brought him a little nearer to a true
goal. Wisdom, it appears to me, will be at least as useful to
us beyond death as on this side.*

I have never known Wisdom to counsel cowardice.

—From the Log of Tros of Samothrace

Dawn heard the roaring begin, as the populace poured into
the seats to make sure none should forestall them by bribing the
attendants. There were frequent fights, enormously enjoyed by
those whose right to their seats was undisputed; and the shouting of the sweet-meat and provision vendors never ceased until
the vast arena was a sea of sweating faces and the equites and

senators began to occupy the seats reserved for them—seats that had been specially protected overnight by raising the wooden wall in front of them.

The spina down the midst had been removed. The Circus was a sea of clean sand glittering in sunlight. Coloured awnings, stretched over the seats on decorated masts threw one half of the spectators into shade, except where hot rays shone through gaps where the awnings were roped together. There was a constant thunder from the canvas shaking in the morning wind. Roaring and baying of starved animals provided grim accompaniment. The blended tumult resembled thunder of surf on a rock-bound beach.

Tros, fettered as before, was allowed to take his place at the hole in the wall, with Orwic chained beside him. Tros asked leave to inspect the weapons, but Nepos, irritable to the verge of madness, snarled at him:

"Govern yourself! I have had trouble enough! I have lost eight good guards!"

There was not an object left, in the enclosure by the gate that opened into the arena, which a prisoner might seize and turn into a weapon. The guards' clubs were fastened to their wrists by heavy thongs. The braziers were set in place behind a grille, where grimy slaves made ready to pass hot irons to the guards; and the first batch of prisoners—they who had staged the outbreak—were hustled in readiness into the irregularly shaped enclosure whose fourth side was the great door that should presently admit them to their death. They all wore clean but very scanty clothing, their own filthy garments having been ripped to rags in the struggle two nights previous; and most of them, acutely conscious of the red-hot irons, managed to look alert, almost eager for the tragedy. They joked. They even laughed. They called themselves the elephants' dinner, unaware yet that the method of their execution had been changed.

But first there was a ceremony in the sunshine. To a great heraldic blare of trumpets all the gladiators marched in through the gate that had admitted chariots the day before and, facing

Pompey in a line, saluted him, one gladiator making a set speech. There were about three hundred armed men, very splendid in their different accoutrements, as dignified and perfect in shape and muscle as so many sculptor's gods.

Another blast of trumpets sounded and a mock-engagement took place—parry and thrust with wooden weapons, wonderfully executed but mechanical. It lasted until the crowd grew restless and began to whistle. Then another trumpet blast and all the gladiators marched out, leaving breathless silence in their wake—and two lone, nearly naked slaves who stood beside a trap-door fifty feet away from the eye-hole where Tros and Orwic watched. Each held a rope in one hand and with the other clung to one of the pegs by which they were to climb from danger.

Trumpets again, and some one swung the dungeon gate, admitting a glare of dazzling sunlight. Slaves passed the hot irons and Nepos' men drove out the prisoners, flourishing the irons behind them and thrusting at those who were last. The great gate swung shut and for a minute the two score looked about them, blinking at the rows and rows of faces. Then the two slaves pulled the trap and jumped clear, one of them missing his grip. He was caught, dragged down and worried by the famished dogs that poured out of the trap yelping for their first meal in nearly a week.

The crowd looked on in silence until two of the prisoners, mad with terror, ran as if to throw themselves before Pompey and beg to be spared. A dozen dogs gave chase, and there began to be a snarl of passion, punctuated by the shrill, excited screams of women, as the Romans felt the vice of it take hold of them. There was a choking roar when half a dozen dogs pulled down the runners; and the roar grew to a din that drowned the yelping when the other dogs all raced toward the prisoners who stood grouped near the dungeon-gate.

It was not over soon, nor easily. The dogs dragged some of the frenzied wretches to the sand and worried them, but there were six dogs to a man, all fighting for the victim's throat and stomach. Two or three men fought the dogs off with their fists. One slew a dog by choking him, and with the carcass guarded himself desperately until a great brute caught him by the arm and pulled him over backward. Utterly bereft of reason by the horror of it as another fifty dogs were loosed out of a trap, the remaining prisoners ran for their lives, until the last one went down under twenty dogs and the two packs started fighting one another.

Men is masks then, representing the infernal regions, came out of a door beside the spoliarium to drag away the mangled bodies. Fifty men in line, with whips and torches, drove the dogs back through the hole they came from, and a dozen men with buckets scattered fresh sand where the blood lay. Then again the crowd stared at an empty rectangle of sand and two slaves, clinging to their pegs, stood by a trap-door facing Pompey's box. There was a gasp of expectation now. Each turn was always more absorbing than the last.

Nepos had herded fifty men and women into the enclosure behind the gate and they were begging to be told what fate awaited them. A woman fainted; they revived her with a hot iron. A man tried to kill a guard who mocked him, so they tore his muscles with the hooks and then, because he could not stand—or would not—they lashed him with cords to two others and so sent him into the arena when the door swung wide.

This time the slaves released three maddened elephants that raced around the Circus before their little blood-shot eyes saw human beings at their mercy—beings of the same sort that had tortured them for three days in the darkened cage. There was a havoc then that pleased Rome to the marrow. Men were tossed over the barrier and thrown back to be finished off. One monster seized a woman in its trunk and beat her head off against the barrier beneath the Vestals' seats. Another chased a woman all around the Circus, seeming to enjoy her screams, and, when she fell at last, knelt slowly on her, as if kneeling in salute to Pompey. The crowd took that for an omen and yelled—

"Pompeius Magnus Imperator!"

There was no capturing those elephants. The maddened brutes were ready to face torches—anything. When they had crushed the last cowering victim and flattened his head in the sand they set off once again around the Circus, pausing here and there to trample on a crushed corpse and to scream back at the mob that roared with a frenzy no less bestial than theirs. The gladiators had to march out and despatch the elephants, and that was the crowd's first taste that day of anything resembling fair fight.

They took the side of the elephants, forever popular in Rome since Carthage fell and Rome learned to amuse herself with monsters that were dangerous to friend and foe alike on battle-fields. A hundred gladiators armed with spears essayed to corner them and kill them where it would be easy to drag out the carcasses, and each time that the elephants charged through the line the crowd applauded madly, disregarding the pluck of the men who knelt and met them point-first—usually to be trampled, even though they thrust the spear home in the monster's belly.

Teams of horses dragged out the enormous carcasses. The men in masks came from the spoliarium with hooks to set under the arms of dead or injured gladiators and haul them out of sight. Fresh sand was strewn, and once again a bare arena sparkled in the sun.

And now the populace's blood was up. They were in no mood to be entertained with any lesser spectacle. The third turn had to be a climax that should glut their appetite for murder—as the men who managed the proceedings well knew—unless they were to yell death-verdicts for expensive gladiators later on. If satiated now with butchery they might let live the wounded men who presently should lie face-upward and appeal for magnanimity; and it took time and money, besides skill to train a gladiator, who, though he were too severely wounded to appear again in the arena, was as marketable as a horse. The fashion of employing gladiators as the personal attendants of even the women of rank had put a premium on wounded men from the arena. And these scarred and grizzled passe warriors, decked out far more gorgeously than in their palmiest fighting days, became expensive luxuries.

So a hundred criminals were herded into the enclosure by the dungeon gate—all "enemies of Rome," as Nepos thoughtfully remarked—and they were all clothed decently to make their death the more spectacular. Nor were they thrust forth as the others had been, to stand blinking and bewildered near the gate. They were herded by Nepos' guards into the very centre of the Circus and there provided with wooden swords with which to make a mockery of self-defence. One man contrived to kill himself with his ridiculous weapon before the guards were out of the arena, and the guards had to hasten retreat at the cost of their own dignity; the master of the ceremonies ordered the traps raised instantly to prevent other victims from cheating the spectators.

Simultaneously, out of ten doors spaced at equal intervals around the arena came tigers, lions, wolves, bears and a great rhinoceros. The latter was received with roars of approbation, which apparently confused him; for a moment he stood blinking at the sunlight, then turned on a tiger suddenly, impaled him on his horn and crushed him against the wooden barricade. The tiger's claws provided all the necessary impulse that was lacking. He began to attack the other animals, but suddenly grew conscious of the helpless mass of humans in the midst of the arena and went straight at them like a avalanche on four legs.

He was violence untrammelled—senseless—an incarnate cataclysm. He impaled his victims, tossed them, trampled down a swath among them, ripped them open, shook the blood and entrails from his eyes and charged until turning so often left him breathless and he stood with drooped head waiting to recover and begin again.

The lions, wolves and tigers were mere supernumerary skirmishers, who picked off victims scattered by the monster. Famished though they were, they dreaded him and kept clear. When he paused at last, and twenty human victims in a group stood back to back to guard themselves against the lions— and the lions sprang in, maddened by the ineffective weapons—the rhinoceros recovered zeal and rammed his weight into the mass, impaling indiscriminately, tossing a great lion in the air and mowing men into a mass of crimson pulp. Wolves tore the wounded. Tigers struck down any who escaped out of the carnage. And the Roman populace exulted as if all Elysium were at its feet.

Then more excitement as the gladiators entered to destroy the brutes that had destroyed the human victims. The extravagance of killing a rhinoceros that was known to have cost enough to feast a whole precinct of Rome raised the whole tone of the orgy in the estimation of the mob; and the big brute slew three gladiators before a luckier one knelt and drove a spear into his belly. Then a dozen others closed in on him with their swords and the horse-teams dragged the carcass out. The last of the tigers was slain by a retiarius with net and trident, after the tiger had wounded half a dozen men.

While slaves were strewing fresh sand and the clamour of the crowd was gradually dying to a satisfied, expectant hum, Tros turned and found Nepos beside him.

"Your turn now," he said. "They are in a good mood."

He released Tros's wrists, then Orwic's, and gave Tros his sword. It was the same one he had left in Zeuxis' house. The Northmen came out of the cage like great bears growling, studying the axes handed to them by the prison guards.

"Lord Tros, these are not our weapons! These are rotten-hafted choppers for a housewife's kindling!"

They appeared to think that Tros had cheated them. Alternatively they were ready to wreak vengeance on the guards, who stood back, ready with their hooked clubs, reaching hands through the grille to receive red-hot "persuaders" from the slaves.

Tros examined an axe. It was the sort of tool the Romans served out to the slaves whom it was reckoned inadvisable to trust with anything too nearly like a weapon—half the weight of the broad-bladed axes that the Northmen used.

"Those are the axes that Zeuxis sent," said Nepos. "There are twelve spears for the Britons. It is too late now for—"

"Too late now for Zeuxis!" Tros said grimly. "Nepos, will you—"

He had all but fallen from the dignity of Samothrace! To have asked Nepos to take vengeance on the Greek would have undone in a moment all the magic Tros knew. The gods, whoever or whatever they are, love him who sees main issues and avoids the byways of revengeful spite. It needed no clairvoyance to appreciate that Zeuxis—characterless rascal—had succumbed at the last minute to the dread that Tros, if not slain in the Circus, might denounce him after all. Let the gods pay Zeuxis.

"It is too late to replace those. Probably Zeuxis' slaves misunderstood him. Can you give us other weapons?"

Nepos, grinned.

"Aye! Tros, you should have been a Roman! Ho, there! Poniards and targets!"

They were long, lean poniards and shields of toughened bronze that clattered on the floor as fast as Nepos' guards could bring them from the storeroom. And for Tros there was a buckler that a Thracian had carried to his death. A wave-edged scimitar a yard long and a wooden Gaulish shield with iron studs for Orwic.

Then the trumpets sounded and the great gate swung, admitting light that dazzled all the Northmen's eyes. They kept the futile axes—thrust the poniards into their belts—and followed Tros, who ordered Orwic out alone in front of him, ten paces in the lead.

"Remember now!" said Nepos, as the great gate swung shut at the nervous Britons' backs.

The Northmen marched in two lines behind Tros, Britons bringing up the rear, Tros keeping up a running admonition to prevent them from thinking their own thoughts and abandoning their discipline in panic. The enormous Circus and the mass of faces, leaning, leering, lusting—the anticipation that suggested ambush and the unpredictable—the glitter, glare and colour, and the hush were likely to have unnerved Tros himself unless he had had men who looked to him to carry himself bravely and direct their destiny.

"So—you will fight as I have taught you when we practiced on the upper deck repelling boarders—Room for a weapon to swing, and no more—ranks closing swiftly when a man goes down—wounded crawl to the centre, keeping clear of feet.— Each wounded man keep hold of his weapon—pass it to any comrade who is disarmed—Swift with the stab; very slow to recover; eyes on the enemy's—ears listening for orders! When the lions come, steady—and step forward as they spring. Then duck and stab!"

They were midway to the centre before a small group of spectators recognized the gallant youngster in the lead. But then, as if some one were organizing a demonstration, they began to shout his name:

"Ignotus! Ignotus!"

Recognition swelled into a roar as Orwic waved the wreath he had received as victor. They who had won money betting on him doubled and redoubled the applause until the whole arena was a-roar with curiosity and new excitement, chang-ing—so it seemed—the very atmosphere. No better man than Orwic could have strode alone to take that thundering ovation; he was to the manner born, and though he walked without the measured Roman dignity, his own was no less captivating. He had won the crowd's mood with a gesture, and the Northmen, ignorant of what was happening, accepted all the acclamation as their own due; Tros could feel their changed emotion as they formed up at his back and stood in line in front of Pompey, with the white-robed Vestals gazing at them from the draped seats of their own enclosure, well to the front, on Pompey's right.

No Vestal made the slightest sign that Tros could detect; they were stern-faced women with their faces framed in white—ap-parently emotionless; four arbiters of life and death. The obliga-tion to attend the sacred flame of Vesta made it always necessary for two to remain on duty to relieve each other. To the right and left of Pompey's box the senators and equites—no inter-est less thrilling would have brought them from their country villas—sat with faces flushed, their attitude an effort to appear calm although every unstudied movement betrayed tense excitement. They were laughing cynically—chattering—their voices drowned by the enormous volume of the crowd's roar.

Pompey was talking to some one who knelt at his side—by his costume a slave, by his bearing a messenger. A dozen gaudily dressed Romans, men and women, who were Pompey's guests, appeared to listen eagerly to what the messenger was saying; not an eye in all that sumptuously decorated box was turned toward the men about to die in the arena. The salute they gave was unreturned, although the mob applauded the raised axes of the Northmen as a new barbaric detail introduced for their amusement. Tros growled to Orwic:

"Ready now! Lud's luck—and a blow for your friends in Britain!" He faced his men; and if he felt afraid they never knew it!

"Ye are my men, and I have come to die or live with you. Do me no shame this day!"

Then, with his men behind him, he followed Orwic to the very midst of the arena; and as he turned he saw that Pompey leaned out of his box to speak to the Great Vestal, who was nearest to him of the four majestic women. The attendant slave-women pressed forward as if to protect the Vestals' privacy. Tros saw the old grey Vestal's lips move. When he shouted to his men again there was a note of triumph in his voice:

"Think you has Odin lost the way to Rome? Does Thor sleep? And is Lud of Lunden rotting in the Thames? Forget you are in Rome, and fight now for your own gods! Steady!"

Faithful to his promise, Nepos had contrived that the lions should be kept in until Tros was ready. He had almost overdone the kindness and the crowd was giving vent to its impatience when the doors were raised at last from five dens and the yellow brutes came hurrying out into the sunlight. There were marks on some of them of hot iron. There was not a second's interval before they saw their quarry and began to creep up, crouching, blinking, stalking for a flank attack—so many of them that Tros never tried to count.

But there was no opening in the solid square of men that faced four ways at once. Tros stood alone, in front, on one side; Orwic on the other to stiffen the Britons, who were not so easy to make battle-brave. And, since they two looked easier to kill, there was a sudden lightning motion nearly too swift for the eye to follow as three brutes at once leaped at each of them, snarling. Then the melee! There was not a second to be spared for rallying the men or for a thought of anything but butchery—axe, poniard and sword out-licking with the speed of light as fifty lions leaped after the first against the solid square. One dragged a Briton down and through the gap three lions leaped in, to be slain by Northmen. Bleeding from a claw-wound, stepping forward with his buckler raised, Tros drove his long sword through a lion's heart and turned to face another, stooping to entice the brute to spring, then straightening himself suddenly and thrusting upward. He could only fight and hope his men were standing firm. He found breath for their battle-cry and roared it:

"Odin! Odin!"

He could hear their answering roar, but it was all mixed up with lions' snarling and the tumult from the mob, until—as suddenly as the assault began—the butchery was over and he turned to see his square unbroken, three men and himself but slightly injured, and one Briton dead. His Northmen grinned at him, filling their lungs and breathing heavily—awaiting praise. He nodded to them, which was praise enough. Three lions dragged themselves away, blood dripping from them, and a fourth, uninjured, raced around the Circus looking for a chance to leap the barrier. The Northmen showed him half a dozen rotten axes broken, but Orwic laughed gaily from the far side of the square:

"Tros, don't you wish those brutes were Romans!"

There was nothing now to make the crowd impatient—not a second's pause. A gate swung open at the end that faced the carceres. Numidians came running in, their ostrich-feather plumes all nodding as they shook their shields in time to a barbaric chant, their long spears flashing in the sun.

Tros turned his eyes toward the Vestal Virgins, but they seemed not to be looking. Pompey was still leaning from his box, apparently engaged in conversation with the Virgo Vestalis Maxima.

There were sixty, not fifty Numidians, and they appeared to have been told their task was easy. Their black, almost naked bodies shone like polished ebony as they began to play and prance to draw the crowd's applause. Groups of three gave chase to the wounded lions and slew them with their long spears, while a dozen others stalked the one uninjured beast and, finally surrounding him, coaxed him to spring, when they knelt and received him on spear-points.

Hurriedly Tros put his Britons in the centre of the square and made them surrender their spears to the Northmen whose axes were broken.

"Watch your chance. Seize the weapons of the fallen enemy!" he commanded. Then, to the Northmen, "Fight as if repelling boarders! If the square breaks, form again!"

He left Orwic on the far side of the square, for the Numidians were circling to attack on all four sides at once. Their leader, a lean Titan of oil-polished ebony with a leopard-skin over his shoulder, yelled, chose Tros as his own objective—

And in a second they engaged, on-rushing like a wind-storm of their native desert—fierce as fire—undisciplined as animals. Their leader leaped, down-stabbing with his spear—Tros's long sword took him in the throat. Crashing above the tumult, he could hear the crowd roar "Habet!" as another black man seized Tros's buckler, bearing down on it to make an opening for two others' spears. Out licked a Northman's axe and bit into a feathered head. As suddenly, Tros's long sword saved the Northman. A poniard, up-stabbing with the heft of all the Baltic under it, went home into encrimsoned ebony, and there was room again—time for a glance over-shoulder.

"Odin! Odin!"

The unbroken square was fighting mad, and through the corner of his eye Tros saw the unarmed Britons crawling between legs to seize Numidian spears—one Northman down, a Briton dragging him—and then a riot-roar as the spectators cheered on the Numidians—a howling onslaught, and the crash of battle in which no man knew what happened, except that the rush ceased and there were black men bleeding on the sand. A third of the Numidians fell back and hesitated, leaderless and numbed by the jeers of the crowd.

"Lord Tros, we stand firm!" cried a Northman, and fell dead. A Briton dragged his body to the centre of the square. The other Northmen closed the gap, their left arms measuring the space to make sure there was room to fight. Then Orwic's voice:

"All over, Tros! They have no more courage. Shall we charge and rout them?"

The Numidians retreated and began arguing, until a few took dead men's spears and, rushing to within six paces, hurled them; but the bucklers stopped those missiles easily and the spectators jeered again, beginning to shout for action, booing, whistling, bellowing "Ignotus!"

"Tros, I beg you, let us charge!" cried Orwic.

But Tros was aware of two things. Pompey was still talking to the Vestal—and the great gate at the end of the arena had been opened. Two long lines of gladiators, helmeted and armed with sword and buckler, began marching in with the mechanical precision of a consul's bodyguard, saluting with a flash of raised swords as the last pair entered and the great gate closed behind them. Tros could hardly make his voice heard above the thundering ovation of the crowd:

"Change formation—into two lines—backs toward the Vestals! Orwic, stand by me!"

He bade them let the wounded lie. The pass was desperate. He formed his double line into a semicircle with its ends retired toward the side where the Vestals and Pompey and all the senators and equites were seated.

"Now ye shall show me what Odin begat, and whether Lud of Lunden raised a brood of men! Behold—those gladiators drive the blacks against us. Slay or be slain! Give ground slowly toward the wall!"

No time for another word. A blast of trumpets. The gladiators, forty of them, separating into pairs with the precision of a guard of honour on parade, came forward at the run, outflanking the bewildered Numidians, urging them forward with gestures, presently stabbing at those in the rear. The Numidians, clustering, not understanding, then suddenly desperate, broke, surged, gathered again, stabbed back at the gladiators—and then fled before them, frenzied, brandishing their spears—stark mad—a whirlwind. And then—shambles!

It was cataclysm without sense or reason in it—slaughter wrought unconsciously, the muscles moving as the heart beat, without signal from the brain—sheer wanton instinct let loose in an orgy of destruction—with the rolling whites of men's eyes, crimson blood on black skin—scornfully handsome Roman faces under brazen helmets at the rear—a deafening din, like a thunder of surf, from the onlookers—the only memory that survived.

Thereafter, no pause, but a change of movement and a measured method in the madness, with a gradual return of conscious will. The gladiators smiled, and that was something. They invited death as if it were a playmate; they inflicted it with scientific skill aloof from malice; they were artful and deliberate, their recklessness a mask beneath which awful energy and calculation lurked. They were as sudden as forked lightning, with an air of having all eternity in which to study their opponents' method.

Tros found himself engaged by one young veteran of twenty-five, bronze-muscled, with a glow of health like satin on his skin, and on his lips the smile of fifty victories. He had the short sword of the Roman legionary and a big bronze shield, short bronze greaves and a gleaming helmet; with the exception of those he was almost naked, so that every movement he made went rippling along his skin.

The moment he singled out Tros and engaged him the spectators began roaring "Glaucus! Glaucus" and it sickeningly dawned on Tros that, though this man might have promised Nepos, the spectators were in no mood to spare any wounded combatant. They were yelling for massacre, cruelty, death, for the uttermost peak of emotion; and Glaucus, all-wise in the signs, with a glance at the crowd beneath the buckler upraised on his arm, confirmed it:

"Est habendum!"

He was still good-natured. Attitude and smile were invitations to submit to the inevitable and receive the thrust under the breastbone that should end the matter swiftly. There was not a trace of malice in his smile when he discerned that Tros refused that easy death. He parried Tros's long, lunging thrust and sprang in with a laugh to crush an instep with his heel and stab before Tros could give ground.

Earth, sky and walls appeared to shake under the thunder of the tumult when the favourite of Rome went reeling backward and fell headlong, tripping over a dead Numidian. He had not realized he had a swordsman facing him—that that old instep trick, and the reply to it, was something Tros learned long before ever a razor touched his face. Glaucus rolled and sprang clear with a cat's agility, and laughed, but he was at Tros's mercy if a pair of gladiators had not cut in to protect him. Melee again; a Northman sprang to Tros's aid. Three more Northmen battle-axed their adversaries and crashed their way to Orwic's side. Tros slew two men. The crowd yelled his praises. Glaucus, venomous at last, called off two other gladiators and again opposed himself to Tros.

There was a sharp command from Glaucus. The other gladiators formed themselves into a phalanx. The expectant crowd drew breath like one thrilled monster, greedy for the coming massed assault—the staggering, reeling line—and then, when Tros should have been separated from his men, the final single combat.

But the art of generalship lies in unexpectedness. Not for nothing had Tros drilled and drilled his crew in deep-sea battle practice. They were used to his roar—obeyed it. Instantly he formed his double line into a wedge, himself its apex, bringing forth a roar of admiration from the crowd, who, loathing discipline themselves, adored to watch it.

Gradually wheeling, with a crabwise movement, sullenly, Tros gave ground, offering his flanks to tempt the phalanx to an indiscretion. And because the gladiators knew Fabian tactics would only annoy the crowd, they shouted and came on, aiming their sudden rush so as to cut Tros off from the arena wall and drive him out toward the centre where he and his survivors could be surrounded.

The spectators stood on the benches and had to be beaten down again. An ocean of sound, as if the very sky were falling, drowned the clash of weapons. Tros moved on the arc of a parabola and struck the phalanx sidewise with his wedge, splitting it diagonally with the fury of a Baltic blast, his Northmen bellowing their bull-mouthed battle-cry.

They burst into the left end of the phalanx. The gladiators lost formation. They tried to re-form and lost seconds doing it. Glaucus, skilfully avoiding Orwic, plunged into the melee, hurling men out of his way, challenging Tros. It was a milling shambles, weight against weight, fury against fury, with the gladiators losing—losing their heads, too, as their numbers thinned. All the axes were broken. Northmen and Britons alike fought now with poniards and spears.

Glaucus reached Tros, sprang at him from behind a gladiator whom Tros slew with a lunging thrust that bent his buckler and went past it deep into the man's breast. That mighty blow left Tros extended, with his buckler useless on his left arm and his sword point in a man's ribs. Glaucus sprang to stab him between neck and shoulder.

"Ah-h-h!"

The crowd roared too soon. Orwic's buckler intervened. Glaucus, springing backward to avoid the Briton's swiping scimitar, tripped over a dead gladiator.

"Habet!"

But the crowd was wrong again; Glaucus was uninjured—instantly on his feet. There were five Northmen and four Britons down. Twice that number of Glaucus' men lay crimsoning the sand. The gladiators realized their case was desperate—sprang back into line again behind their leader.

Instantly Tros re-formed his wedge. He did not dare to take his eyes off Glaucus for more than a second, but he spared one swift glance at the Vestals. The Vestalis Maxima was still talking to Pompey, who leaned forward from his seat, apparently engaged in heated argument; his face was flushed. There was something unexpected happening. The spectators seemed aware of it; they swayed; there was a new note in the tumult.

But there was also a new move in Glaucus' mind; he spread his arms and shouted. Instantly his men split in two divisions and attacked the wedge on either flank, Glaucus watching his chance to charge at Tros when the weight of the assault should have driven the Northmen back a yard or two and left him unprotected.

For a breath—ten—twenty breaths the wedge held—until suddenly the Northmen lost their heads and charged to meet the onslaught, breaking line and bellowing their "Odin! Odin!" as they locked shields against the gladiators' and opposed sheer strength and fury against skill. As swiftly as leaves whirl and scatter in the wind the tight formation broke up into single combats.

And now, again, the crowd went frantic. Glaucus, favourite of fortune, winner of a hundred fights, had met his destiny at last! Tros had at him in silence, grimly, minded to make swift work of it—ears, eyes, passion concentrated.

There was a blare of trumpets—but it might have been a thousand miles away. There was a man's voice pitched against the thunder of the crowd—but it was a voice heard in a dream. There was a yelping, snarling anger note in the crowd's increasing tumult—but that only matched Tros's own dissatisfaction with the gods, who had provided him no better opportunity than this to save the day. He had no desire to kill Glaucus. He knew he must, and anger substituted for desire.

Glaucus sprang like a leopard—feinted—turned aside Tros's lunge on his buckler—ducked in to get the advantage with his short sword at close quarters. The quick stab missed by a hand's breadth. Tros's next stroke shore away the crest of Glaucus' helmet, the terrific impact hurling back the gladiator on his heels. There was never a doubt about the outcome from that second.

Glaucus fought a losing battle with the desperate determination of a veteran—cunning, alert, experimenting with a hundred tricks, now giving ground, now feigning weariness, now swifter than a flash of lightning. Twice he drew blood. Once, with a whirlwind effort that brought tumults from the crowd, he forced Tros backward against a writhing gladiator's body and then, buckler against buckler, almost tripped him. But the effort spent itself and Tros's strength overwhelmed him. Glaucus' own blood trickled in his eyes from where the long sword had shorn the helmet-brass and bit into his scalp. He shook his head, like an embattled bull and sprang in blindly trying to smash down Tros's guard with his buckler. For a second they were breath to breath, and he spat in Tros's face, stabbing furiously, until Tros hurled him backward and the long sword licked out like a tongue of flame.

The sword was swifter than the eye, yet thought was swifter.

"Habet!"

The crowd's yelp was like a thunder-clap. But swifter than a year's events that flash by in a dream, was the vision of Nepos' face—the memory of Nepos' voice—the thought of Glaucus' willingness to wound and then ask mercy for his victim. Between syllable and syllable of "Habet!" the point lowered and went lunging into Glaucus' thigh.

"Down with you!" Tros beat him to the sand with a terrific buckler blow. He set his foot on him. Glaucus tried to squirm free.

"Lie still!"

Now he became conscious of the trumpet blasts, and of the man's voice pitched against the din. The crowd was screaming savagely for Glaucus' death; they lusted for the last refinement of mob-cruelty, the fun of turning on their favourite, condemning him as he appealed for the mercy he had so often begged for others. Tros raised his sword and glanced at Pompey's box. The triumvir was gone! The box was empty! Some of his Northmen were cheering. He could not count how many men were killed; his own head swam, but through the corner of his eye he saw the dungeon door was open. Nepos and his attendants were dragging wounded men into a group. There were thirty or forty simultaneous fights going on among the upper rows of seats, and officials were swarming up over the barriers to enforce order; others were already driving the spectators out through the exits at the rear. But the Vestals were still seated, although their attendants seemed to be urging them to go. Tros threw up his sword and asked for Glaucus' life. All four Vestals waved their handkerchiefs. The next he knew, Nepos was nudging him.

"Down on your knees!" commanded Nepos, signing to his men, who set their hooks under Glaucus' armpits and began to drag him away.

Tros knelt. The Vestals waved their handkerchiefs again. "That is enough for me," said Nepos. "Swiftly!"

The men in masks were dragging out the dead. One was killing wounded gladiators, drawing a heavy sword across their throats, but Nepos would not let him kill Tros's wounded men. Orwic, bleeding and breathless, came to examine Tros's wounds, but Nepos was impatient. The crowd was raging.

"Come!" he commanded. He appeared to think Tros knew what had happened. "Bid your men carry their wounded. Swift before your gods reverse themselves!"

The dungeon guards hustled them out as swiftly as the wounded could be dragged and carried. The great door of the carceres slammed shut behind them, deadening the angry tumult of the crowd.

"That is the first time in the history of Rome!" said Nepos. "What gods do you pray to? I myself would like to sacrifice to gods who can accomplish that!"

Tros answered sullenly:

"Eleven good men dead—and all these wounded! Rot me such a lousy lot of gods!"

Nepos brought a doctor, whose accomplishment was cauterizing wounds with red-hot iron and was bitterly offended because Tros preferred the pine-oil dressing that the druids had given him and which he kept in his haversack. Tros dressed the Northmen's wounds, then Orwic's, then his own.

"There is magic in this," he said, offering the flask to Nepos. "I will give you what is left of it. Tell me now what happened."

"Julia died!" said Nepos. "Didn't you hear the announcer? There came two messengers, and one told Pompey, but another told the Vestals. Pompey would have let the games go on, not daring to offend the crowd, but the Vestals said shame on him and—so the guard near Pompey's box told me—they threatened to predict a great disaster to the Roman arms, and to ascribe the blame to Pompey, if he disobeyed them. They thought a deal of Julia. So did everybody. Rome will have to go in mourning. I will bet you fifty sesterces that Pompey will do all he can to keep the news from Julius Caesar until he can get ready to defend himself. The link that kept them from each other's throats is broken."

"And what now?" Tros asked.

"You are free, my friend. The Vestals ordered it. But not yet. I will keep you in the dungeon until darkness makes it easier to pass unrecognized."

There was wisdom in delay, particularly as Tros did not want to be seen escaping down the Tiber. But it was hardly an hour before Helene came and sent a message by Nepos.

"Speak through the gate with her," he advised, and came and listened in the shadow where the great steps turned under the entrance arch.

"Tros!" exclaimed Helene, her lips trembling with excitement, "you would do well to make haste! All Rome knows the Vestals have released you. Zeuxis is afraid of you; he knows Conops came; he has warned one of Pompey's men that your ship will try to pick you up in Ostia. The gallopers have gone to warn the captains of the triremes! If you try to go by chariot to Ostia they will find excuse to bar the road against you; they will certainly seize your ship! But I have permits to take stage to Gaul. None will expect you to take that route. Leave your men. Come with me!"

Tros wondered whether it was she or Zeuxis who had contrived that danger to the ship—even whether it was true at all, although he knew that either of them would be capable of doing it. Helene was as treacherous as Zeuxis. He could read determination in her eyes. He had to invent subterfuge, and suddenly.

"Here are half of the pearls I owe you," he said, pulling out his leather pouch. "Take them. Give Zeuxis this." He produced the ivory tessera. "Tell him, I denounce hospitium; from this hour we are enemies, to the death unless he can explain how he sent my Northmen rotten axes. You shall have the other pearls I owe you—after I reach Britain—after Caesar manumits you. Go tell Zeuxis."

"You will come by road to Gaul?"

"If there is no other way. I must see to my men. They are good men. The gods would rot me if I gave them no chance; also some of them are badly hurt. I have arranged to send them down the Tiber. If all goes well they may find some way of escaping to their own land. Meet me one hour after dark down by the fish-wharf near the bridge. I will be free to answer you then. Bring Zeuxis, but see that he doesn't betray me again. Make him believe I love him and would welcome a fair explanation. Manage so that I shall find him where he can't escape—down there beside the fish-wharf in the dark. I think the gods would not approve if I should miss my reckoning with Zeuxis."

"You and your gods! I would give ten gods for your little finger! So would Caesar!" She nodded, and went to do his bidding, careful not to stay too long near the dungeon gate because of loiterers—and because there was a bad stench coming through the entrance tunnel.

"You will kill Zeuxis?" Nepos asked, taking Tros's arm as he returned into the dungeon. "Better let me have him crucified. I can contrive that easily."

"Friend Nepos, will you do me this last favour, that you let me attend to Zeuxis?"

It was pitch dark when the party filed out of the dungeon with the wounded Northmen leaning between comrades and one carried on a stretcher in the midst. The streets were nearly empty. Whoever was abroad at that hour took care to avoid

so large a company of stalwarts, who were very likely gladiators carrying a drunken master home. The slaves at the city
gate were playing dice beside a torch and hardly looked up.
Nearly all the porters near the bridge-foot were asleep. The
long, shadowy fish-wharf, built of wooden piles, appeared deserted as Tros led the way down creaking wooden steps. He
saw the men whom Conops had brought, all sitting glooming
by a bonfire built of broken crates below a low shed, with their
oars like a gridiron's shadow leaning up against the shed wall.
And he saw the boats, their noses to the bank within a stone's
throw of the men. For one long, hopeful minute he believed
he had escaped Helene.

But she stepped out of a shadow suddenly and took his hand.
"Tros, here is Zeuxis! He supposes he is to meet a man who is
willing to murder you for half your pearls!"

She pointed into shadow. Tros sprang. He dragged out Zeuxis, squealing, shook him like a rat until his breath was gone, then
gave him to two Northmen to be gagged and bound. The men
by the bonfire recognized Tros then and ran to greet him; he had
hard work to prevent them from making an uproar.

"Man the boats! Silence!" They threw the Greek into the first
boat as it nosed the wharf. When that was done, and all his men
were loaded in the three boats, he turned on Helene suddenly.

"Are you alone? Are you safe?"

"I have servants yonder. Are you coming? What will they do
with Zeuxis? Drown him? Sell him into slavery?"

"He comes with me to Britain," Tros said grimly. "I am taking him to save you from his tongue. If his affairs don't prosper
in his absence, perhaps Caesar may recompense him! Farewell,
Helene! You may look for manumission and the pearls when I
have said my say in Caesar's ear!"

He jumped into the foremost boat, but she seized the painter
and tossed it cleverly around a bollard. He could have cut it with
his sword but hesitated, wondering what treachery she might
do yet if he should leave her feeling scorned. She solved that
problem for him.

184

"Tros," she said, "they have ordered out the triremes!"

"How do you know?" he demanded. Whereat she laughed a little.

"Tros, you are lost unless you come with me to Gaul!"

"So it was you who suggested triremes, was it? You who told Pompey to capture my ship? Well, we shall see!"

He cut the painter with his sword and left her standing there. He could see her figure, like a shadow, waving, until the boats swept out of sight around a bend, and the last he heard of her was his own name rolling musically down the river.

"Tros! Tros! Turn while it is not too late! Tros!"

Danger was as nothing to the thought of an entanglement with her! Lions had not scared him half as much! Escape from the arena had not brought as much relief as leaving her behind! All the way down-Tiber, as he urged his men and beat time for the oars, he exulted at having saved her from betrayal by the Greek, but more at having saved himself out of her clutches. But he still had to save his ship. He still had to save Caswallon and his Britons. Row! Row!

They passed by Ostia at midnight, seeing nothing but the watchmen's lanterns and the low line of the receding hills on either hand, with here and there a group of shadowy masts in-shore. As dawn approached they rested on their oars and let the longshore current bear them northward as they keep all eyes strained for the three great purple sails. Orwic was the first to see them, yelling and waving his arms in the boat ahead. Tros was the first to see two other sails, a mile apart and a mile to seaward of his own ship, that appeared as dawn sent shimmering light along the dancing sea.

Sigurdsen was standing in to search the harbour mouth. The triremes had put out to sea in darkness and hard worked to windward of him. They were closing in now under oar and sail to force him into Ostia or crush him on their boiling bronze beaks.

"Row! Row!"

By the time Tros stepped on to his own poop there was not

a quarter of a mile between the three ships. The triremes' oars were beating up the sea into a white confusion. They were coming along two legs of a triangle before a brisk breeze.

"Out oars! Drums and cymbals!"

Tros took the helm from Sigurdsen and put the ship about.

"Let go halyards! Downhaul!"

The three great purple sails came down on deck. The trireme captains mistook that for a signal of surrender. They slightly changed course so as to range alongside, one on either hand. Tros set the drums and cymbals beating.

"To the benches, Conops! Half-speed, but splash! Make it look like a panic until I give the word. Then backs and legs into the work and pull!"

The Liafail, tin-bottomed and as free from weed as on the day Tros launched her in the Thames, began to gather headway. The trireme captains saw she meant to try to escape between them. Judging her speed, they changed helm simultaneously, leaning over in the wind and leaping forward to the shouts of the oar-overseers, their rams awash in the rising sea. The Liafail's oars splashed as if the crew were panic-stricken, until Tros threw up his right hand for a double drum-beat.

"Row!" Conops echoed him.

There were seconds while the issue hung in balance—seconds during which Tros dreaded that the trireme captains might have speed, too, in reserve—but he could see the weeds under their hulls. Or that they might have manned their arrow-engines—though it was not probable that they had had time enough to get their fighting crews on board. He beat time, setting an ever faster oar-beat, doubting his own eye, mistrusting his judgment, believing he had overrated his own ship's speed and under-guessed that of the triremes. Wind and wave were against him.

But his great bronze serpent in the bow laughed gaily, shaking its tongue as it danced on the waves. Too late, both the trireme captains saw he had escaped. They changed helm, tried to back oars, let go sheets and halyards—and crashed, each beak into the other's bow, with a havoc of falling spars and breaking timber and the oars all skyward as the rowers sprawled among the benches.

"Catapult?" asked Sigurdsen. "They are a big mark. We could hit them with the first shot."

Conops came on deck to watch the triremes rolling, locked together, sinking.

"Arrows?" he suggested, fingering the 'paulin housing of an arrow-engine.

"Let be!" Tros answered. "Spare them for the sake of Nepos and the Vestal Virgins!"

For a while he laughed at the absurdity of coupling the Roman headsman and the Vestals in one category. Then:

"Have we wine aboard? Serve wine to all hands. There's a long pull and a hard blow to the coast of Britain. May the gods give us gales from astern and no scurvy!"

Britain: Late Summer

I perceive that, even as the seasons and the years, and night and day make war on one another, there will be conquerors and conquered, until Wisdom reigns. But I believe we enter into Wisdom one by one. A herd hates Wisdom. I perceive that conquerors can conquer fools; they are already the slaves of avarice and suchlike vices, and among the avaricious Avarice is King. A wise man's conquest is himself, to the end that the gaining gales of Wisdom may fill his sails and, blowing him clear of the shoals of ignorance, storm him toward new horizons.

—From the Log of Tros of Samothrace

A row of bonfires on a beach glared fitfully. The skeletons of ships and a mystery of moving shadows on a white chalk cliff suggested through squalls of rain a battlefield of fabulous, enormous monsters. The bonfire flames were coloured by the sea-salt and by copper fastenings that men were raking out as swiftly as the timber was consumed; the figures of the men suggested demons of the underworld attending furnaces where dead men burned their baggage on the banks of Styx. A half gale blew the flames irregularly. A tremendous thunder and the grinding of surf on shingle sang of high tide and a gradually falling sea.

Under a rough shed made of ships' beams with a mass of sand and seaweed heaped to windward Caesar sat, pale and alert, with a list of the ships on his knees. Two veterans guarded the hut, their shields held to protect them as they leaned on spears and stared into the rain. A tribune, cloaked and helmeted, sat on a broken chest near Caesar's feet, attending to a stream of very precisely worded orders, that were being written on a tablet by a Gaulish slave as fast as Caesar could dictate them.

"That will be all now. Work will begin at dawn," said Caesar, taking the tablet from the slave and frowning over it in the un-steady light from a bronze ship's lantern hanging from a beam. "Curius, will you address the men at daybreak and assure them, that though Caesar accepts disaster he is not resigned to it. Tell them that a difficulty is an opportunity to prove how invincible Caesar is. The fleet is broken—but by the sea, not by the human enemy. It will be seen how swiftly Romans can rebuild it. And now see who is out there in the dark. I heard a voice."

"Wind, Imperator."

"I heard a voice. Whose is it?"

Decimus Curius got to his feet with an air of not relishing the weather. He was sleepy, and stiff from exposure to storms. He drew his cloak around him, shuddering as he stepped into the darkness. Presently his voice called from where a campfire shone on one plate of his armour:

"There is a man who says his name is Tros of Samothrace. He is alone."

Caesar's eyes changed, but the slave, who watched narrowly, detected no confession of surprise; only the lean right forefinger went to straighten his thin hair, after which he adjusted the folds of his tunic and cloak.

"You may bring him in," he said.

Tros loomed into the lantern light; the tribune at his side, though helmeted, looked hardly half as big.

"It is a bitter wind that blows you into my camp as a rule!" said Caesar, "but in this instance the omen arrives after the event! My fleet already has been wrecked. What other misfortune can Tros of Samothrace invent for me?"

"I am the messenger of destiny," Tros answered and Caesar stared at him, as it might be, curiously.

"Is your ship also broken on the beach?"

Tros answered with a gruff laugh.

"My ship rides the storm. It will wreak no havoc with that remnant of your fleet that frets its cables off a lee shore. I am an envoy, subject to the usages of truce."

"Provide him with a seat," said Caesar. The slave pulled up the broken chest under the lantern light.

"You interest me, Tros. You are a very circumspective man for one so deaf to his own interests. How often have I offered you my friendship?"

"As frequently as I gave opportunity!" Tros answered. "I am not your friend. I said, I am the messenger of destiny. I wish to speak with you alone."

The tribune, close behind Tros, pointing at his long sword, shook his head emphatically. Caesar smiled, the deep, long lines around his mouth absorbing shadow, making his aristocratic face look something like a skull. He nodded.

"You may leave us, Curius."

The tribune shrugged his shoulders.

"Caesar, fortune has not favoured us of late," he protested. "You heard him with his own mouth say—"

"Curius, when I let fear control me, I will not begin with enemies who candidly profess their enmity! You may leave us, too," he added, glancing at the slave.

Still standing—peering once or twice into the darkness to make sure the tribune and the slave were out of earshot—Tros looked straight at Caesar and repeated the one secret word that the Vestalis Maxima had whispered to him. Caesar looked almost startled, but he made no comment beyond signing to Tros to sit down on the chest.

"Have you conquered the Britons?" Tros asked.

"Very far from it," said Caesar. "Their chief, Caswallon, is an excellent general with a sort of genius that needs time and persistence to defeat. Their chariots are ably handled. So is their cavalry, and I am very short of cavalry, which makes it difficult to bring the Britons to a pitched engagement. But we will do better when the storms cease and the leaves are off the trees. You may say I have defeated them in one sense. Their army is scattered. But they are able to raid my long line of communication and to harass my foraging parties. I have seen fit to withdraw my army to the coast and to await reinforcements from Gaul. Meanwhile, there is this misfortune to my fleet. So—now that I have satisfied your curiosity, assuage mine. What do you think to gain by knowing all this?"

"I am here," said Tros, "to turn you out of Britain!"

Caesar smiled.

"I admire you confidence, but I think you misjudge my character. When I invade, I conquer. If you have nothing else to suggest—well, I suppose what is left of my fleet is at the mercy of your ship, since you say so, but—I can imagine worse predicaments. Surely yours is equally unpleasant!"

"I am an ambassador," said Tros.

"So I understood. You made use of a word that tempted me to speak you very frankly. Why not discharge your embassy instead of talking nonsense?"

Tros sat. With an elbow on his knee, he leaned forward until his face was not a yard from Caesar's. He spoke in a low voice, slowly and distinctly:

"These are the words of the Virgo Vestalis Maxima: 'Bid Caesar turn his eyes toward Rome! Bid him look to Gaul, that when the time comes he may leave Gaul tranquil at his rear!'"

"You bring me dangerous advice!" said Caesar. But his eyes had changed again; he seemed to be considering, behind a mask of rather cynical amusement, calculated to make Tros feel he had blundered into too deep counsels.

"Julia is dead," Tros added, turning his head away, as if the statement were an afterthought. He had been eight-and-twenty days at sea. He thought it probable Caesar had that news already. But the corner of his eye detected absolute surprise. Caesar leaned and gripped him by the shoulder.

"Are you lying?"

"That is for you to judge," Tros answered. "Are you a leader of men and need to ask that?"

"How did they keep the news from me? I have had despatches—"

Tros laughed. "If I were Pompey I would take good care to keep it from you until my army was as powerful as yours! But I am glad I am not Pompey. I foresee the end of that proud—"

"Very noble Roman!" Caesar interrupted, finishing the sentence.

Tros sat motionless. The Roman imperator stared into the night beyond him, seeming to read destiny among the shadows and to hear it in the dirging of the sea. The very pebbles on the beach cried, "Caesar!" The surf's thunder was ovation.

"It is not yet time," he said at last. "I will conquer Britain."

"Nay, Caesar! The very gods are warning you! Twice running they have wrecked your ships!"

"Unless memory deceives me, it was you the first time," Caesar answered, showing not the least trace of resentment. "Generalship, Tros, consists in following an advantage instantly—which is why I doubt you now. You were blind then to your opportunity. Shall I believe you have turned suddenly into a—what is it you called yourself?—a messenger of destiny!"

"Caesar!" Tros stood up and raised his right fist, holding his left palm ready for the coming blow of emphasis. His amber eyes shone like a lion's in the lantern light. "Thrice I might have slain you! If I cared to deal treacherously, all your legions could not save you now! But I am here to save the Britons, not to do cowardice. Any scullion can stab. And I despise not you, though I despise your aim. You are resolved to conquer Britain for your own pride's sake and for the lustre it may add to your famous name. But choose between Rome or Britain. What shall hinder Pompey from arousing Gaul against you and then taking the dictatorship? Is it plunder you crave? I have deposited a thousand pearls with the Vestalis Maxima for you, to make that breastplate for the Venus Genetrix—a thousand pearls, each better than the best that Pompey took from Mithridates and was too ungenerous to give to the Roman people!"

He smashed his fist into his palm at last and Caesar blinked at him, smiling, moving a little to see past him and to signal to the tribune not to run in and protect him.

"We are not electing a people's tribune, Tros! Sit down and calm yourself."

But Tros stood, knotting his fingers together behind his back to help him to subdue the violence of his emotion.

"Pride is it?" he asked. "You shall boast, if you will, you have conquered the Britons! You shall show those pearls in Rome in proof of it! The Vestal has my leave to give them to you when you turn away from Britain. It is the Britons and their home-steads I will save. If you wish to say you conquered them, you have my leave—and I will add Caswallon's if he will listen to me!" "Where is he?" Caesar asked, very abruptly. "I defeated him at the Thames, where he defended a ford with more skill than one might expect from a barbarian. Since then his army is di-vided into independent groups that harry my communications and I can not learn where he is."

"I doubt not he expects me. I have sent a man ashore who will find him and bid him meet me at a certain place," said Tros. "If I should go to him and say Caesar accepts that trib-ute of a thousand pearls in the name of the Roman people, and is willing to make peace and to withdraw his army, I am sure I can persuade Caswallon to permit the legions to em-bark unhindered. And for the rest—if you crave a few chari-ots to adorn your triumph, and a few promises not covered by security—perhaps even a brave man's oath of honour that he will not encourage rebellion in Gaul I can arrange that. Otherwise—"

He paused, and for at least a minute each man looked into the other's eyes. Then:

"Otherwise?" asked Caesar.

"I believe," said Tros, "that you will rue the day you entered Britain! It is easy to befoul your honour by one crook of your finger, that would doubtless bring a javelin into my back out of the darkness—"

"No," said Caesar, "I have taken you entirely at your word. You may go as you came."

"Go you, also, as you came!" Tros answered. "That man I set ashore has told the Britons how the matter stands in Gaul and Rome. Tomorrow's dawn will see that news go spreading through the forests—and away northward to the Iceni—and westward to a dozen other tribes. It will be a long war then, that your ship-less legions will be forced to wage—if they will conquer Britain for you—while Gaul rises against Rome—and Rome gives Pompey the dictatorship!"

"I begin to suspect," said Caesar, "that I underestimated your ability. How soon can you meet Caswallon?"

"I will take my ship around the coast and up the river, to the place where she was built, and see him there," Tros answered.

"Very well. Will you go to him, at last, as Caesar's friend?"

"Not I! I am neither friend nor enemy. I have brought you a Greek named Zeuxis."

Caesar thought a minute. Then suddenly: "Oh, that rogue—the contractor? You may have him. He might make a good servant if properly whipped."

"And you owe nine pearls to a girl named Helene."

"You may have her also."

"Keep her. But manumit her."

"She has served you? Very well," said Caesar. He made a note on his tablet. "Tros, there may come a day when I shall badly need an admiral."

"Aye, Pompey has the allegiance of the Roman fleet. But you shall struggle with him lacking my aid. What shape is the earth? Square? Round?"

"I would like to know," said Caesar.

"I, too. But I will know! I will sail around the world! My father, whom you tortured, prophesied that one day I should serve you. I have done it, though it was none of my wish. But he said, when I have served you I shall have my heart's desire. If I owned Rome and all her legions, Caesar, I would leave them to whoever lusted for such trash, and sail away. I shall have

sailed around the world before you die in Rome of friendless-
ness and a broken heart!"

"Each to his own view," said Caesar. "You seem to prefer
what is beyond your view. But I think you will die nevertheless,
and no less turbulently. I would rather conquer what I see. That
seems enough. Come back, however, if you should have that
good fortune, and tell me all about your voyage."

"Caesar," said Tros. "I hope for both our sakes not to meet
you again until after death. Eternity—"

"Oh, do you believe in that?" said Caesar.

LEONAUR

ALSO FROM LEONAUR

AVAILABLE IN SOFTCOVER OR HARDCOVER WITH DUST JACKET

THE COLLECTED SCIENCE FICTION AND FANTASY OF STANLEY G. WEINBAUM: INTERPLANETARY ODYSSEYS—Classic Tales of Interplanetary Adventure Including: A Martian Odyssey, its Sequel Valley of Dreams, the Complete 'Ham' Hammond Stories and Others.

THE COLLECTED SCIENCE FICTION AND FANTASY OF STANLEY G. WEINBAUM: OTHER EARTHS—Classic Futuristic Tales Including: Dawn of Flame & its Sequel The Black Flame, plus The Revolution of 1960 & Others.

THE COLLECTED SCIENCE FICTION AND FANTASY OF STANLEY G. WEINBAUM: STRANGE GENIUS—Classic Tales of the Human Mind at Work Including the Complete Novel The New Adam, the 'van Manderpootz' Stories and Others.

THE COLLECTED SCIENCE FICTION AND FANTASY OF STANLEY G. WEINBAUM: THE BLACK HEART—Classic Strange Tales Including: the Complete Novel The Dark Other, Plus Proteus Island and Others.

DARKNESS AND DAWN 1: THE VACANT WORLD *by George Allen England*—A Novel of a future New York.

DARKNESS AND DAWN 2: BEYOND THE GREAT OBLIVION *by George Allen England*—A Novel of a future America.

DARKNESS AND DAWN 3: THE AFTER GLOW *by George Allen England*—A Novel of a future America.

CARSON OF VENUS VOLUME 1: PIRATES OF VENUS & LOST ON VENUS—*by Edgar Rice Burroughs*—Two full length novels.

JOHN CARTER OF MARS VOLUME 1: THE PRINCESS OF MARS & THE GODS OF MARS—*by Edgar Rice Burroughs*—Two full length novels.

PELLUCIDAR - THE INNER WORLD VOLUME 1: AT THE EARTH'S CORE - PELLUCIDAR—*by Edgar Rice Burroughs*—Two full length novels.

BEFORE ADAM & OTHER STORIES—*by Jack London*—Includes the novel Before Adam + The Scarlet Plague A Relic of the Pliocene When the World Was Young and others.

THE IRON HEEL & OTHER STORIES—*by Jack London*—Includes the novel The Iron Heel + The Enemy of All the World The Shadow and the Flash The Strength of the Strong The Unparalleled Invasion The Dream of Debs.

CLASSIC SF FROM LEONAUR
AVAILABLE IN SOFTCOVER OR HARDCOVER WITH DUST JACKET

SF7 CLASSIC SCIENCE FICTION SERIES
INTERPLANETARY ODYSSEYS
by Stanley G. Weinbaum

Classic Tales of Interplanetary Adventure Including: A Martian Odyssey, its Sequel Valley of Dreams & Others

SOFTCOVER : **ISBN 1-84677-060-2**
HARDCOVER : **ISBN 1-84677-070-X**

SF8 CLASSIC SCIENCE FICTION SERIES
OTHER EARTHS
by Stanley G. Weinbaum

Classic Futuristic Tales Including: Dawn of Flame & its Sequel The Black Flame, plus The Revolution of 1960 & Others

SOFTCOVER : **ISBN 1-84677-062-9**
HARDCOVER : **ISBN 1-84677-072-6**

SF9 CLASSIC SCIENCE FICTION SERIES
STRANGE GENIUS
by Stanley G. Weinbaum

Classic Tales of the Human Mind at Work Including the Complete Novel The New Adam, the 'van Manderpootz' Stories & More

SOFTCOVER : **ISBN 1-84677-048-3**
HARDCOVER : **ISBN 1-84677-055-6**

SF10 CLASSIC SCIENCE FICTION SERIES
THE BLACK HEART
by Stanley G. Weinbaum

Classic Strange Tales Including: the Complete Novel The Dark Other, Plus Proteus Island and Others

SOFTCOVER : **ISBN 1-84677-049-1**
HARDCOVER : **ISBN 1-84677-054-8**

AVAILABLE ONLINE AT
www.leonaur.com
AND OTHER GOOD BOOK STORES

CLASSIC SF FROM LEONAUR
AVAILABLE IN SOFTCOVER OR HARDCOVER WITH DUST JACKET

SF4 CLASSIC SCIENCE FICTION SERIES
DARKNESS & DAWN 1: The Vacant World
by George Allen England

SOFTCOVER : **ISBN 1-84677-027-0**
HARDCOVER : **ISBN 1-84677-034-3**

New York City – the end of the 3rd millennium. Buildings in ruins. Central Park a jungle peopled by sub-humans. A huge black shape moving across the night sky. Civilization has vanished along with humankind. Into this hostile new world two survivors of our enlightened age awaken from 1000 years of slumber - to fall victims to a world gone wild? - or to give mankind a second chance?

SF5 CLASSIC SCIENCE FICTION SERIES
DARKNESS & DAWN 2: Beyond the Great Oblivion *by George Allen England*

SOFTCOVER : **ISBN 1-84677-028-9**
HARDCOVER : **ISBN 1-84677-036-X**

The distant future - exotic flora and fauna thrive - savage tribes of cannibalistic sub-humans fight for dominance. New York is a place of little hope! The last vestiges of humanity set out across America's devastated landscape in search of their dream, enticed onward by a mysterious and vast black chasm 500 miles deep - does the future threaten extinction for mankind? - or offer one last chance of redemption?

SF6 CLASSIC SCIENCE FICTION SERIES
DARKNESS & DAWN 3: The After Glow
by George Allen England

SOFTCOVER : **ISBN 1-84677-029-7**
HARDCOVER : **ISBN 1-84677-038-6**

Near the Great Lakes, 1000 years from now. Below our planet's surface tribes of albino warriors eke out an existence in a hostile environment. They tell stories of a golden age; but such tales are mere myths - until a man and a woman with god-like abilities arrive and promise to lead them towards the surface, towards the light and to a new life of plenty.

www.ingramcontent.com/pod-product-compliance
Lightning Source LLC
Chambersburg PA
CBHW050534260626
47157CB00004B/1595